# Riders of
# Deathwater Valley

*Other Five Star Titles*
*by James C. Work:*

Ride South to Purgatory
The Tobermory Manuscript
Ride West to Dawn
Ride to Banshee Cañon
The Dead Ride Alone
A Title to Murder: The Carhenge Mystery

# Riders of Deathwater Valley

## A KEYSTONE RANCH STORY

## JAMES C. WORK

**Five Star • Waterville, Maine**

First Edition
First Printing: September 2005

Published in 2005 in conjunction with Golden West Literary Agency.

Set in 11 pt. Plantin by Elena Picard.

Printed in the United States on permanent paper.

**Library of Congress Cataloging-in-Publication Data**

Work, James C.
    Riders of Deathwater Valley : a Keystone Ranch story / by James C. Work.—1st ed.
        p. cm.
    "Five Star Western published in conjunction with Golden West Literary Agency"—T.p. verso.
    ISBN 1-59414-160-6 (hc : alk. paper)
    1. Ranch life—Fiction.  2. Cattle theft—Fiction.
I. Title.
PS3573.O6925R63 2005
813'.54—dc22                                      2005014201

# Riders of
# Deathwater Valley

# Foreword

Some say it was the *old* West, while others say it was the *real* West. Still others speak of a time that happened *out* West.

*Old* suggests something that happened a time long gone, during an era of history no longer clearly remembered. The old West lives on mostly in stories and nostalgic legends. The word *real* implies something a bit different: it suggests there was another West out there somewhere, a non-fictional West, a set of people and circumstances being continually rediscovered by historians and documentary television.

And what does the term *out* West mean? Well, ever since the first Europeans dumped English tea into Boston Harbor and climbed the Appalachians to gaze inland, people around the world have thought of out West as a place of new opportunities, new beginnings, new adventure.

Images of the American West have been handed down from generation to generation in three forms. This novel, *Riders of Deathwater Valley*, like its predecessors in the Keystone Ranch series draws upon all three kinds of stories: facts, folk history, and myth.

It's a fact, for instance, that during the 1880s and 1890s smokeless gunpowder became widely available in America. There was an obvious advantage to using gunpowder that did not produce a thick cloud of smoke and heavy concussion. It was also more powerful than the old black powder. However, many of the guns in use were not designed to withstand the increased pressure of smokeless powder and so continued to be used with black powder. That's a fact. It is another fact that by the 1880s most of the vast buffalo herds of the Great Plains were gone and that only their bones remained to be picked up by bone scavengers who sold them to be ground into agricultural fertilizer.

It's a fact that where the high plains rise across Wyoming and flow up into the foothills of the Rocky Mountains there are thousands of square miles of sage-covered hills sufficient to conceal a man, a troop of men, or a whole village of people. These hills rise and roll and dive into secret arroyos and cañons, sometimes leading to little-known openings in the mountains. Coming to that far Western limit of the high plains, after crossing miles of sage hills, a rider could struggle to the top of a dry, rocky slope pitched like a roof only to find himself looking down over a sheer cliff on the other side. This is the geological phenomenon known as a *cuesta,* a steep uplift of land ending in an abrupt drop off. *Cuestas* occur in long parallel ridges along the foothills. In between them are found flat, fertile valleys that are protected as if surrounded by fortress walls. That's a fact.

Folk history, which may or may not be based on fact, offers us legends of bad water, poison water, lost towns such as Hole-in-the-Wall where forgotten people led dismal lives, and even of settlements cut off from civilization by avalanche or flood. Wandering hermits, Indians with strange powers of prophecy, kidnappings, and lost children—these also have their legends. Among them is the story of an outlaw band that really existed. The leader's real name was James Riley, but he was called Doc Middleton, and his gang ranged the high plains country between the Niobrara River of Nebraska and the foothills of Wyoming. Their strategy was to steal entire herds of horses from ranchers, leaving the ranchers no way to pursue them or go for the law—such law as there was. The Middleton gang specialized in robbing remote ranches, the more remote the better. Having rounded up all the horses as well as any other livestock they wanted, they would vanish into the endless sage hills. They didn't play favorites, either; they were liable to descend on a small homestead and take the settler's few horses or mules or milk cow, or they might raid Indian camps and make off with whole herds of ponies.

Farmers and ranchers rarely tried to stop these marauders, fearing that Doc and his boys might double back and set fire to the whole place. The law rarely chased them very far, fearing (with good reason) that the Middleton gang might purposely lead a posse into the endless maze of sage hills and then ambush them. It was also to Doc Middleton's advantage that law enforcement agencies were inadequately funded and had insufficient manpower. Jurisdictions were often vague, prompting some sheriffs and marshals to let the lawmen in the next county handle the pursuit.

> There are about fifty men engaged in this nefarious business of horse and cattle stealing, who have headquarters on Turtle Creek. They are freebooters—bandits, like those of Italy and Spain. No United States marshal dares to penetrate that nest, although they can have, if they wish, the whole United States Army to back them.
>
> Adoniram J. Leach, quoted in
> *The Luckiest Outlaw* (1974)
> by Harold Hutton

A great many efforts have been made to capture Doc Middleton, but as yet he is still at large. He has had many escapes and adventures and is regarded as the luckiest outlaw who ever infested the Western frontier.

Cheyenne *Daily Leader*, April 8, 1879

*Riders of Deathwater Valley* is not about Doc Middleton and his gang, but does draw upon that legend for the sake of authenticity.

Facts and folk history can make good novels. Even better is to have a way to tie them into a good myth. Many are the myths of fighting men, ranging back in time to Joshua and David, to Hector and Achilles, to Sir Galahad and on down through the corridors of time to Zane Grey's Lassiter or Owen Wister's Virginian. I am particularly interested, this time, in men who rode horses into battle. To narrow it down even further, I decided to focus on the *code* of the horseman, and one particular aspect of it.

That aspect addresses this question: if being mounted on a horse gives a man a sense of pride and honor, a sense of being set aside and superior to other men, what happens when he is *dis*mounted?

A mounted man carrying weapons. A mounted man who shares a code of honor with other horsemen. Throughout history he has appeared in many forms. He was among the Roman legions, he was a Japanese Samurai, a medieval French *chevalier*, a Spanish *caballero*, or an English *cavalier*. Whatever his epoch and whatever his nationality, he shared something with all the others: a sense of obligation and pride owing to his special status among the people. He felt he had betrayed that status and obligation if he was to travel on foot or in a common vehicle. If you would like to see the modern vestige of this traditional mythic horseman, look at today's real cowboys. Their massive buckles and leather

10

chaps and vests are remnants of the armor worn by knights in the days of chivalry. The Leatherman knife on the belt and the rifle rack in the pickup are his weapons on display, direct descendants of the dagger, lance, and battle-axe. They know there is a cowboy way of doing things. And they hate being picked to drive the honey truck when it's time to clean up horse manure. Some cowboys I know have never ridden in the back seat of a car, and never will if they can help it. There's that old song, "The Dying Cowboy", in which the cowboy asks his pals to tie his corpse in the saddle and point the pony West—even dead, he would rather not ride in a hearse. A man on a horse, they said, was more than a man. And a man on foot was less than a man.

This is called a myth, but not in the sense of being false. It is a story whose origin lies somewhere far back in the mists of time, and it is a story that defines and explains one group's social behavior.

One myth about a horseman, a mounted warrior, whose sense of self-worth is put to the test when circumstances force him to dismount from his horse is *Lancelot: or the Knight of the Cart*, a tale from the legends of King Arthur. It was written down somewhere between 1177 and 1181 by a French writer named Chretien de Troyes. To get into an enemy's castle stronghold and rescue his lady from her abductor, Lancelot comes to a point where he must dismount from his horse and step into a peasant's cart, which will take him safely through the enemy's gates. Once he has done that, no matter how many ladies he saves or how many villains he kills, no matter how many risks he takes, his reputation is stained. "There he goes," people say, "the knight who once rode in a woodcutter's cart!"

He is no longer "the finest knight that ever was." He had become "the knight who rode in a cart."

# Chapter One

"At the end of this time he invited unto him all soever
of most prowess from far-off kingdoms. . . ."
*History of the Kings of Britain*, IX 11
Geoffrey of Monmouth

Gwen Pendragon buttoned the front of her dress with deliberate slowness. She sat down at her mirror and brushed her
hair just as slowly, stopping every few strokes to clear long
blonde hairs from the brush. She knew that she was stalling,
delaying the inevitable moment when she would have to go
downstairs, smiling, to breakfast.

She was a little tired of having company. She told herself
it had been only three days, at the same time reminding
herself that some of these people had come an awfully long
way to get Art's help and his advice. She told herself it
would be only a few more days, three or four at the most,
and their guests would be on their way back to their respec-
tive homes.

It wasn't that she and Art were cramped for space, or
that these guests were unpleasant people. Not at all. And
usually she enjoyed having company. But this particular
gathering wasn't like the usual lively bustle and hubbub
where everyone kept busy as if it was a week-long garden
party. This was different. The men spent most of their
hours in Art's office or sitting under the big cottonwood in
serious conversation, trying to come up with a plan for

13

dealing with the rustler problem. When they weren't doing that, Art was taking them on little excursions to look at new livestock or some of the Keystone Ranch improvements.

Gwen's responsibility was to keep the women and their various children entertained, but her heart just wasn't in it. For example, she couldn't seem to remember names. She confused Jonas Robbins's wife with Mrs. Robinson, and couldn't keep their little boys' names sorted out at all. She knew the widow Nellie McCarthy and her son Jim, of course, from the time they had homesteaded on the northeast corner of the Keystone home ranch, but since Nellie was now running the small livestock operation on her own, she spent most of her time talking with the other owners.

Mrs. Halptmann . . . was she the one with blonde hair? She had a small daughter, but so did Mrs. Ashe. Mrs. Webster, now, what was her first name again? Sometimes, it didn't matter so much to know names. Sitting with a group of them and chatting over knitting and needlework, for instance, Gwen felt less pressure. It was when she happened to be alone with one of them, either in the house or out on the porch, or in the yard somewhere, that she felt that uncertainty about names. Art laughed about her concern, but he didn't understand how tense it made her, walking around, trying to make everyone feel at home, even while trying desperately to recall their names, not to mention the names of their husbands and children.

Bob Riley was sympathetic. For Gwen's sake, he took it upon himself to keep the children entertained. He learned their names. Gwen thought it a little bit strange that Art would let his home ranch foreman play with youngsters while he and the other ranchers discussed the problem of horse thieves, but, on the other hand, Bob was sort of a child himself at times. He had a gentle, even temper and wonderful tolerance for children's horseplay.

Well, Gwen told herself, everyone would soon be headed back home, returning to the H Bar C, to Saxon's Holme, to the Silver Cliff Ranch, the P Bar T Ranch, the Lazy A and Plum Creek Ranch. Meanwhile, she would smile pleasantly, sit in the parlor or on the porch or in the kitchen while the women talked about recipes and dress patterns, described the cities they had seen, and aired their opinions about the future of the territory.

There was one visitor she was always aware of, a man whose name and face constantly clung to her thoughts like a sandbur in a silk stocking. She fervently wished he would go away and she fervently wished she could just ignore him. Flynt Malin had showed up on the second or third day of the meeting, saying he'd come from a place called Gorre Valley where the horse thieves had been active. He'd heard about the gathering of stockmen at the Keystone and thought he'd join in and see what the other ranchers were figuring to do about it. Art and the others knew nothing about him. Gwen reminded Art that she had gone into town—nearly two months ago—and a man hanging around the livery had stared at her and seemed to follow her wherever she went. She was almost certain he was this Flynt Malin person. She hadn't liked the way he looked at her.

"I could tell him to leave," Art said.

"No," Gwen said. "They'll all be gone soon enough. I know how hard you're working to bring all the territory people together. Just let it go. And Arthur. . . ." She usually used his full name whenever she was about to suggest something he might not like.

"Yes, sweetheart?"

"Don't you have a new pair of boots in your closet?"

Art looked down at his comfortable old boots. They were

clean, even had a coat of wax polish on them. True, there was a small patch on one side and that scar where his axe had slipped one day, but they were the most comfortable ones he could ever remember having.

"I'll change after lunch," he said.

"While you're at it," Gwen went on, "you might put that shirt in the basket with the other rags I use when I braid rugs. It's getting a bit disreputable."

"Even with my coat on?"

"Even with your coat on." She smiled. "You *are* the most important man at this gathering, you know. You do need to look the part, darling."

While changing into a stiff new shirt, Art thought about Malin and decided to let him stay. Maybe Malin would manage to become so obnoxious that the other ranch owners would agree that he should go. That would be better than Art doing it on his own and maybe kicking up a grudge and making it look like he wanted to run everything on his own.

"Gorre Valley. I've heard of that place," Simon Webster was saying. "Down my way there's a rumor that foreigners and all kinds of range bums end up wanderin' into that Gorre Valley and never comin' out again. They say it's full of down-and-outers, a bunch of sodbusters gone broke."

"That's the place." Flynt Malin sneered, looking around the gathering to be sure he had all the attention. "We call 'em the cripples. *Hombres mancos.* My old man . . . you heard of Henry Malin? . . . he has 'em on the books at his store. Hell, they every one owe him a year's wages. Can't farm, can't raise stock, just run up bills. Some of 'em went and started a little ol' town of their own, tryin' to get away from my ol' man's ledger books, but it's just as hopeless as

16

they are. None of 'em will ever get outta debt or outta the valley till the day we haul their worthless carcasses out to the graveyard."

Art looked concerned. "Surely we could do something about that. That doesn't seem right. With the territory growing like it is, we need families just as much as we need good manpower. And all of us here have been immigrants, coming into the West."

Malin snapped shut the clasp knife with which he had been trimming his fingernails. The trimmings were scattered at his feet on Gwen's polished floor.

"Tell you somethin', Pendragon," he said. "You do that. You figure out a way to pay off their bills for 'em, move all those hard luck cases, an' find some kinda work they could maybe do, and me and the ol' man would even *help* you get 'em out of the valley."

Malin cocked one leg up over the other so he could use his knife handle to knock small chips of dried mud from his boot heel. The men were listening to him and he loved an audience.

"Y'know how they get stuck there?" he went on. "One poor bastard drifts in with his family and his junk in a busted wagon, see. Then he finds another poor bastard already there, an' he says . . . 'I heerd you was from Wales,' or such like . . . and the other, he says . . . 'Yes, I was a coal miner,' and the other says . . . 'Damn, so was I,' and purty soon they're jabberin' away in some damn' foreign language, and then the settler decides he's among friends, so he throws up a shack next door. There ain't any work for him, but he's tired of driftin'. Next thing y'know you got you a whole *pueblo* of 'em livin' together, helpin' each other starve to death and none of 'em has the guts to leave."

Adolph Hauptmann scowled. He was pretty close to the

17

old country himself and it troubled him deeply to think any of his fellow Germans was squatting somewhere like that, some not even knowing English. His impression of Malin was quickly soured as well.

" 'Course there's a good part," Malin went on. "If y'need a outhouse hole cleaned out or a ditch dug on a day hot as hell, there's always some damn' dirt-poor nester ready to grab a shovel and earn two bits. And some of their daughters . . ."—he looked up from his boot and gave the other men a knowing grin—"two bits can always get ye a peek. Or more."

Sitting in the next room, Gwen overheard Malin's ugly remarks and for the hundredth time wished he would go back to where he came from. Ever since he had arrived at the Keystone, she had felt his eyes on her. When he first had walked up to the porch where she had been sitting with two of the other women, he had looked her up and down, deliberately, unblinking, taking his time. That evening, from her bedroom window, she saw him lolling against the rail fence in the front yard, watching the house as he smoked his cigarette. While the other men met together and planned ways to deal with the horse thief problem, Malin often would be somewhere nearby, watching the house. Gwen found herself peering cautiously through the curtains before venturing out, just in case he was waiting. Afraid to go out of her own house—thinking about it brought a sense of hot shame to her cheeks!

One morning, she went out onto the east porch, as she usually did, to stretch and take deep breaths of the clean morning air, and there he was, watching. And that afternoon, she narrowly avoided a direct face-to-face encounter with the man. She was hunting eggs, making the rounds of straw piles, places under sheds, and behind bushes where she knew the hens would lay. She thought she had glimpsed Malin out of the corner of her eye as she turned around the corner of the grain bins. And when she bent over to feel beneath a pile of hay where one hen always left an egg or two, she sensed someone watching from behind. Forgetting about the eggs, she straightened up and hurried around the corner and back toward the house, listening hard in case she might hear footsteps behind her.

It made her mad! Angry, upset, furious. Every time she went outdoors she went with her fists clenched so hard her nails dug into her palms, all because *he* might be out there with his lecherous sneer.

She didn't want to tattle to Art about it. Art was trying *so* hard to have people get along and work on problems together. Malin was just another guest, she told herself, and soon would be gone with the rest of them. Meanwhile, if he tried anything, she would deal with it herself, and it made her even angrier that she hadn't said something to him already.

*If only Link wasn't away, he would deal with Mister Malin.*

The thought had hardly left her clenched teeth before it made her angrier still. Since when did she need help confronting a low-life person like Malin?

It nagged at her all morning. She'd fled from him, that leering Malin. Worse yet, to her way of thinking, the first solution that had come to mind was to call on another man to do something about it. A man who clearly didn't care *what* happened, since he had ridden off on some little month-long errand of his own. What had become of her, that she wanted Link Lochlin, of all people, to come hurrying to her aid? It was high time she started behaving like the mistress of the Keystone and not just "that young thing the boss married."

19

Gwen stood in the front window, looking out at the foothills. An idea began to form. She could play hostess to Art's guests and give herself a respite from the place all at the same time. And it was nearly dinnertime; she would ask Art about it while they were eating.

It was only May but already rather warm for so many people to gather in the dining room for dinner, so the midday meal was set on tables in the back yard. It seemed like more of a picnic, everyone talking at once and the children teasing one another, unable to sit still. They were nearly ready for dessert when she finally got Art's attention away from his guests.

"I was thinking, darling," she said, plucking a loose thread from his sleeve.

"Yes?"

"Tomorrow morning, why don't I take the ladies . . . those who would like to go . . . and their children, and drive up to The Tanks for an outing? The change of scenery would do us all good. There really isn't that much to do around here, with you and the men sitting around talking about livestock and rustlers and posses and all. Up in the hills, the ladies could pick flowers, the children could play in the water . . . it would be fun, don't you think?"

Art agreed. The chain of man-made ponds ten miles up in the foothills among tall old cottonwoods was one of his favorite places to relax. Redstone cliffs sheltered the thick grove of trees, and the trees in turn sheltered the clear stream as it fell over one dam and then another. The grass made a soft green carpet. He and Gwen sometimes went there to spend a night or two by themselves in the silence far away from the bustle of the home ranch. To him it was always a place to recover his energy. The Tanks was a place

20

for him to get away from all the details and decisions and see things in clearer perspective. Good memories there, too.

His sudden laugh brought a quizzical look to Gwen's face.

"What is it?" she asked.

"Nothing." He grinned. "I was just remembering the day I threw you in the water, that's all."

She smiled as well. She had not been smiling at the time he had done it; in fact, she had come out of the pond like a wet cat with its claws out. But the aftermath of his prank. . . . There in the sun-warm grass. . . .

"This isn't the place to talk about it," she whispered. "What about my idea?"

Art kissed her cheek even though some of the guests were watching.

"I think it's wonderful, just like all of your ideas." He smiled, patting her hand. He pushed his plate away and began to rise. "I've got a few minutes here, so why don't I ask Bob if he'd line up a couple of buggies, or the mud wagon, and get him to find a couple of horse wranglers to go along. . . ."

Gwen took his arm and pulled him back into his chair. "Let me do it, dear," she said. "*All* of it. I do really need to."

Art looked into her eyes and saw that he *would* let her do everything. He saw the need there, just as he saw the tiny sparkle of anticipation.

The word spread quickly among the guests. Sarah Dunlap said she'd help pack a lunch. Davy set out in search of the McCarthy boy and together they talked the wranglers' cook out of a shovel and lard can for fish worms. Bob Riley said he had a fishing line they could borrow. One woman feared her little daughter was coming down with

21

something, so she thought they'd better not go. Riley, followed by four excited children, went striding down to the carriage barns to make sure the mud wagon would be ready to go in the morning. They giggled as he lifted them up, one by one, into the wagon and had them sit on the front seat, then the second seat, then the third and fourth seats.

"Now," he said in his most serious tone, "how many could we fit on each seat?"

"Four," said one little boy.

"No, six of us!" said a little girl.

"Four fat ladies," the little boy retorted.

"Like *your* momma," giggled another boy.

"You take that back!" the first boy yelled, tumbling over the back of the seat to grapple with his mother's detractor.

"Hey, hey!" Bob said. "Enough. No fights. Now who knows arithmetic?"

Four hands shot into the air.

"Four seats. How many people will the wagon hold?"

"Can I ride a horse, instead?" the second boy asked. "Somebody could have my place."

"I don't think so," Bob answered. "I'll have my hands full enough with you all in the wagon, let alone galloping off across the hills in all directions. Now come on, we need to figure out how many will fit in this wagon."

Her name is Sarah, Gwen thought. It was already working. With something to *do* at last, she was actually remembering names.

The two women went into the kitchen together and found Flynt Malin there. He was drinking lemonade, straddling a chair backwards. His eyes were following the hired girl's every move. She was trim and reasonably attractive, Mary's new assistant, Hannah, but that did not give Malin license to leer at her. Gwen acknowledged him with polite diffidence, then turned away to speak with Mary.

"Missus Pendragon," Mary whispered, "it's *too* much! He walks in and politely asks for some lemonade. And I give it to him, then, instead of taking it outside the way one of the other men would, he sits down uninvited and tries to chat with Hannah. It's too much."

"I know, I know," Gwen whispered. "I'll get Mister Pendragon to speak to him. I don't think he knows how to act in a nice house, or around women like us. I think he comes from a very crude, primitive kind of place."

"Now," Gwen resumed in full voice, "I'm taking some of the ladies and their children on an outing up in the hills tomorrow. We're going up to The Tanks. We'll need a few lunch baskets, plates, silverware, that sort of thing. Sarah has volunteered to be in charge of lunch, so could you and Hannah show her what we have, and help get it ready?"

"Well," Mary said. "Now, let me see! Since they won't be eating dinner here at the house, you can take some of the potato salad I was fixing. We can slice some of the cold roast from yesterday. There's plenty of apples and carrots. We've just made pie you could take, too. Let me see, what else . . . ?"

Mary stepped into the food pantry, followed by Sarah and Hannah, leaving Gwen alone in the kitchen with Malin. He gave Gwen's figure an insolent look, then stood up and slid the chair out from between his legs. On his way out the back door he set his dirty glass down on Mary's dough board, a violation that none of the Keystone hands would have dared. Malin left the porch, headed for the giant cottonwood where the other men were sitting in the shade together, but then he slowed his steps as if he had another idea. He turned and went instead to the stables where he ordered the hostler to saddle and bridle his horse.

"He needs exercise," Malin said, tapping his quirt impatiently while waiting for the man to finish with the bridle. "So do I. Too much talk around here to suit me."

"Lot of jabber can wear a man down some," the hostler agreed.

"Thought I'd ride up toward the hills. Somebody said somethin' about some tanks up there. Seems like a curious place to put cattle tanks."

The hostler pointed west. "That direction. They ain't stock tanks like you'd think, though. They just call it The Tanks. It's a place where Mister Pendragon dammed up a creek into a bunch of ponds long time ago. The west road takes a fork after the gate, and the right hand track kinda follows along the creek up to it."

Without a word of thanks to the hostler, Malin swung up into the saddle and jabbed his horse into a lope. He rode toward the foothills, across a hayfield and a grass meadow, opening a gate and letting it drop. He turned south along a low ridge, like he'd decided to go that way instead, but, once he was out of sight on the other side, he doubled back and headed for the dark green line of trees in the next valley. Before long he was on the wagon track following the creek into the wide cañon.

"Well, looka here!"

"We wondered when you was comin' back."

"Hey, Flynt. You git tired of all that soft life already?"

The camp smelled of horseshit and unwashed men. Flies buzzed at the empty tin cans lying next to a fire ring overflowing with old ashes and chunks of charred wood. The three men who spoke were sitting on the log of a tree they had chopped down. Two other men sprawled, snoring, in the shade of a stained wagon sheet rigged between two trees. They wore only their long-handled underwear, and their gun belts hung from an axe driven into one of the trees.

"Anybody been here?" Flynt said.

"Nah. Banks is out there keepin' watch, just in case."

"Yeah? Y'notice he didn't see me ride in. Probably asleep."

"Anyway, nobody's been here. Quiet as a church."

"That's gonna change." Flynt came down off his horse and picked up a rock. "Army!" he called out.

He chucked the rock at the two sleeping figures and hit one of them. The man called Army struggled to his knees and rubbed his eyes. A third man came out of the trees, buttoning his pants as he walked.

"Army, get the hell over here. Steve, go get Banks."

"Here's the deal," Malin said when they'd all gathered. "Down at the fancy-dandy Keystone, there's a buncha upstandin' stockmen and family men all talkin' about how they're gonna get a posse up and go after the horse thieves. The U.S. Army ain't gonna help 'em until they have proof, and that damn' marshal hasn't got men to spare, so he went and gave Pendragon a free hand. He's the one we gotta worry about."

"Not the ranchers?"

"Hell"—Flynt sneered—"some of 'em haven't shot a gun in years. Too busy raising brats and growin' flower gardens. No, it's Pendragon and his boys that could give us problems. But I got a plan."

The eight men listened as Flynt described The Tanks and tomorrow's outing.

"I scouted it all, see?" he said. He swept a patch of dirt with the sole of his boot and picked up a stick to draw a crude map in the dust. "Here's that string of ponds, a good ten miles from the Keystone. Now, up over here . . ."—he drew a line leading southwest from the circles that indicated The Tanks—"I found a trail right on over the hogback. Not much of a trail, but it'll be quick. Instead of headin' out onto the flats and ridin' for home, we sneak up over into that next valley, follow it down, ride hard, and we'll be back in Gorre before they know it."

"Be pushin' the horses some," one growled. He had a new horse, one he'd stolen just a month prior, and he was being careful with it.

"Yeah? Well, you ain't exactly been makin' 'em work this past four days. Get this camp cleaned up and get packed. We ride down there at dawn."

"So y'figure if we grab this bunch of women and kids, they'll back off and leave us alone?"

"Sure. We get to Gorre with 'em and nobody'll dare follow. Not without an army. Then we make a deal, see. They can't get in to get their families, but we let a few get out now an' then. In return, they drift off an' leave us be about our business. Pretty soon, give 'em a winter or two to think about it, an' they'll forget all about us. They'll figure they was lucky to get the kids and women back. They'll figure the best thing to do is just wait."

"Could get ourselves shot up doin' it," Army said under his breath. "Me an' Slick saw those Keystone boys shootin' at North Platte, y'remember."

"With nine of us?" Flynt said. "This is a damn' picnic they're on, I told you. Just a bunch of women and kids, maybe a couple of wranglers. They won't put up much of a fight, 'specially when we jump 'em all of a sudden like. Them are good odds, Army. Where's your backbone?"

"I still don't like it," Army complained. "I think we're

askin' for trouble. What's gonna keep that Keystone bunch from followin' us into Gorre and wipin' us out?"

"If they do, we wipe *them* out. We wipe 'em out, and that's gonna be the end of anybody tryin' to catch the Malin gang. Everybody'll figure that if the Keystone couldn't get us, nobody can. Worst thing that can happen is that they'll get past us and get their women and kids back, but they'll be so shot up, they'll think twice before botherin' us ever again."

Flynt stopped arguing. He dismissed Army and the others with a wave of his arm and walked to the narrow stream to wash the dust off his face. He thought about that Pendragon woman. He thought about how he'd seen her at her window one night, in her white nightgown and with her gold hair all down. Damn! He reached into his crotch to adjust his Levi's. Pretty soon, he thought. Just like those stupid tarts he kept around at Gorre, she'd pretty soon be parading for him and wearing damned less.

Under the shade of the cottonwood tree back at Keystone headquarters, the stockmen sitting around Art were surprised when he suddenly jumped to his feet. Then they turned and saw the reason. A figure was walking toward them: a lanky cowboy with a tan hat worn high-peaked and flat-brimmed, Mexican style. He also wore short, close-fitting chaps and his Levi's were tucked into high boots. He took long strides and walked tall.

Art hurried to meet the new visitor halfway, grasped him by the hand, and pounded on his shoulder. He led him back to the group seated in the shade.

"Here's somebody I don't think I told you men about." Art smiled. "My nephew. We call him Pasque. When he worked here, he always rode the hills in the springtime, looking for those little pasque flowers to put in his hatband. Then he ran off to New Mexico to get himself married into a big *hacienda*. How the hell you been, Pasque?"

The cowboy dropped his wide brimmed hat into the grass and settled himself into an empty chair. John Keaton poured a glass of lemonade and handed it to him.

"*Muy bien, gracias.* Well, I'm good, Art! I got that Godinez layout goin' like a top. Hired two of Elena's cousins and darned if one of 'em didn't turn out to be a natural foreman, a real *mayordomo.* He's so good at runnin' things, I figured I could get away for a while and buy some more stock. So here I am!"

The men seemed glad for something to talk about other than horse thieves, and the sun went on down across the sky as Pasque talked about life in New Mexico and they told him about stock they had for sale, or stock they knew about. But, inevitably, the conversation returned to the livestock problem.

"As a matter of fact, I heard about it," Pasque said. "Stopped in Live Oak. People there seem kind of worried you're going to start a war over it. Some of them got relatives in Gorre Valley. They say it's a regular fortress . . . well, it's like Robber's Roost. Only one way in, and guarded all the time. Suicide to ride in there."

"We heard that, too," Keaton said.

"The hotel man at Live Oak told me that some local muck-a-muck, some ex-Army *politiquero* organized a militia to invade the Gorre Valley and they didn't even get past the first set of guards. Of course, *none* of them was a *Keystone* rider!" Pasque laughed.

"I think it's going to come down to just that," Art said, without returning the laugh. "Our neighbors, here, came all this way to see if the Keystone could head up a raid on the

28

place. I just wish Link was here. We could use *your* guns, too, if you weren't a married man and had to get home."

"Talking of Link," Pasque said, "Evan Thompson said he saw him on the road. Might be here tomorrow, next day."

"Evan Thompson!" Art said. "Where'd you see him?"

"Oh," Pasque said casually, "down at the southwest gate. Where that kid started the grass fire a few years back. He's on his way here."

"He's coming here? Did he say why? You know what I mean. Did he say anything to you? Is anything wrong?"

"We talked, if that's what you want to know. We had us quite a chat. He wanted to know all about what I'd been up to since the last time he saw me."

"Nothing about this bunch of rustlers, though? Nothing about that?" Art asked.

"He sort of said he thinks there's some kind of trouble coming."

"That's pretty damn' vague."

"*Sí.* Oh, and the last thing he said was for me not to worry about the water, whatever that means. I got an idea it's something to do with me and Link. Maybe like the old days, no?"

"*Hmm.* Well let's go up to the house. Your Aunt Gwen'll be glad to see you. If you gents will excuse us. . . ."

"Sure thing," Frank Saxon said. "It's time for my nap anyway."

Art and Pasque walked along together across the wide yard.

"So what are you riding these days?" Art asked.

"Don't even look at 'em." Pasque laughed. "My plan is to pick up some fine horses around here somewhere, so I just rode a couple of old culls up here. Figured if they lasted the trip I could just turn 'em loose on the range."

Art nodded. "Makes sense," he said. "So, the blacksmith is down at the southwest gate?"

Somewhere deep in Art's mind was the nagging thought that this whole string of events felt unnatural as hell. The thing worked away at him inside his head like a worm chewing its way out of an apple. Here was Pasque all of a sudden showing up, *and* riding worn-out horses. He'd never known Pasque to leave home in the springtime, and never knew him to use anything but the best of horses. And the blacksmith was coming to the Keystone. Even Gwen had started acting edgy. Then there were all these ranchers and stockmen, hard men with plenty of determination. Strangely, for all of that determination, they were unable to grab hold of a plan to wipe out the rustlers.

Art felt caught between two fences. Seeing Pasque again reminded him of earlier days, times when he and the boys were a law unto themselves, when all the little ranchers and settlers looked to the Keystone for help. With a handful of good men, he'd ride hundreds of miles to chase down an outlaw and recover somebody's livestock. But now things were different, with all this population coming into the territory. Now he had neighbors scarcely a half day's ride from his fences. It was getting to be like a community, where everyone needed to act together in the common interest, which took far more time and discussion than he was used to.

Something, Art thought, something seemed to be brewing. The blacksmith would know what it was.

# Chapter Two

The random grim forge
"Felix Randal"
Gerard Manley Hopkins

Evan Thompson hauled back on the lines and set the wagon brake. He waved one massive arm, signaling his son to drive the other wagon around so they could set up with the tail-boards facing one another. They had camped here in the same place behind the Keystone wagon barns often enough that their old wheel tracks in the grass could be seen even with the sun straight overhead.

Guests were usually greeted upon arrival at the Keystone headquarters ranch, but the blacksmith was not an ordinary guest. His appearances were sudden, but never unnoticed. Nonetheless, no one rode down to the meadow until he put his teams on picket ropes, stretched the big tarp between the wagons for shade, set up the forge and anvil, and prepared a meal. Afterward, Thompson would light the forge and the boy would begin pumping the bellows. Seeing the column of smoke ascending, Art Pendragon would ride down to welcome him to the Keystone.

Whenever the blacksmith was camped there, the place took on a sort of timeless serenity. The sparkling little stream quietly went meandering down the meadow. The boy brought buckets of water to the barrel strapped to the side of the wagon and anyone who drank a dipper of it said they had never tasted water so sweet and cool. The shade underneath the willows and trees that grew along the stream seemed so calm that a man might lie down there and sleep forever.

The blacksmith knew why the Pendragons loved their valley. But as he watched the boy pumping at the bellows and saw the fire glow begin to spread deeply into the coals, he could also see what was wrong with the Keystone: it looked finished.

Finished. There stood the wagon barns, the distant smithy and carpenter shop, then the granaries. There were the two long bunkhouse buildings and the two foremen's houses complete with tie rails and porches. Nearer the main house stood the livery barns and hay barn. And then there was the big house itself with its green yard and hospitable shade trees. All finished, a community unto itself, a peaceful stronghold set into the brown expanses of the high plains.

Art Pendragon had matured well, but he was still too young for such finality, such completion of a dream. The blacksmith could look into Art's eyes and see what Art wanted to become just as he could look at a piece of glowing steel and see the shape it would take. Deep inside Pendragon burned the idea of doing so much more, of helping to create a whole region where ranches and farms and villages would flourish. He was one of those rare men who could envision himself as part of a new civilization, a new world between the mountains and the Missouri.

As for the woman . . . the blacksmith gazed steadily into the glow of the forge. She seemed not to know how intensely her own fires might burn, given the opportunity. Or what those fires might consume. His wedding gift to Pendragon had been a warning about her: her love may prove uncontrollable, he told him, and one day it will come between you and your best rider.

So far, however, the fates had left them in peace to enjoy their valley together. She remained loyal to Arthur, beautiful and passionate. Protected by the courage and guns of the Keystone riders, Gwen Pendragon had yet to face anything that could threaten her, anything that might turn out to be stronger than she.

The boy rested on the bellows.

The blacksmith went to the wagon for one of the metal bars, the bars that he bent and welded into links of the great chain he was forever forging. He tested the cold steel with his great hands. It would make a strong link. Or it could be the one that would ultimately fail. All chains contain that one inevitable link that breaks when the strain reaches the limit of the metal. There was no way to gauge the chain's strength until that limit came, just as there was no way of knowing which of the links would be the one to fail.

Evan Thompson knew as surely as he knew anything that the Pendragon metal was about to be put to the test. They would not sit and watch their lives peacefully drone away into old age and death. Such was seldom the natural order of things.

For Art Pendragon the arrival of the blacksmith's wagons brought the finishing detail to a perfect picture. There by the recently painted barns, in a wide green field, Evan Thompson loomed over his anvil. Red sparks showered from his hammer's blows and the music of steel on steel rang like a church bell calling through the valley. When he wasn't repairing a plowshare or fashioning new fireplace dogs or performing any one of his thousand bits of magic with metal, the giant would be found hammering a cherry-red steel bar into an oval.

At times, with the fire of his forge banked and the bellows silent, the blacksmith sat with visitors and talked. It took the better part of an hour for him to catch up on Keystone happenings, before Pendragon's conversation wandered around to the question of why Thompson was there. Art knew that Evan Thompson's visits were anything but random. And Art was not the only man on the Keystone who had learned to respect the blacksmith's mysterious way of showing up whenever there was some danger in the air. Art, Kyle, Link, even Emil—for each of them, at one time or another, Thompson's forge had strangely been the starting point of a hazardous undertaking.

"I see you have visitors this month," the blacksmith said. "I recognize most of the outfits."

"Big meeting," Art said. "They're all people who've lost livestock to a sneaky bunch of brush riders. We've been tryin' to figure out how to do something about it. They hit fast and take whole herds, then just disappear into the sage flats. Our problem is that they hole up in some godforsaken place back in the foothills 'way south of here."

"Yes," the blacksmith said. "South and somewhat west. You haven't yet learned where it is." It was not a question but a statement.

"Yes and no. Sort of . . . mostly through hearsay," Art said. "Don't know why none of my men has ever come across it."

"No reason they should," Thompson said. "Until now."

Art looked at the big man seated on the bag of coal. Having known the blacksmith for so long, he did not need to ask the meaning of those two words.

"Have you seen it? Big place?" Art asked instead.

"Big valley. Room for nearly anyone who'd want to be there."

"When were you there?" Art asked.

"First time was many years ago. Back when Henry, the elder Malin, was still young. Before the younger Malin came along. You've met Flynt. Henry always wanted a son who would be well respected. Hoped he would marry a nice girl and raise some fine grandchildren. But young Flynt took to rustling, instead."

"Malin's with that gang?"

"Flynt is the leader of that gang," the blacksmith said.

"The hell he is!" Art exclaimed. "Why, he's here right *now!* He told us about Gorre Valley. Said he raised livestock near there and knew about the rustlers. Said he heard about the meeting, thought he'd come see what was up. But you're sayin' he's the one in charge of them! The bastard probably came here to spy on us. A lot of damned nerve he has!"

"I take it you don't care much for him," Thompson said.

"Hell, no. Neither does Gwen. Most people just thought he was obnoxious, but we never figured he was one of the rustlers himself."

"The son of Henry Malin right here on the Keystone," the blacksmith mused.

"So what's the old man's story?" Art asked. "I expect he's the one behind the rustling operation?"

"Henry? No. Henry is just a man who wandered into Gorre Valley years ago looking to get some land and start a settlement. Young, as I said. He bought a shack and some land from a trapper called Jim Mulford. Mulford was nobody important, just another trapper who got tired of wandering from winter camp to winter camp. But once he got to Gorre, Mulford lost that itch he had of owning his own place, so he sold out to Malin and drifted off. Now and again, I used to see Mulford dragging his footsteps back to Gorre Valley. Finally died sitting against a boulder, looking down at Gorre."

"Gorre's what they call the town?"

"Yes." The giant blacksmith picked up a piece of coal that had rolled out of the bag and turned it over and over in his hands. "There's three towns," he said. "Gorre sits right plop on top of a spring where the stream begins. That's why Mulford wanted his cabin there. He dug it out and laid up rocks to make a stock tank where he could get his water. That's the main reason Malin bought it and started to build a town around it."

"So water's pretty scarce up there?"

"No. There's other creeks and springs enough. Malin would've done better to let that particular stream alone. The water's worse than bad. My horses wouldn't drink it, and neither would I."

"So you were there. But you didn't stay? Not much for a blacksmith to do there, I guess. Or maybe they already have one."

"They do have a smith, more's the pity. Every town needs a smith. But he's a gloomy man. His forge sits dusty and cold most of the time."

"Why pity?"

"It's no place for a smith to be. Look what a smith does. He mends a wagon trace, shrinks a tire to a wheel, puts an edge on your axe and shovel. He'll make you a chimney jack to hang your pot over your fire, build shoes for any horse to take you anywhere. It all depends on having hope, Pendragon. All for hope. You hope to put meat in that pot. You hope to take your wagon to town loaded with your harvest. You chop wood and your mind is already looking toward the day you'll be sitting in front of the winter fire.

"Or take horseshoes, for instance. You don't need 'em unless you're looking at going somewhere, hoping to find better pasture or see a friend. Or you ride out a-courting, eh? You and your bride will need a blacksmith's nails for the house, his hinges for the doors, his firedogs for the fireplace. You even need his hoops for your water bucket."

"No need for those things in Gorre, then?" Art asked.

"A need? Yes, I suppose so. There always seems to be a need for the things a blacksmith makes. But in such a place, there's no joy in making them. It's a valley with no hope left in it, so there's little satisfaction to running a smithy."

"So, except for being cattle rustlers and horse thieves, they don't have any future down there?" Art asked.

The blacksmith tossed the lump of coal into the glowing forge.

"Pendragon," he said, "all of us have a future. It's just that some futures tend to come out better than others."

There was no breeze, yet Art suddenly felt a chill in the air all around him, and he shivered despite the heat from the forge.

There came a silence between the two men, and in that silence a lark sang in the meadow to the south. To the north, a black bird of considerable size flew straight and level and very fast, right across the tops of the trees.

"You were sayin' there were three towns," Art resumed.

"Gorre itself, that's the hell town. Four saloons, two still in operation, where you can find a crooked card game or a gunfight or an easy woman any hour of the day. Two stores Flynt took over from his father, both filthy. One livery at each end of town . . . one of them buys so-called 'breeding' stock, most of it stolen, the other buys 'found' cattle and sells 'em to the butcher. There's a barber, hardly ever sober. You already know how they rustle horses.

"Then there's the second town, Getaway. Some residents of Gorre built it to get away from Flynt's crooked ledgers and his gunmen. Two buildings built to be mercantiles, one of them empty. Sheriff's office, except no sheriff ever showed up to use it. A small bar, but nobody has money for drinking. People come from their houses and open up these stores every morning. Then they sit in them, sometimes sweep a sidewalk, but nobody comes to buy anything so they lock up about dinner time and go home again. There's even a church, but it was never finished. Nothing in it to steal, but it's all boarded up."

Thompson's wife came with a bucket of cold, clear water. The blacksmith offered Pendragon the dipper, and Art accepted it.

"Now, that third town," he continued, "that's much the same story. . . ."

"Hold up a minute," Art said, passing the dipper. "Go back to the water. What were you saying earlier about the water?"

Thompson drank deeply, letting cold water drip into his beard and smiling as he wiped it away with his hand. "Deathwater."

"Deathwater?"

"That's the story. You go there and you think you've found your settling-down place. But something happens. Father Nicholas and I used to talk about it. Ask Christollomay, next time you're in town and she's there. She knows about it, too."

"The fortune-teller," Art said. "So what happens with this water?"

"Well, whatever it is you seek, and I mean whatever you seek the *most*, it seems to die there. Some say it happens as soon as you reach the valley. Some say it happens after you drink the water. I'll tell you something just as odd . . . that water isn't fit to quench steel. You put your hot iron into a bucket of that water and it sizzles and hisses and steams, all right, but that water won't put a temper to it."

"*Hmm.* You know, I'm findin' this pretty strange. Seems like you're sayin' the water itself somehow takes away hope from a person, but other times it brings 'em what they want. Only it's the wrong thing they want?"

"It goes beyond strange. It's like the lotus flowers Odysseus's men ate. Have you read Homer's story about Odysseus's companions? After eating lotus they didn't have any interest in going home. No more ambition, no hopes, no future. Nothing. I told you Henry Malin wanted a respectable son who had a nice wife and good children . . . well, look what he got instead."

He took another dipper of cold water. Before sipping from it, Thompson turned east and poured a little onto the ground. He also turned north, then west, then south and did the same thing, and Art knew that the blacksmith was paying respect to the Great Circle of the Plains Indians. Thompson believed in the power of the Six Directions.

"Don't forget the circle," Thompson said after he had drunk from the dipper. "Let's see . . . where was I? . . . oh, the other town. No name to it, but they call it End Of Track when they talk about it. One man has a store there, another has a kind of livery and feed store. There was a café, but it's just a shell now. The place sits on a graded gravel bar, right out in the full sun. Not a tree would grow there. The railroad built a track bed and town site, thinking if they put in a spur line the place would turn into a real community. They gave up on it, of course, but at least they left a good roadbed. Nice and level. It stretches clear down to the river."

"What river's that?" Art asked.

"Gorre River. Around here they call it the Book Cliffs River, once it leaves the mountains. It runs through one end of the valley, rippin' and roarin'. Between the rapids and the gorge, nobody even tries to get into the valley that way. At one point you can see what's left of a railroad trestle across the gorge, but there's just rails still spiked to a few rotten ties and beams. I don't know if the steel holds up the ties, or the ties hold up the steel. Couple of high towers . . . real shaky now . . . and rails hangin' off of them."

"And you say nobody leaves this place."

"Not a soul. Old man Malin, he'd probably let them go. But Flynt's a different story. He's got gunmen, mean like him, and they like a steady supply of meat and goods and women. One family started to leave End Of Track once, I heard, because Flynt started paying attention to their daughter. I heard the whole family came floating, face down, out of the mountains on the river."

"Where's the way in, then?" Art asked.

"Not along the river," the blacksmith said. "The direct way is to take a road that runs through a gap in the *cuesta*. And then it goes through another gap in another ridge behind that one. The whole valley is walled in with hogbacks and *cuestas*. You remember El Corredor, down in New Mexico. The time you and I met up at Chupadero? The Gorre Valley is like that. No way out for fifty miles or more."

"Except these gaps."

"Except the gaps. Malin has outposts there, little stone blockhouses hidden up in the rocks so you can hardly see them. He has men living there, watching the gaps night and day. With a great many men you *might* be able to fight your way through the first one, but then there's a second one. And it would slow you down long enough for him to collect all his other riders to massacre you."

"Flank him, then?"

"You could. A man might make a long ride around through the mountains and come into the valley that way. Or else find a river crossing far upstream. The problem is there's people living all over, scattered in the mountains and along the river. They're so afraid of Malin's men that they might run to tell him the minute they saw strangers. Plus the fact that lots of them would be caught in your crossfire. You might even find frightened women and old men shooting at you."

"If that *is* where the rustlers come from," Art said, "it sounds like we should get the U.S. Army to go in there. Some of the ranchers suggested doing just that. I guess you heard about that decree out of Washington, though."

"That the Army isn't authorized to make civilian arrests or assist local law officers. Yes, I heard."

"Politicians!" Art spat.

"Pendragon." Evan Thompson laughed, his voice a low boom like a distant peal of thunder. "Time was when you and your riders would go charging in there like devils and hell take the consequences! Any one of your men was worth ten or twenty outlaws. I wonder if the Keystone isn't getting soft these days. But enough about that. Come break bread with us."

"All right. Thanks."

Waiting at the table the woman had set up in the shade of the tarp, Art tried to stretch his toes in his new boots. They were stiff and confining. And, damn it, so was the collar on this new shirt. "Time was when you'd go charging

41

in," the blacksmith had said. *Well,* thought Art, *maybe it's all in the past now. The time has come for everybody to pull together and do these things like civilized society.*

It was a workingman's meal of heavy stew and thick bread. There was some talk about the weather, the prospects of a good hay crop, new settlers Thompson had met in his travels, and the state of the territory in general.

"While I'm here," the blacksmith said, "I think I'll start forging that iron fence you want around your graveyard."

"No hurry," Art said. "There's only the one grave."

"So far," Thompson said. "So far."

Art looked up in surprise at the blacksmith's words. Looking past him over his shoulder, he could see the little grave far off on the slope of the hill. It was probably only a trick of the shadows, but Art thought he could also see a newer, fresher grave there as well.

"*Please* stop! Oh, won't you please stop! You're killing him! Can't you see? You're killing him!"

The man driving the wagon sneered and drove faster, whipping the lines to one side so the wagon would lurch.

The woman wailed, trying to steady the unconscious figure on the floor with one hand while she clung to the swaying seat with the other. The outlaws had slid him in under the seats and the women hardly had time to pillow his head on a folded blanket before the wagon started. The woman next to her sobbed incoherently.

"*Please!*" the first woman screamed. The jolting wagon and the clouds of dust hammered the air from her lungs, but she gasped and went on screaming.

"Murderers!" she cried. "Stop, stop, stop!"

The man on the front seat only looked over his shoulder again and grinned, showing broken and yellow teeth. He turned back at the team and went on lashing them with the lines to keep up with the others who rode ahead. Four captive boys were being pulled along with the outlaw riders, their hands bound to their saddle horns. The women in the wagon pleaded with the driver to stop, too frightened to let go of the seats and sides, too choked with dust to see clearly. The only one who didn't cry out each time the wheels struck a hole or a rock was Gwen Pendragon. With her right hand she kept a firm grip on the steel frame of the bouncing seat. She leaned forward to steady the man's head with her other hand. She could see that his wounds had stopped flowing, but she did not know whether he was alive or dead.

Lather flew from the nearly spent horses when Flynt Malin yelled for his men to slow up. They were well into the endlessly rolling flat country now, a plain stretching away from the foothills. It was a land so seemingly infinite that it could hide hundreds of men and animals in miles and miles of gullies and arroyos, low swales and sloughs that could swallow up uncountable riders.

He spit a mouthful of phlegm over the horse's shoulder. Their old strategy had worked again. Study the layout, make sure of surprise, figure an escape route, then sweep in and grab all the stock in sight. Then keep pushing and pushing before any pursuit could even get organized. Put the better part of a day between you and whoever tried to follow, and the endless miles of sage and yucca would hide you completely. It worked perfectly with the Indian ponies and it worked perfectly with remote ranches, getting away with all their horses and leaving them no way even to ride for help.

Capturing the picnic bunch had been just as easy. Two of the Keystone cowboys had made a run for their horses to grab guns, being stupid enough to start shooting with women and kids around, but they were easy. Now one was dead back there and one was probably dead in the wagon.

Army rode up beside Malin.

"Purty slick, I'd say," he said.

"Slick as hell! Nobody left behind to ride for help."

"Yeah. Just like always. By the time somebody misses 'em and rides out there to check on 'em, then goes back to get help, we'll be long gone. Long gone!" Army laughed at their cleverness.

"Not so many horses, though." Malin laughed, spitting again. "But good ones. Good as those Indian ponies we got once. Hell, *that* was a good one, wasn't it? Got in there, stole their whole damn' herd, got away clean."

"I tell y', Flynt," Army said, "this plan of yours is sure goin' to work. With those damn' Keystone boys backin' off and stayin' on their own range where they belong, we'll be sellin' stock anywheres we want to and stealin' us some more on the way home!"

"Yeah. You get back there and make sure none of them females jump outta the wagon. Banks!"

"Yeah, boss?" the other outlaw replied.

"Keep on movin' south to that outcrop 'way out there, then up to the hills to get around it. I'm goin' up higher with the field glasses and make sure we ain't bein' followed."

With the wagon slowed down to a steady bumping pace the women's cries of confused terror quieted to a chaotic murmur of hopeless indignation and fearful submission. Gwen spoke up and assured them that the Keystone riders would be coming after them before nightfall. All we need do, she said, is to be calm and strong and to stay together if they possibly could. That, and minister to Bob Riley, if he

44

is still among the living. For his sake, she told them, they had to bear up and act like the frontier women they were.

The outlaw driving the wagon heard it all with a curled lip. *They'd be "frontier women" soon enough,* he thought. *The old one and the fat one'll find themselves doin' more washin' and cookin' than they ever did before. The two slim ones, they'd probably end up bein' wived to some of the men.* And he almost felt sort of sorry for the pretty one with the yellow hair, the one who seemed to think she was the queen. *Flynt'll be addin' her to his collection, all right. She'd be paradin' around his place in her drawers before the week was out, showin' off them nice legs for him.*

*And as for them little boys, they'd pretty quick be findin' out what it was like to have to work for a livin'.*

# Chapter Three

Whither away . . . and what thy quest?
                    "A Passer-By"
                    Robert Bridges

Four ranchers sat on the porch, drinking Art's whiskey. The late afternoon sun threw a long silhouette of the windmill across the lawn and three children danced, laughing, as they tried to step on the shadow of the moving blades. These children and two others had protested against riding all that way in a "bouncy ol' wagon" when right here at the headquarters ranch they had chickens to chase, a creek to play in, and bigger barns for hide-and-seek than any they had at home.

Mr. Harris sipped his whiskey and said he could smell supper cooking. Jonas Robbins said that if the Keystone meals got any better, none of them would ever want to go home. Simon Webster looked out toward the foothills and said he wished the women would get back so they could eat.

"Still early," Art said, squinting at the low sun. "Shouldn't any of you boys be hungry yet."

Pasque rose and walked to the edge of the porch and leaned against a post to study the line of hills. Art joined him.

"Something the matter?" Art asked.

"¿Quién sabe?"

"What do you mean? Saying it that way, I mean."

46

"The blacksmith. Now Aunt Gwen's late in getting back, and that oily Malin *hombre* has gone off somewhere. I think Evan Thompson wants us to know there's a problem headed our way. Something's in the air."

"Well, what do you think we ought to do?"

"You know, I think I'll just saddle up and ride out there a ways."

"I'll come along," Art said.

"No. You stay with your guests. I'm just restless, probably. I'll just take a little ride and probably meet the wagon comin' back in."

While Pasque was tightening the saddle girth, he thought about taking a rifle with him. Instead, he tossed his saddlebags across the back of the saddle and tied them on. He never rode without a few provisions, like a packet of jerky and a couple of cans of beans, some extra shells for his Colt and whatever other possibles had found their way into his saddlebags. But there was probably no need for a rifle.

Although the horse was hardly a good one, it managed a respectable trot down the road and they were soon out of sight of the Keystone headquarters. The road brought back some pleasingly soft memories for Pasque, for when he was working for Uncle Art he had frequently ridden along this very same road. More than once he'd ridden all the way into the foothills just to look for those pretty purple flowers. Sometimes he had gone flower picking when he was supposed to be working.

A couple of miles brought him up onto a low rise from which he could see another mile ahead, but there was no sign of the mud wagon and the horses that had gone out from the Keystone that morning. Pasque rode the next mile, then another. He stopped on another rise of ground and reached into his saddlebag for his little brass telescope, a betrothal present from his father-in-law, *Don* Diego Godinez. With it he could see almost all of the road leading into The Tanks. He could see the tops of The Tanks cottonwood grove, barely visible as dark green above the hills.

Turning to look south, Pasque spied a far off rider just approaching the southwest gate. It was a long way distant, but the stiff, tall figure, riding with his hat level to the horizon, looked familiar. Pasque turned back to scan the road to The Tanks one more time, saw no movement, and so turned his horse toward the approaching rider. Near the bottom of the hill, he stopped to use the telescope again. No doubt about it. It was Link, returning from his trip.

In fifteen minutes they were together, just inside the gate where the new kid had burned the grass. Pasque wondered if Garth would ever live that down. Link's first question, of course, was why Pasque was in that part of the country and not down at his own New Mexico ranch with his pretty wife and . . . kids? Pasque admitted to two *niños*.

"So what brings you back to the Keystone?"

"I was looking to buy some horses to take home. Something special. I brought some nags like this one and wanted to see if anyone in the area happened to have a small bunch of good Quarter horses. But when I got here, Uncle Art was in the middle of his big meeting about your problem with the *bandidos,* so I thought I would stay around and meet people, maybe be able to help out."

"What *bandido* problem are you talking about?"

"Pretty bad one, from the look of things. It's this gang that preys on isolated ranches and line camps. Uncle Art, he is for rounding up the Keystone riders and going to find them, but he also wants to get the other ranchers involved in it. Be more democratic and. . . ."

"Civilized?"

"*Si,* that is probably the word. But you can see it almost makes him loco to be sitting and talking all the time when he wants to be out there with his six-gun shooting the bad ones."

"So, I guess you're just out for an evening ride, then? Maybe we could ride into the ranch together," Link said. Pasque could see in Link's face that he was tired from a long trip.

"My thought was to meet up with Gwen and some of her guests. They took a picnic to The Tanks this morning and didn't get back yet."

"Oh. In that case, I'll ride along with you. It's not too much farther," Link said. He patted the neck of his big black horse. "Ol' Messenger has had a long day, but I guess he's got a few miles left. OK, boy?"

Back trailing the way Pasque had come, they arrived at the road alongside the creek that meandered among the swales. The sun was down behind the tall cottonwoods when they rounded the corner and saw The Tanks ahead. Drawing closer, Link leaned across Messenger's shoulder and examined the ground.

"Damn, but there's a lot of horse tracks here," he said. "Look at this. Looks like a dozen horses or more, going every which way. And some of them were in a hurry! Look at the way the ground is torn up there!"

Where the road branched into The Tanks grove, they saw how the wagon's tracks went in but didn't come out. The trail was clear: a large wagon had entered the grove and then its tracks went on west toward the foothills, followed by several horses. Maybe the picnic group had decided for some reason to go farther than the ponds and the grove. But then Pasque saw the wagon robe caught in a bush and food hamper upset on the ground. The two riders turned off the road and into the shadows.

They found Bob Riley's sorrel standing back in the trees with one leg broken and oozing blood. There was more blood on the saddle. Not far away they found young Oliver Keaton dead from a gunshot wound in the chest. His hand still clutched a small pocket pistol.

Suddenly the silence seemed to reach out into the shadowy stands of trees surrounding them, the quiet heavy air itself seeming to probe and listen for the sound of a breaking twig or a rifle being cocked. Without a word, they dismounted and cautiously moved out in two separate directions to search the groves. They found nothing, heard nothing. By the time they rejoined at the place where Oliver Keaton lay, Link's rage and apprehension was pumping the hot blood into his brow. Gwen had been here. Keaton was dead. Where was she now? Who did this?

Pasque also felt hot fury rising in his brain and he shook his head violently to clear it away before it could blind him. He, too, felt the dread and the unknowing.

"We'd better cover Keaton," Pasque said, breaking the thick quiet.

"Yeah," Link said. His eyes were on the unfortunate young man lying in the grass. He turned to ask how many others had been with the wagon, but Pasque had walked back to the clearing and returned with the wagon robe. Link picked up Keaton's gun and folded the hands across the chest. He and Pasque covered him with the robe.

"His gun's empty," Link said, handing Pasque the pistol. "Looks like he made a stand here. See the trees?"

Pasque looked. Fresh gouges in the tree bark showed where heavy-caliber bullets had ripped through the grove.

"How many people were there?" Link asked.

"I'm not certain," Pasque replied. "Aunt Gwen, maybe

five or six other women. Four or five children. Bob Riley. And him." He indicated the corpse.

Link silently turned away to walk back to where Riley's crippled horse stood. Pasque heard a single shot. Link came back to the clearing, replacing the spent cartridge as he walked, and the two men still did not speak. Instead they made a circuit of the place, looking at the remains of the outing. A picnic basket lay shattered from having been stepped on by a horse. Two blankets spread on the grass had been ridden over as well. There was a woman's shawl snagged on a wild rose bush, and plates and drinking glasses scattered everywhere.

"What do you figure went on here?" Link finally said.

"I wish I could remember how many rode out here with the wagon. From the ranch, I mean. Somebody rode in here with a lot of men and took them. The tracks are all messed up, but there must have been ten horses that came in here. And like you said, they were riding fast. Look how the hoofs dug up that grass over there."

"Bastards."

"*Verdad.* You know, *amigo,* our next move should be to look around for anybody else. Might find Bob Riley back in the trees somewhere."

Reluctant, Link agreed. He was burning to be on the trail of the wagon, but he knew it had a long head start. He also knew they had to make sure nobody was lying among the trees somewhere, maybe wounded. He went one way and Pasque went another, making a slow and careful search of the grove up and down the little creek. Finding nothing, they put a second blanket over the corpse and anchored it with heavy stones.

"We had better get back to the ranch," Pasque said. "Not much daylight left, and Art won't want Keaton lying up here overnight. We could take him back on one of our horses, but I think it's faster to leave him and come back. Don't you?"

"Your horse is fresher than Messenger. You take Messenger and go get help. Leave me yours, plus all the ammunition and gear y'can spare me. I'm gonna follow their trail. All night long if I have to. You get back to the ranch and start out tomorrow at daybreak with the men. Art can send men and a wagon up here tonight to get Keaton."

"This isn't much of a horse, you know."

"Good enough. Messenger can get you back to the ranch pretty quick. Yours looks like it could walk all night."

"Link, my friend, do you think it's a good idea to go ahead all by yourself following a bunch the size of this one?"

"Look, there's no use both of us going back to the Keystone. I'll follow the trail as far as I can, then I'll make smoke or leave some kind of sign for you and the others. You know how these bastards vanish, once they get a head start. A couple of years now they've been disappearing with whole herds, somehow. He'll get there fine," Link said, patting Messenger's neck. "Just let him set his pace. He's done a fair share of miles today."

"We'll be behind you soon as we can," Pasque said

The thing was done in a matter of minutes—Link's saddle changed for Pasque's, Pasque's extra two cans of beans and box of .44 cartridges, a small brick of matches transferred to Link's saddlebag.

"I'll leave sign," Link said. "This might be the best chance we've ever had to find out where those outlaws get to."

"*Vaya con Dios,*" Pasque said.

"Take care," Link replied.

Pasque put Messenger into an easy trot, looking backward more than once at the tops of the cottonwood trees and at the gathering evening over the mountains. The long line of clouds across the southern horizon and the blue-black line of haze along the northern rim of the prairie coupled with the silhouette of mountains made him feel he was riding across a circle, a circle of infinite scope.

Pasque had gone two miles, maybe a little more, when he was met by a Keystone wagon coming up the road at a pretty smart clip. Dick Elliot was handling the lines. Pasque didn't know the cowboy with him.

"Art thought the picnic party might need another wagon," Dick said. "Figured they broke down, they were so late getting back. Any trouble?"

"Big trouble," Pasque said. "The worst kind of trouble. I am very happy to see you fellows. Somebody attacked the people at The Tanks. They're gone!" He turned around and rode alongside the wagon. "It was outlaws. Those horse thieves, we figure. The ones that the meeting is all about, no?"

"We? I thought you came alone?"

"Link is up there. I met him coming back from his trip. He's on their trail right now."

"Anybody else?"

"Nobody left. They got Oliver Keaton."

"Dead?"

"*Si*. Nobody else up there. We think whoever it was took the wagon and the women and kids and everything."

"Missus Pendragon?"

"Her, too."

"What's happened to them? My God, man, there must have been a dozen women and children in that group.

53

You're telling me they're all *gone?*"

"*Si*. Taken away."

"What about Riley?" Dick asked. "He was with them."

"No sign of him. Somebody did a lot of shooting up there, but Keaton's the only one we found. We'll get him in your wagon and get back to the ranch with the news."

"My God!" Dick said. "We ought to go after Link! He's riding straight into trouble. If that bunch of outlaws is the size you think it is, I'm bettin' they set a couple of men to watch their back trail. That's what I'd do."

"*Si*. But he's too far ahead now for us to do anything about it. Let's get Keaton loaded up and back to the ranch."

*Vaya con Dios*, Pasque had said in parting. *Go with God.*

The gods with whom the lone rider now traveled took shape in phantom shadows stretching out from clumps of sage. They lurked in murky ridge-line tangles where twilight made rabbitbrush and yucca turn steely gray like smoke puffs. These gods played cruel tricks on the horseman, first showing him the wagon tracks plainly and deeply in the sand, and then hiding all trace of wagon and riders in a maze of brush. He found the tracks again, lost them again, used up some of the last remaining light looking for them, found them again. Finally he was lost in a waste where every opening through the sage looked like another trail. With trails seeming to run this way and that way, behind as well as ahead of him, Link felt the dark overtaking him. Dismounting, he half dragged and half led the horse to the highest skyline he could see, hoping maybe he'd spot a campfire.

Miles away, but in the wrong direction, there was a glimmer of firelight that rose and fell and finally went out.

Otherwise, there was only the dark, only the silence, only the owl who hunted the brush on hushed wings for wasteland mice scurrying along their own tiny paths among the yucca and sage. Link unsaddled in the dark and tied the horse to a bush, then lay down to sleep beneath his saddle blanket. Either in his dream, or in the half-dreaming moments before sleep, he imagined her face. She was watching him, her eyes bright with love and her lips moist and half open. And in this dream, what was he doing? He was destroying her assailants right before her eyes, his Colt roaring out their deaths and his fists chopping down the ones who were not worth a bullet. He was the best fighting man he knew, the best that she knew, and the hour was coming when he could prove to her just how much she could need him. Wherever he found the bastards who had taken her, he would make them know more fear than they ever imagined could exist.

He knew how it would be. Just as it had been when he rode into Kansas and as it had been afterward, when he rode out of Kansas to find the Keystone Ranch. There in the stillness of the lonely sage flats Link asked himself how it had all begun. So many men he knew had found homes of their own, and families, and peace. Why was it that for him it went on and on, over and over? The blacksmith always said that there were patterns in it. And Link could see the pattern. He could see it clearly. What he couldn't see was how it ended.

There was barely enough pre-dawn light to see by when Link struggled to his feet and tried to stomp the feeling back into his legs, whipping his arms back and forth in an effort to warm himself. As soon as his hands stopped shaking, he built a fire and hunkered down next to it to warm a can of beans. And by the merest kind of luck, a burning twig under the can snapped. When the can began to teeter toward the flames, Link made a' sudden grab to save it. His abrupt move meant that the rifle shot missed him by inches.

He clawed his Colt from its holster hanging on the saddle horn, then bellied into the sand as hard as he could, scanning the brush for some kind of sign, something like a drift of gunsmoke rising up. Still too dark to see anything. A second shot came, hitting the horse. The animal cried out and lurched to rip its tether free, and, before he could do anything about it, Link saw it running off into the pre-dawn gloom.

He took a chance and fired back at the place where he had seen the muzzle flash, almost hoping it would draw another shot his way. And it did; it missed, but he yelled as if he'd been hit, rolled out into the thickest part of the sage around him, and held his breath, waiting.

He waited and no one came. He waited and listened as the light gray sky along the horizon turned to pale blue and as the bushes and grass and hillocks and gullies reassumed their daylight definition. But no one came. Finally he crawled off, bellying along in a direction away from his fire and saddle until he got onto a little bit of rising ground and could lift his head to look around. Nothing. Nothing but the flat pale green expanse of sage stretching to the horizon in three directions. In the fourth direction there were just the softly rounded swells that seemed to flow out of the foothills. And the hills themselves.

Link walked cautiously back to his fire. He saw no one else in all of that empty sage flat. No more shots were fired. It was as if the thing had never happened.

He lifted the cold can of beans from the ashes and tilted it back to let the beans slide into his mouth. Then he buckled up the saddlebags and threw them over his shoulder. He would have put his saddle up in the crotch of a tree until he could come back for it, but there were no trees. As for the horse, there was only the broken sage branch and deep prints of hoofs churning the ground in panic next to dark splotches on the sandy soil. Blood and tracks.

Link followed the tracks.

There was a good reason that Link had not seen any further sign of his ambushers: they had left almost as soon as they heard him yell. They rode away in the pre-dawn gloom at a hard trot, so it was still morning when they walked into the smoky, low-ceilinged dining room of the only hotel in the town of Ehre's Hole and found Flynt Malin just finishing his breakfast.

"So?" he asked.

"One man, boss. Only one man followin' us. An' he kept losin' the trail. We watched 'im till it got dark."

"Where's he now? Dead?"

"Mebbe. First, we got his horse. It went limpin' off, and it was hit pretty good. Then we got 'im. Heard him yell."

"You didn't check?"

"Hell, it was gettin' light and we was hungry. We figured without no horse he wasn't goin' nowhere, and with a slug in him. It would 'a' took another couple hours to sneak up on him and then maybe he'd bushwhack us."

Malin finished his coffee and got to his feet. "Tell you what," he said. "Slick and Army just took some food to the women and their brats down to the stable. We're goin' to start for Gorre in less than a half hour, and I want you two to get back out there and find that rider and finish 'im. Matter of fact, I think I'll send Slick with y'to make sure y'do it."

"All right, Flynt. But first we'll get ourselves somethin' to eat."

"No, you'll do like I *tell* you first. Soon as Slick gets here, you get back out there in the brush an' you finish the job right. And be sure y'check around for anybody else."

Slick and the two gunmen stood on the porch of the hotel watching the Keystone mud wagon and its escort of five outlaws leave the other end of town. When it was out of sight, they looked the other direction at the dusty narrow road slanting up the hill and back out onto the sage flats. Their three horses tied to the rail were asleep. The saddles looked cold and were about the least inviting thing they could think of. There was a long silence as one of them sat down to tighten one of his spurs and another picked flecks of peeling paint from a porch baluster.

"Know what I'm thinkin'?" Slick finally said, looking off toward the hill and the road. "I'm thinkin' why wear out my horse huntin' the damn' brush for some wounded cowpoke on foot."

"Yeah?"

"Thinkin' one of two things. Either he makes it, followin' our trail, and ends up right here in town, or else he don't."

"I'm bettin' he don't. When Steve pulled the trigger, I heard him yelp. He's bleedin' out there, you bet."

Slick scowled at the interruption. "I'm thinkin' we'll just get us some more breakfast and a pot of coffee and set ourselves right here in the shade and wait for 'im. Give him, what? Till noon or better to show up?"

"Give 'im all day, to be on the safe side. I'd sure admire to spend th' night in a hotel bed like you done. We didn't sleep much last night."

"*Hmphh,*" Slick snorted. "That was Malin what slept in the hotel. I slept outside the stable where we had them women and kids locked up. Damn' sobbin' all night. Kept me awake is what it done."

"Look, Slick, we ain't et since last night," the other one said. "You don't mind if we get us some breakfast?"

"Go ahead. Send that cook out here with my coffee."

The man called Slick adjusted the dirty blue scarf he always wore and eased himself into one of the wooden chairs on the porch. He tilted it back against the wall and waited. He thought about Malin and his "problem" with women and he had to chuckle about the idea of three men guarding his back trail just so Malin could get a pretty woman to his place. *And that was just so's she'd parade around for him in her under-drawers or less. Everybody knew Malin wanted women in the worst way, but couldn't do nothin' much about it. And, by God, that was Malin's problem and not his. Wasn't worth spendin' a day out in the hot sun searchin' the bushes for some shot-up cowboy. Just as easy to sit in the shade a while, just in case he'd come limpin' down the street, then kill the bastard and get on back to Gorre. If he was worth killin', that is.*

Link walked for miles carrying the saddlebags and keeping his head down to watch the tracks he was following. Besides the saddlebags, he was also carrying the weight of his rage. It simmered in him as he slogged across the monotony of the sagebrush wastes, simmered and hardened until it was a thick lump all through his chest. And his boots were punishing him with blisters.

More than anything, he was now angry. First at Art for letting those women and kids go so far from the ranch when he knew there were outlaws in the territory. The idea of those outlaws kidnapping women enraged him even more. And he was angry as hell with himself for not finishing it all clear back at North Platte where he had encountered those three bastards the year before. They were the same outlaws, he was sure of it. Part of the same bunch, anyway.

Art Pendragon, sitting on his ranch, trying to organize a bunch of ranchers, holding meetings and talks while there were still cesspools of lawless bastards running around taking livestock any time they wanted to. *Once I get my own place going,* Link thought, *you won't see* me *sitting on my hands.*

He walked on. Here he was and he had to keep on going, tired and dirty and dragging along through miles of this damned sagebrush.

Suddenly Link found the horse's tracks again. He found the poor animal standing in a small clearing in the brush with its head drooping, miserably trying to graze on the thin dry grass. The wound in the shoulder looked very bad, but at least the blood had stopped flowing. It might live through the day, but he didn't think so. Link walked up to it and spoke gently while he patted it on the neck and nose, quietly taking up the lead rope. Together they started again through the flat and featureless sage, the horse limping along after the limping man.

Less than a mile farther, Link smelled smoke and stopped to look around. A thin line of white smoke seemed to be rising right out of the ground 100 yards ahead of him. He left the horse and went forward, gun ready. The sage plain broke open suddenly to show a deep arroyo at his very feet. At the bottom there flowed a tiny sluggish creek, hardly more than a trickle of water. Crouching warily, he moved along the edge in the direction of the rising smoke until he could see a small campfire next to the water—just a campfire burning away down there on the empty sand and nothing more.

When he went back and picked up the horse's lead again, the animal took a step and nearly crumpled to the ground. But it still followed him, its eyes glazed and its steps uncertain. They walked west along the rim of the arroyo as Link searched for a way to get down into it. He had lost the outlaw tracks a long way back, but he knew the direction they were going and it seemed certain that he would need to cross this steep gulch in order to follow them. He finally found it, some way past where he had seen the campfire, a side arroyo that offered a steep way down.

Link looked back down the arroyo toward the campfire. Where there had at first been nothing but empty sand, there were now two people and two outfits. Link had never seen any outfits like those anywhere. All his life he'd never seen anything like them.

The draft animals were mules, bigger than the mules usually found in this region. These were tall, skinny, Missouri-type working mules. There were three of them. One was hitched to an old-fashioned Spanish *carreta* with big heavy wooden wheels and high sides made from poles set on end, like pickets. On each of the four corner posts of this lumberous cart hung a buffalo skull. He couldn't tell what was in the cart, but it looked like a roll of canvas and a bunch of grain sacks. The mule was hitched to the cart between a pair of long poles and the harness was a crazy tangle of old ropes, bits of rawhide, and twisted cloth all tied together.

The other two mules were hitched to an even stranger rig. The hind mule stood between two bent shafts and the front mule was simply tied to the cart by two long pieces of rope reaching back from its hames to the wagon.

The cart itself, or wagon or whatever you'd call it, looked like an Indian travois with shafts more than twenty feet long from the mule's shoulders to the ground behind him. Somebody had decided to add a pair of old wooden spoke wheels to this travois, heavy ones, so the whole thing looked like a two-wheeled wheelbarrow being pulled backward. Like the first cart, it had high sides made of rough poles lashed together with rawhide and bits of wire and rope.

This second cart was half full of bones. The whole outfit stunk to high heaven.

Link slipped and slid down the steep bank, dragging the horse after him, and walked toward the two people who seemed almost as mismatched as their conveyances. The man was a holdover from the old days of the mountain men, tall, but stoop-shouldered with rheumy eyes, wearing grease-stained buckskins. Much of the fringe was gone from his leggings and hunting frock and the leather was worn so thin in places that his white skin showed through. The possibles sack hanging from his wide leather belt had once boasted a circle design of quillwork, but time and accident had worn gaps and breaks in it. He had the look of a man who had seen many a fur trappers' rendezvous in his time, but it must have been long before Link was even born.

The woman was an Indian nearly as bent and age-worn as the man. Like the man she seemed an antique holdover from an earlier time. Many seasons had creased her face and the winters had long since turned her hair to snow. But her eyes were clear and bright and her doeskin dress and moccasins were clean and decent to look upon. A wide sash of quillwork leather went over her shoulder, and from the belt around her waist hung a knife in a deep sheath.

The ancient mountain man peered through his watery

eyes at Link and waved for him to come on up to the fire. "Been lookin' for ye to show up," the mountain man said. "Hyar's coffee, an' thar's meat bilin' in the pot. Set yoreself down, if y'care to."

"You knew I was coming?" Link said, dropping the lead rope and advancing toward the fire.

"*She* did," the mountain man said, nodding toward the woman. "Th' way she figgers it is thet her people's gods sent y'. Or they come with y'. No matter . . . hyar's meat, an' th' water skin's just there yonder."

# Chapter Four

"And the midst of the valley was full of bones."
Ezekiel 37:1

The first faint light of dawn found the Keystone Ranch in a state of alarm and confusion. Many of the ranchers hadn't slept since the boys had brought Keaton's body in, along with the news of the kidnapping. A couple of those whose wives and kids were missing had saddled horses in the dark and headed out with lanterns, only to return in frustration after realizing they had no idea where they were going. Other men built a fire out by the corral and stood by it, shivering in their coats and stamping their feet, each man arguing his own plan of action.

The sun was nowhere near ready to rise when lantern lights began to wink on in the windows of the two bunkhouses where the guests had been staying, and in the kitchen of the main house the stove was already hot as Mary and Hannah made coffee and stirred up large bowls of pancake batter.

Art was wearing his Colt when he opened the side door. He stepped out onto the porch, leaving the door standing open as a signal that his neighbors should come to breakfast. The morning was chilly and the air had no scent of moisture anywhere in it.

The first men in the door directed their argument at him.

64

"Art, what we gonna do? Your boys said it looked like maybe twenty or thirty outlaws took our women and kids. We were figuring we could count on a dozen of us, plus some of your riders."

"That's the way I was thinking, too," Art said. "We'll eat, get enough supplies together, and head out. We need to keep organized, not let anybody go running off on his own."

One of the ranchers whose wife and daughter were safe in bed over at the bunkhouse spoke up. "It seems to me we need to make this more like a military expedition. I know you all want to ride out there like a big posse and rescue your people, but you need to stop and realize we don't know where they are or where they're headed. It won't do us any good to tear off through the hills, wearing out our horses, wearing ourselves down, not getting anywhere."

"Go on," Art said, picking up a mug of coffee from Hannah's tray and leading the way into the dining room.

"I vote for sending two men on good horses to trail your man Link. They can mark a clear trail for the rest of us to come along. They can travel light and fast. We'll be behind them with more men, more supplies. And then I think we need to get some men, maybe with wagons, to come along after us and bring tents, food, ammunition."

Some of the others argued, but in the end they saw the logic of the plan.

"It'll take some time to get all that organized," Art said.

"That's right," the other one said. "But in the end it'll save us time. While your people are getting things ready, you can get the scouts started."

Art said very little more as they rapidly ate breakfast, and, after he was finished, he rose and went out to get things going. The first man he ran into was Pasque, who was just doing up his cinch.

"Do we ride?" he asked Art.

"Pretty soon," Art said. "You ready?"

"I can leave right now. What's going on with the group?"

Art shifted his gun belt and hitched up his Levi's. "They decided to send some scouts out after Link, then follow with the main body of men. And a supply train behind that."

"This does not sound like the old days!" Pasque exclaimed.

"Yeah," Art said. "To tell the truth . . . and don't let this go any further . . . I don't much like having a damn' committee tell me what to do. I'm worried sick about Gwen. And the others, of course. This standin' around, makin' plans, just grates at me. Webster even wants to wait until we can notify the Army or the territorial governor."

"Where do they think they took them?" Pasque asked.

"Gorre, of course. But Ashe made a good point about not headin' straight for there. The raiders hit his place last winter. He had to walk to the next ranch for a horse, and him and three others followed the tracks. But the rustlers had wandered around and backtracked and it didn't look like they even headed south. He's afraid we'll all get out there in a bunch and wear out the horses following the wrong tracks, or else we'll go tearing into Gorre and find out they aren't there, anyway."

Pasque checked his cinch and rebuckled the cheek strap. "Link said he'd make smoke or leave some kind of sign so I could follow him," he said. "And I'm not really part of this bunch. I don't have to wait around."

"You talk like you're leaving without us. I told the others we shouldn't let anybody run off on his own."

"Sorry, Art, but Aunt Gwen's out there and I'm going

after her. I'm certain to find Link's trail. I'll probably catch up to him by nightfall."

Art clapped the young man on the shoulder. "You're a good man, Pasque," he said. "God, I wish I could go with you."

"It is the way it is," Pasque said. "Somebody has to be *mayordomo* now. It's important. You're the one. But I can find Link for you and we'll do everything we can to get your wife and the others back again."

"Go ahead then, but take care," Art said. "Best take it easy, find out what's what. If it turns out the outlaws headed into Gorre, I don't want you goin' in by yourself. You wait for us. If you find Link, tell him the same thing."

"OK," Pasque agreed. He would agree to anything if it meant getting away from this pack train posse. "I'll mark my trail for you. *Adiós.*"

"Limber up yore Green River, cowboy, an' dig in. Young pronghorn shines near ez good ez buffler hump."

Link and Two Nose sat cross-legged on the ground with the pot between them. After the fashion of the old fur trappers, they took turns stabbing their hunting knives into the pot for chunks of meat. The woman brought hard bread to dunk in the broth, and, as she handed it to Two Nose, she spoke to him in a language Link did not recognize.

The mountain man finished chewing his hunk of meat, then pointed his Green River butcher knife at the wounded horse. The animal was barely standing. It looked as if it would lie down at any moment and never rise again.

"Crows Woman says yore cayuse is dyin'," he said. "Her people puts a heap o' stock in hosses. Says she oughta take it an' send it to jine its ancestors. She'd do it th' sacred way, y'unnerstan'."

67

Link looked at the horse and at the old woman, standing there wrapped in her dignity and silence. Finally he spoke. "Go ahead," he said.

Without another word she walked to the sick horse and spoke softly to it as she picked up the lead rope. She led it slowly down the arroyo along the little stream until they were out of sight around the bend.

"What's her people?" Link asked.

"Crows Woman?" the old man replied. "She be Arapaho. Standing Hollow Horn's people, long gone time ago. 'Most all gone under now."

"Not speak English?" Link said.

"None of 'em 'Rapahoe do, far's I kin cipher. One did oncet, feller name of Niwot. Left Hand? He'd talk English good as me. Rest of 'em never parlayed it 'tall. All gone to the grandfathers now, ennyways. An me, *waugh!* I'm prob'ly th' only true mountain man left above ground, yup."

"I appreciate the grub," Link said.

"Ye do, eh? But how y'favor the *stink?*" Two Nose smiled. "Y' must be hungry, if y'kin eat with thet smell in th' air. Thet bone wagon's got 'nough atmosphere about it to make a coyote sick."

It was a terrible, nose-twisting, eye-watering smell that came from the cart's cargo, even though the two men had chosen a sitting place upwind of it. It was the kind of smell you never seem to get rid of once you've gotten it in your nose. There was spoiled meat in the smell, meat that maggots wouldn't touch, and there was moldering hide and hair in it as well, worse even than the stench of hair burning. It got in the nose and worked its way clear back into your skull where it lodged under your eyes and wouldn't leave.

"Bone collector, are you?" Link asked. "Long haul from here to a railroad, ain't it?"

Link had come across bone piles at rail sidings during his trips—mountains of cattle and buffalo bones waiting to be shipped to factories to be ground into fertilizer. A couple of times he had encountered the wagons of bone pickers, those highly odorous individuals who scoured the grasslands for animal skeletons. But he had never seen one with an Indian wife, nor with a hybrid travois for a cart.

From downstream came a softly heard whinny and a long, sighing noise as the spirit of the horse rose out of the arroyo to go run with the ponies of the Arapahoes in their ghostly eternal herds. At the sound the men looked up, then went back to eating.

"Vision woman, her," Two Nose said. "Started 'way back upon a time when she first adopts a black scantlin' from a passin' wagon pilgrim, an' gits a medicine dream sayin' she's to raise the cub like he wuz her own. But he's no sooner growed big 'nuff to get hisself a name than he up an' follers 'nother vision inta th' mountains. Some seasons after, we're gone to trade at Pueblo an' she gets a dream sayin' most of her people was wiped out. Never seen the tribe again. We two packed our possibles an' lit out. What's it gone now? Near twenty year, mebbe? Allus lookin' fer th' black papoose with th' one eye."

"Black, you said?" The mountain man's story hadn't been as clear as it might have been.

"*Waugh*. Little negra fella left fer dead by one of them wagon trains. Blacker'n a lickerish stick. Crows Woman mothered 'im till he's purty much half growed. Howsomever, he went an' got hisself crosswise to the Arapaho spirit woman an' had to hump it fer the hills. Never seed 'im ag'in."

Link kept his eyes on the meat pot, the brim of his hat hiding the fact that Two Nose had startled him. He thought he had an idea where Two Nose and Crows Woman might find a black, one-eyed man who had gone to the mountains. But he would keep quiet until he was more certain. He was curious about this spirit woman, too, but for now it seemed sensible to just keep quiet or change the talk to something else.

"Now you're collectin' bones, instead of trapping," Link said. "Or maybe doing some trading?"

"*Was* a trader, thank 'ee. Tried m'hand at trappin' when I first come inta the country, but trappin' don't shine with this ol' coon. Wadin' them frozen cricks, hunkerin' in winter camp till yore jints freeze, poor bull fer meat . . . *waugh!* Me, I takes to tradin', instead, an' purty soon winter found me cached with th' Arapahoes. Warmer lodges y'ain't about to find. Antelope stew and plenty. Do enough tradin' to keep a man in 'baccy and DuPont, what else y'want?"

"Hard work, though, collecting bones," Link observed

"Doin' it 'cause of her medicine," Two Nose said, nodding at the Indian woman who had come back to the fire. With eyes so dark they seemed fathomless, she stared into Link's face until he sensed she was trying to find something in his thoughts, probing his mind for something she already knew was there. But she kept her peace.

"Big vision she had, two, mebbe three moons after th' massacre. Three days an' nights it took her jus' to see th' whole of it, so she says."

"What kind of vision?" Link asked, spearing another piece of meat for himself.

"Y' heerd of Six Grandfathers?"

"Maybe."

"Arapaho powers. Six Grandfathers livin' in the sky somewheres. Crows Woman an' me is comin' back with trade goods an' a dream tells her that most of her people is massacred. We lights out to other direction, like I said, and she goes to slashin' herself for grievin', then commences fastin' for grief. Never heerd such a wailin' as she done. Outta her head nigh on four nights, like ol' Bill Williams th' time he et them purty night-bloomin' flowers down on the Heely. Afterward she tells me the Grandfathers come to her, from th' sky y'unnerstan', an' told her what to do."

Two Nose was finished eating. He wiped his knife on his buckskins before sliding it back into its deep sheath, and then leaned back on an elbow to pick his teeth with one finger. "They give Crows Woman the gift of knowin' where buffler bones be a-layin'," he continued. "All over the peraira, all up in th' hills, everywhere. We finds a set o' bones, an', quick ez fire comes to flint, she knows everythin' about that buffler . . . what herd they was from, how they went under, all of it. Even knewed y'was comin' to help us git some more bone, *waugh!*"

There was only quiet in the arroyo. Only quiet. The woman stirred a pot over the fire and moved about the camp, but there was no sound from the stirring and no sound of a footfall. The small trickle of a creek went on flowing away, but hushed into silence. The mules stood dozing in their harness, soundless. Two Nose seemed to pause as if letting the silence sink in as part of his story, then broke into the quiet again.

"Yore a-wondering what she does with 'em bones? Waal, I'll tell 'ee. We finds only them as was the *big* animules, y'unnerstan, those as was leader bulls and grandmother cows like them heads y'see on the cart yonder. Gathers up their bones. Then we carts 'em off to a place she knows, only I don't go all th' way inta it. Me not bein' The People, y'unnerstan. She goes the last bit alone. She lays out them

71

bones an' skulls an' puts 'em all back togither jus' like they was a herd still livin'. Crows Woman tells me there's hunnerds and hunnerds o' buffler lyin' in that place, all pointin' east, all there. It must surely be a sight, all them buffler skeletons all put back to gither in a herd."

"What's it for?"

"Hah? I ast that, too. Accordin' to Crows Woman, there's gonna one day come a sign o' some description, mebbe some big Indian honcho who's a-goin' to come along with great powers, y'unnerstan, some time . . . this here's a prophecy, y'unnerstan . . . an' he's gonna make all them buffler rise up an' thet whole herd's spose'd to start a-walkin' east, gatherin' up more ghost buffler as they goes, tramplin' over the whites and their square houses. She got a vision of all the buffler bein' back and tramplin' down the cities an' all the whites bein' gone. Her spirit people, medicine folk, all o' 'em been layin' out buffler bones fer many a winter."

"And I'm supposed to help with that?" Link asked incredulously.

"Yep. No 'sposed about it. Ye'll do it. This here hoss learnt long moons back not to fight th' rope when it comes to 'Rapaho medicine. Crows Woman says ye'll do this er that, and y'do."

Two Nose signaled the end of the meal and conversation by issuing a loud belch. Link stabbed his knife into the sand to clean off the grease and then wiped the blade on his boot before putting it away.

Crows Woman gestured for the two men to join her next to the fire. She put branches of green sage on the embers to make a thick, pungent smudge. She showed Link how to gather smoke between his cupped hands and how to wipe it up and down his body as if bathing in it. He followed her example, but it didn't help much. The stench of decaying bones and rotting meat still clung to every part of him.

"Nothing personal," he said later as he watched Two Nose and Crows Woman roll out their blankets under the larger of the two bone carts, "but I think I'll sleep upwind a ways."

"Figgered ye would," Two Nose chuckled. "Couple days er three an' y'won't notice the smell ennymore."

"Couple days?"

"Well," Two Nose said, "y'need ter git inta Ehre's Hole, didn't y'say?"

"Don't think I *did* say."

"Thet's where yore friends cached the last couple o' nights. Y'kin pick up their trail there. Thet's where we're headin'."

Link was up at first light and out of the arroyo on his own, following the dirt track road that would lead to Ehre's Hole. Maybe Two Nose Thomas and Crows Woman had the rest of *their* lives to get there, but he had no time to lose. He walked with determination, watching for any kind of sign of a horse he could catch. By the time the sun rose enough to warm his back, however, his blistered feet were so painful that he could only limp along.

Behind him he heard the sound of heavy wooden wheels and stepped out of the track as Two Nose came lumbering up, driving the lead cart, Crows Woman following in the hybrid travois. The mules seemed to drop off to sleep as soon as Two Nose brought them to a standstill.

"Git up an' ride!" he called. "Ye'll git used ter the smell in no time a-tall."

"Where's that town you talked about?" Link asked.

Two Nose pointed off at an angle to the road. "Yonder,"

he said. "Road cuts 'round the hill here. Town's thet direction, though."

"I figure I'll take the short way across through the brush, then," Link said. He limped off into the sage and yucca, leaving the carts to plod along the road.

At mid-morning they caught up with him again, sitting on a rock, trying to wrap a foot with a strip of cloth cut from his shirttail.

"Better git up an' ride," Two Nose repeated. "Ye kin cut acrost the brush ag'in, if thet's whar yore stick floats, but y'still got you a longish way to walk."

"Your road seems to take ten miles of switchbacks just to go two," Link said. "I'm doing all right the way I am."

Again he resumed walking through sand and among the bushes, watching out for the pointy spikes of low-growing cactus. *Any horse,* he kept thinking. *If I find any horse in that damn' town, I'm taking it one way or another.* He came into an opening in the sage, a place where the grass stood instead of the monotonous drab brush. A sort of animal trail led in the direction he wanted, but it was so overgrown that it was hard to see. He made good time, but his feet were paying a terrible price for it. His socks felt sopping wet, but whether it was with blood or with the juice from his busted blisters, he didn't want to know.

By the time Link limped and stumbled down the hard slope and encountered the bone wagon again, he was done. His pride lay somewhere back among the yucca, along with the stubborn self-reliance that kept him staggering along under the hot sun. No longer did he smile grimly whenever he felt the weight of the Colt on his hip; no longer did he mentally rehearse the coming showdown when he would shoot the men who abducted Gwen. Now he thought only of an end to the pain and the heat and the hunger. He was ready to pay the price, whatever it might be. But *if*, he told himself, only *if* by paying that price could he continue on. There was no question of quitting, no matter how bad it got.

This time Two Nose said nothing. When the mules stopped, Link wordlessly climbed up onto the hard plank of a seat on the cart and held on as Two Nose clucked to the animals and the cart resumed its lurching and swaying along the dirt track. In the late afternoon they stopped beside a sluggish stream where the mules drank as if they had never seen water before. Link soaked his feet. Two Nose and Crows Woman conversed in low tones, then came to where Link was seated on the stream bank.

"Nearly there," Two Nose said. "Crows Woman's gonna git you fed an' outfitted, an' I'm a-goin' on ahead inter town to scout 'er out."

Link wanted to protest, but couldn't find a reason. Riding on the cart, punished by the pain in his body, surrounded by the stench, lulled by the rocking and bumping, he was in a daze like a man who's been sitting in a saloon and drinking for so long that he can't remember why he should get up and go.

Two Nose slung his shooting bag over his shoulder, picked up his antique long rifle, and walked away with the long and purposeful strides of a far younger man. Crows Woman brought Link a gourd filled with a kind of cold soup with chunks of meat in it. She brought pemmican and a chunk of hard bread and slices of a tough white root like a turnip, only with the texture of a manila rope.

After he had eaten, Crows Woman dug around among the stuff in the smaller cart and came up with a parfleche bag from which she withdrew a pair of hand-stitched deerskin pants, saggy and stained and much in need of patching.

She took out a stinking brown serape or poncho, a worn-out buckskin hunting frock, a pair of reasonably intact moccasins, and a long wide sash that once had been red. Now it was more brown, like the color of dried blood.

She held them out to him one by one, these pieces of clothing, so that he would see what they were. And he saw what she was after. The very thought of it almost made his gorge rise hot in his throat, but it made sense. She was offering him a disguise, a way to ride the cart right into the middle of town without being challenged. If it worked, and Gwen and the others were still being held there, he might be able to take the whole gang before they figured out who he was. So he put aside his California pants, his store-bought shirt and boots, his Stetson and all, and donned the smelly leathery rags of Two Nose Thomas. He had to admit that the soft moccasins felt better on his sore feet. Crows Woman took a square of gingham trade cloth from the parfleche and tied it on his head like a kerchief. But she was dissatisfied with how he looked and so she again rummaged in the cart's cargo until she located a wide-brimmed hat, the shapeless floppy kind favored by old mountain men and young farm boys. It hid Link's eyes effectively; even his nose was lost in the shadow of the brim.

"*Waugh!*" exclaimed Two Nose when he returned. "Injin moccasins an' all! I'd a-took ye fer a one o' Bent's boys, so I would. Ye look fit to set at meat with eny hibernaut as ever lifted Pawnee ha'r or drunk Towse lightnin.' "

"The pants are too long," Link observed, but Two Nose just laughed.

"Thet's the mountain way to wear yore leggin's," he said. "Draggin' behint like thet, they wipe out yore tracks!"

Two Nose was still laughing at his own joke as he took

the bread and meat proffered by Crows Woman. Between bites, he told about his scouting trip to town.

"Waal, didn' I Injin m'way thru the gulch 'round all them buildings en such! Come out to other side an' doubled back down th' street like as if I was jus' strollin' in from out them hills yonder. Slick ez ba'r grease! Went right up to the liv'ry an' out thisaway like ez if jus' passin' through."

"See anything?" Link asked. "Big passenger wagon, maybe, like a coach without a top to it? Women and kids in nice clothes, anything like that?"

"Nah. Tracks lead out, to other side o' town. Good wagon tracks follered by shod horses. Headed toward Gorre, I figger. Nobody left 'cept the booshways and sech. Them, and a rear guard."

"Hah?" Link said.

"Thar's three skunks they left bchin' at the hotel. I seen 'em. Stopped to the livery, kinda casual-like, askin' after eny cayuses fer sale, y'see. Fella says no, nuthin' fer sale. I says it looks like plenty o' tracks in the dirt fer havin' no hosses, an' he says ez how there was a buncha riders . . . and that wagon . . . left yesterday. Three of 'em stayed, sez he." Two Nose stuck a piece of meat in his mouth and chewed thoughtfully. "I seen 'em, directly I shambled past thet hotel. *Vacho hombres* like yoreself, givin' their haunches a rest on the porch an' smokin' roll-ups. Figger they're keepin' a eye on their back trail a while."

"Three of them," Link repeated, drawing his Colt from under the ragged poncho and checking the cylinder.

"Shootin' 'em might jus' not be yore best play, I'm thinkin'."

"Hah?"

"This here hoss, he's jus' a ol' trader an' trapper an'

*mebbe* he don't know his own scat from grizzly snot. But sometime, a-huntin' up in th' hills, I'd come acrost a lone aniymule and figger I'd kill it an' git me one good wolf robe er a painter hide er a bear skin. Then the ol' dream gourd would git to workin' and I'd cipher a while. I oughter track thet loner back to the den instead, an' git me th' whole passel. Mebbe you'd oughta better make these here two-legged coyotes think nobody's follerin' 'em. Then foller 'em. Thar's even a slick way to do it . . . you and Crows Woman go inter town an' pay 'em no mind a-tall, jus' go on about yore bizness, an' I'll take to other rig 'round town se-cret-like an' watch th' road. 'Tween the two of us, we'll purty soon savvy where they're headed."

"I'm not real clear on what our business *is*," Link said.

"Medicine tells Crows Woman they's a granddaddy buffler thar. Wandered too close to town, y'savvy, an' the booshway put lead through 'is lights an' butchered him out. The bones ez in a gulch whar they throws all the ol' bones an' such like."

"Why don't you and her just go in and get them, then?"

"An ol' grayback with nuthin' but a Green River an' a ol' front-filler Hawken, comin' in with a squaw? The squatter in thet cabin'd run us off fer sure."

"Why would he treat me anythin' different?" Link asked, looking down at his own sorry rags.

"He ain't always been cached up in a shack on thet gulch, y'savvy. Time was he rode fer yore own outfit! Yes, sir! Before yore time. But he'll reckon y'fer a companyero right enuf, soon's y'tell 'im yore a Keystone waddie."

"How come you know all this?" Link asked.

"Crows Woman an' me, we fust come here two seasons back an' got run out ag'in. Went on about doin' bizness

78

elsewheres, but she keeps prayin' and talkin' with the Six Grandfathers an' by-an'-by she tells me . . . 'Two Nose, soon a *wasichu* rider comes to take the travois for the old one.' Old one's thet buffler, y'savvy. 'He will know the bent one,' she says to me. An' by bent one she's meanin' thet ol' cowboy a-livin' there. Then she gets her a dream and sees how the ol' boy hez a mark on his riggin', an', when she draws it in the sand fer me, I whoops out . . . 'By the bull barley! Thet be the Keystone Brand, so it does!' So she knows you're the one, all right. Y'best haul yoreself back inta yore royal chariot ag'in and we'll get 'er done."

Once more Link felt he would do anything, face any kind of odds, rather than climb into the swaying seat of the putrid-smelling bone wagon. It was against all he had ever known about himself since the first day his father had lifted him into a saddle. There's just things a horseman don't do, the older cowboys told him. He don't walk if there's a horse anywhere nearby. He don't ride little donkeys. He don't ride lame or sick horses. And the only time he drives a team is when it's needed to carry feed to the herd in wintertime or to spark a pretty woman.

He belonged to a frontier aristocracy, a select group of men who were master horsemen and who seemed born to the gun in a world of cattle and horses and little else except far open spaces. Cattle raising may have been only a business, but it had its own rigid social order. At the top of it were men such as himself, men who attracted natural respect wherever they went. They knew each other instantly when they met and others knew them, too.

Below Link and his peers in this ranking were cowboys who the trail drive cook might ask to go in search of firewood, or ones the foreman might select to go search for strayed horses. On the next level were other men, competent with horse and lariat, who were either young and inexperienced or had flaws concerning liquor or gambling or women. These were given the task of riding the green off the spookier horses in the cavvy yard; around the ranch they could expect to find themselves stretching fence and cleaning ditches.

It was not that the top hands ever refused to do any sort of work. Indeed, they might volunteer to do so. If it was needed, they would climb up and repair a windmill atop a high tower or strip off shirts and pitch in to dig a pit in order to bury some unfortunate animal. But it was understood that no one would *ask* such duty of them. When men of Link's caliber volunteered to take a team and scraper to help with the springtime ditch work or lasso a log and drag it to the cook wagon, it was regarded as a thing that should be done, even looked upon as a generous gesture coming from a noble spirit. It enhanced rather than diminished their reputation. When men—and women—spoke of "honor" and "code", when they spoke in respectful tones about the very best of Western men, it was about men such as Link that they spoke.

They wouldn't recognize him now, covered in evil-smelling cast-off leather and rags, hiding his face under a torn and shapeless old hat—itself reeking like sour milk—traveling into a town on a bone cart. Back on the Keystone there was a honey wagon with which the stable boys hauled manure, the most degrading job on the ranch. But compared with this bone wagon on which he now rode, the Keystone honey wagon seemed like a hero's chariot.

Following Two Nose's scheme, Link got into the cart again and Crows Woman drove it to a small house near the edge of a gully behind town. In a rocker on the porch of that small house sat a small old man sucking on a cold pipe and staring off into the sage flats. Crows Woman drove the creaking, jolting old wagon past the place and downwind a good distance before bringing the mules to a halt. Link jumped down to walk back to the house. Between the unfamiliar moccasins and his torn-up feet, he limped along like he had aged into a cripple himself. The old man seemed not to have heard the rattling din of the bones bouncing in the cart, nor did he seem to pay the smell any mind. It was not until Link said the word "Keystone" that he blinked and moved his head.

With agonizing patience, Link carefully primed the conversation. Ten minutes went by as the old man recited his story of coming out from Missouri to be a cowboy. While his monologue droned on, a few townspeople showed up at the edge of the dirt street to stare at the bone wagon and the Indian woman on it. They held their noses and fanned the air with their hands. Link went on listening, saying very little, trying to sneak glances at the people in case he could spot the outlaws among them.

More time passed. Link steered the talk around to the bull buffalo that had been killed near town some two or three years ago. The old man told of seeing the great herds of buffalo as a young man, of hearing the thunder of their hoofs as they ran the prairie. He spoke of stampedes, of outlaws, of Indian attacks. He recalled the time young Pendragon came along, he said, with nothing but an axe and a cap-and-ball six-gun. The old cowboy seemed to recall all manner of things, even things that had to have taken place long before he had been on the prairie.

Finally there came an opening, a chance for Link to mention the buffalo again and ask if the Indian woman might look in the gully for its bones. They're sacred to her people, he explained, but the old man just eyed him with deep suspicion.

"You come all this way jus' to help some Injun collect bones?" he said.

"You bein' an old Keystone rider, you probably already know what I'm doin' here," Link replied. He did not point, but with a slight movement of his head and with a flick of his eyes he gave the old man to understand he was indicating the knot of townspeople standing not too far off. "Outlaws took Mister Pendragon's wife and some women and children," Link whispered. "Some of 'em might be right here in Ehre's Hole. I need to track 'em back to their place."

"Any more Keystone riders comin'?" the old man whispered back. Link thought he saw a glimmer in the old eyes.

"Plenty of Keystone riders," Link said. "It might be a few days, though."

Crows Woman, seeing Link and the old man in quiet talk for so long, got down from the wagon and began making trips into the gully and bringing back bones to place in the wagon. Some townspeople edged closer to look down at her as she sorted through the pile of animal débris.

Three men showed up to cast sneering glances down at Crows Woman before stepping out away from the other people to watch Link talking to the old man. The three stood with their hats pushed back and their thumbs hanging in their gun belts. The one they called Slick seemed particularly curious about the figure in the filthy leathers who had ridden in on the bone wagon.

"Reckon who that is?" he said to his confederates.

"Nope."

"You remember me and Army tellin' about the time we went to North Platte, when we got a can tied to our tail by a cowboy?"

"Y'mean when y'went after the whole town's horse herd and came damn' near gettin' yourselves caught?"

"Yeah, but we got away. But the day before, we was havin' our little fun showin' them city feather merchants how real cowboys can shoot, and a couple of goody-goody bastards spoilt it all. Busted my gun, shot my hand, everything. Well, right over there I think we're lookin' at one of those sons-of-bitches that done for us."

"What makes y'think so?" his companion argued. "I figure that stinkin' horse turd over yonder is nothin' but a down-an'-out bunch-quitter, prob'ly a drinker. Why else do that kinda work? Just a range bum. Worse'n a range bum, if y'ask me."

"Could be he got himself fired. Sure does look down on his uppers. You jus' wait till he tips his head up. It's that big black mustache. He carries a lot of muscle for a range bum, too. Pretty sure it's him."

"If it *is* him, y' gonna call him out?"

"Let's see what kinda fun we can have with him," Slick said. "We got all the time in the world, ain't we? We still gotta wait around to see if that one we shot out in the brush shows up."

# Chapter Five

There is but one road that leads to Corinth.
*Marius the Epicurean*, Chapter 24
Walter Pater

One of the three rustlers spat on the ground, wiped his mouth with the back of his hand, hooked his thumb back into his gun belt, and began to taunt the man they saw as a fallen cowboy. He was not just another pitiful derelict of the cattle range; to them he represented an affront to "real" range riders such as themselves.

"Didya see what that one mule jus' dropped behint 'im?" he said loudly enough for everyone to hear him. He wasn't looking at the mule. He was looking at the foul-smelling creature standing in the dust of the road.

"Them mules must not been feedin' too good lately," said the one called Banks. "That's 'bout the sickliest-lookin' pile o' shit I ever seen."

The third man, Hodge Perkins, spoke in a high-pitched voice that seemed to wheeze out of his nose. "If this was *my* town, now," he whinnied, "I'd make thet squaw there clean up that mess an' git rid of it. Somethin' like that on the streets jus' plain puts people off, that's what I say."

They stood nervously, tensely, looking back and forth at one another for support and looking at the little knot of townspeople for approval. There was no disapproval from that group and no reaction from the stinking, crippled-looking figure in the filthy poncho. And so they went on.

"How do y's'pose it'd be," said Banks, "for a man to be ridin' behind ol' long-ears all day long, waitin' for the next load to drop?"

"Don' want to know." Perkins giggled. "No *real* man'd ever sit on sich a outfit as thet. But I know I'd druther watch thet mule's butt all day then to have to look at thet homely ol' squaw. *Thet's* for sure."

The other two guffawed at their comrade's wit.

"I'm surprised she don't make him ride with them bones," said the one named Whyte. "That smell'd make a maggot give up on meat an' go to eatin' grass. Mebbe he needs to git stripped down and dunked in the horse tank." Whyte laughed again and looked around quickly to see who all was enjoying the cleverness of his wit.

"Puttin' him in th' horse tank'd likely make the hosses sick," Perkins added.

More laughter. Whyte and Perkins were taking their lead in this game of verbal abuse from Slick Banks, partly because he was more or less the leader and because he had run into this man before, or so he said. Of the three of them, he was the most likely to know how far to push. Banks, uncertain whether the bone-collecting bum was carrying a gun, made no move to start a gunfight. He preferred to stand and taunt.

"Is that broken-down mule pullin' one of them fancy new sulky carts y'hear about?" he asked his pals. "I heerd that Easterners was drivin' such contraptions, but I never seen the like."

"You oughta move in and get you a closer look at it, Slick," Perkins snickered.

"Not *me*," Banks said. "Eny closer to thet gawd-awful stink and I'd have to burn my clothes. What in hell do you s'pose would make a man ride on such a contraption as that? Looka them wheels. Must 'a' been hacked outta a tree by Noah hisself."

Link turned with very careful slowness, keeping his face hidden in the drooping brim of Two Nose's old hat. His neck burned under the rough wool of the poncho and his hand itched for the butt of his Colt. But he kept his head bowed and shoulders slumped. He kept his eyes on the dirt at his feet as he hobbled toward the cart like an old deaf cripple who only wanted to be left alone.

"Hey, bone picker!" Steve called. "Tell me sumthin'! You hump yore squaw right there on top o' the bones, or do y'crawl under it when y'wanna go at it? Which way smells better for y'?"

Steve's sidekicks chortled loudly, and he grinned back at them, reveling in their approval.

Link's eyes glared hot beneath the hat brim where they were hidden from the three tormentors. Under the dragging legs of the leather pants his toes curled hard through the soles of his moccasins to get a grip on the soft ground. His right hand became a stiff claw inside the poncho as his fingers opened over the butt of the Colt. All down his back and along his legs his muscles tensed, ready suddenly to twist around into a crouch with his gun blasting. His mind already saw the three rustlers stretched out, kicking in the dust.

In another few seconds the range would have been free of three undesirables, had Crows Woman not called out to him at that moment.

*"Was'che'oha!"* she shouted from the gully.

Without relaxing a muscle and without taking his hand away from the gun, Link forced his head around to look down at her. She was struggling to carry the buffalo's skull, a massive thing with thick curving horns. She rested it against her leg and waved for him to come help.

"Reckon thet purty li'l squaw of your'n *needs* somethin'," Steve said loudly, unaware he had been a split second away from death.

"Better run and go see, bone picker!" Hodge Perkins wheezed. "Don't keep 'er waitin'! She's liable to lodgepole y'if y'dally eny!"

"C'mon, Hodge," Banks said. "C'mon Steve. Let's git goin'. The stink from that pile of shit's 'bout to gimme a headache."

Link's fingers closed down and felt the pattern in the pistol grips and the cool steel of the frame. The hand caressed the metal lightly, taking comfort in it, lingering over it. The gun seemed to whisper to his hand: "*Now!* Take back your honor!" Link was frozen in the moment, his hand saying one thing and one thing only. His mind fought for control by throwing out images of *other* men, men worse than these, the men who were taking Gwen Pendragon and her friends away to God knows where. His trigger finger curled into the trigger guard and his thumb felt for the familiar curve and roughness of the Colt's hammer. His mind said *later* and showed him another time for revenge, a better time and a better revenge. So in the end he did not draw his gun and fire. These three had to remain alive so their trail would lead him to Gwen and the others.

He did not turn his eyes upon them. He let them walk away oblivious of the fact that they had been on the very verge of bloody death. Now ignoring them, Link stepped over the edge of the gully to slip and slide down to the bottom. There he took hold of one of the great thick horns as Crows Woman took the other, and together they hoisted its weight between them and struggled back up the bank.

She took care not to drag it through the dirt, although it would have made the job easier. Easier, but not fitting. It was not the Indian way to allow any remnant of the sacred bison to be dragged in the dirt.

Banks, Steve, and Perkins started back toward the town's main street—its only street, come to that—but looked back in time to see Link and Crows Woman straining to lift the huge bison skull into the wagon. Overcome with sudden bravado, or perhaps with lingering resentment of his treatment back at North Platte, Banks turned back and walked up to them with his gun in his hand.

"You!" he said. He was certain that this stinking specimen in front of him was indeed the man from North Platte. His brain was having a hard time figuring out what had changed him, but something sure had. Liquor, most likely. But it was the same man, the same swaggering Keystone cowboy who had taken his gun away from him and knocked him to the ground in front of dozens of other men. Seeing him fallen on hard times infuriated and pleased him all at the same time.

"Now thet y'got yore smelly bones, I want you an' yore ugly squaw to climb back on yore pile of junk and whip up them damn' stinking animals and git th' hell outta my sight." For emphasis he cocked the hammer and aimed the revolver at the center of Link's chest. "Right now, I said. Git up there inta yore cart, squaw man."

Link didn't look up to stare into the mocking eyes, but he did look at the hand holding the gun and saw it quivering. It could flinch on the trigger—just once—and Link would be nothing but a pile of rags twisting and holding his guts in the middle of an uncaring street. He couldn't make himself stop staring at the muzzle of that gun until he put one hand on the rough wooden wheel and steadied himself. His legs and arms hauled him up into the cart where he crawled on all fours over the bones until he was all the way in, all the way to the front of the jumbled mass. There he turned around to sit with his back against the crooked poles while Crows Woman gathered up the lines and climbed onto the seat and slapped the sleepy mules into movement.

"Let's git the hell back to Gorre," Banks said to the other two, fully loud enough for Link to hear him. "They ain't gonna be any Keystone riders follerin' us. Reckon they ain't such a tough outfit no more. Probl'y all of 'em gone to farmin' er makin' ladies' hats."

Their laughter burned into Link's mind. *So you're headed for Gorre,* he thought. *Well, go and be damned. The next time I hear those laughs, I'll kill you.*

They walked off to collect their horses, casting backward glances at the reeking pile of rags sitting under his big shaggy hat atop the pile of bones. Link tried to plan their deaths, deaths that would be long in coming and echoing with their wails of unspeakable fear. But his mind betrayed him; he could make images of the Colt recoiling hard into the heel of his hand as it spit fire and lead, but instantly the image would drift off into empty blackness. It was if the hand holding that gun belonged to some other man, in some other time, and had nothing to do with him.

Another hand reached through the palings and touched him. Link looked up. It was the old Keystone rider. He had left his rocker on the cabin porch to walk alongside the cart. The hand reaching in to touch Link was wrinkled and scarred and soft from age.

"You all right, then?" the ancient rider croaked in a broken voice.

"Hah?" was all Link could say.

" 'T'ain't so bad, after a time," the old man said. "People give y'odd jobs, invite y'to meals sometimes. You'll be all right. After a time, people jus' fergit you're there. Makes it easier then, livin' with it. Not bein' a rider enymore, I mean."

Crows Woman looked straight ahead, holding the lines. Leaning with bowed necks into the makeshift harness, the mules dragged their awkward load back to the road and out the other side of town. The heavy hand-hewn wheels jolted down into the ruts and the slow swaying rhythm of the cart resumed. After a few minutes the three outlaws came past, deliberately quirting their horses to churn up a choking dust. They laughed and whooped and spat at the creature in the cart. But they didn't stop to torment him, and Link was grateful for that. His mind had gone as numb as his reflexes. He knew that Gwen and the others were now far beyond any help he could give.

Somehow he had to get a horse and get himself cleaned up and put on his own clothes again. He knew everything he needed to know, now. The cart had served its purpose and he could be done with it. But he had not counted on it making him lose so much. Link tried to shake off the gloom, tried to straighten his back and sit erect. He had to concentrate now on getting a horse.

They had just barely driven far enough to be out of sight of the town when Two Nose Thomas's own cart suddenly pulled out of a draw and intercepted them.

"How y'be?" he said as casually as if it was just another chance encounter. "Now thet them coyotes is gone, mebbe we kin stop an' bile coffee. This hoss's meat paunch ez hollerin' fer fodder."

Two Nose left his cart and went into the brush for dry

twigs, which he heaped up next to the road. He mashed dry grass into a little nest, filling the nest with dry leaves he crushed almost to powder. Then with a few deft swipes of his flint striker, he set the leaves and grass to smoldering and blew into it until it flared up. Crows Woman got out the coffee pot and filled it with water from a skin she had hanging on the travois. Link only sat on his pile of bones in the cart and watched them. Two Nose kept up a steady monologue as he worked, but Link listened with little interest.

"Waal," Two Nose said as he hunkered next to the little blaze and watched the flames lick the sides of the pot, "hyar's a hoss as hez been a-doin' bizness like a booshway, ain't he! Back thar 't edge o' town, didn't he jump a farmer what hez a purty fair horse an' saddle rig fer sale? 'Course, y'need to git sixty dollars American, lessen yore cipherin' on makin' 'er a moonlight trade. An' thar's more news, yes, sir. Didn' thet same corn shucker offer this ol' coon a swaller o' alkyhol if I wuz to make a dicker 'come' fer thet hoss? Thar we be, tradin' drinks o' his corn likker . . . an' *didn'* it warm th' innards! . . . when lookee hyar! Up comes 'nother o' them dirt-diggin' terrapins from th' next farm over, and 'Say,' sez he, 'this hyar's a day fer visiters, fer certain sure. Dang, if there ain't a fancy rider in th' booshway's store, buyin' supplies and askin' after a tall *hombre* with a black mustache and six-gun.' "

Link looked up, startled. "Who . . . ?" he began.

Two Nose stirred the grounds of the coffee and reached for a cup. "Wantin' to keep an' eye skinned fer enythin' lookin' like a friend, this hoss ankled back to the booshway's real easy-like and took him a look at thet stranger." Two Nose filled a second cup and offered it through the bars to Link, who still sat motionless in the cart. "Fancy-lookin' character *he* was," Two Nose continued. "All kinda silver doodads on his vest an' a big ol' silver hatband on his *sombrero*. Had them big ol' spurs with jinglebobs on 'em, *waugh!*"

*Pasque?* Link thought. *Sounds like Pasque.*

"*Waugh!*" Two Nose said again. "Thar he be, shore as my firestick has a hindsight!"

Along the road at a nice easy trot came the very man himself, spurs jingling. It was Pasque. He was not riding Messenger but one of the ranch horses, a strong buckskin. Link stared at him, and then looked away in humiliation.

Pasque smiled and touched his hat at Crows Woman and Two Nose and started to go around their carts, but then his eye fell on the figure hunkering in the travois cart. Through the palings the shadowy lump looked to be little more than a pile of old hides carelessly tossed there—until it raised its head and gazed at him from under the shaggy hat.

His friend's face told Link as much about his own appearance as if he had looked into a mirror.

"*Dios!*" Pasque said. "Link? Link! What in the name of . . . ? What happened to *you?* It *is* you, yes?" Pasque suddenly looked back at the old mountain man and the Indian woman and his hand went to his gun as his horse danced sideways from the strange-smelling thing in the cart.

"Are you hurt, *amigo?* These two are taking you . . . where?"

"Hullo, Pasque," Link said. "They're just helpin' me, that's all. Was tryin' to get to Gwen and her friends."

"Where *is* Gwen? Have you seen her with the others?"

"They're gone, I guess," the shabby figure mumbled. "Looks as if the bastards took 'em up to that Gorre Valley place. Left a rear guard back in that town there."

"And you dealt with them? I did not see anyone in town

who did not seem as if he belonged there. How many did you kill? Were you hit?"

Pasque could not believe he was really talking to Link Lochlin. But he was.

"No," the raspy voice said. "I let 'em go on by. Two Nose's idea, there. There's three of 'em. They just came by here less than a half hour ago, headin' west. We figured . . . me and Two Nose . . . we figured we'd let 'em lead us to Gorre. Where's Art and them?"

"Who is to know? I hoped they'd be here by now. Art must be champing at the bit to be here, but there are the others, *verdad?* No doubt they hold him back. Some of them wish to organize a regular army to attack the place, which takes much time. Much time."

"How'd you find me, then?"

"You? Oh, I tracked *you* to where you made a fire in the sage. I, too, stopped there for several hours to build a good smudge fire to show them where to come. But no sign of them did I see. I took even more time to mark my trail, following you and leaving marks for them. Finally came across your horse dead in the arroyo. *My* horse, I guess it was. Never seen anything like that."

"Hah?"

"The way you killed it. Or somebody killed it."

"What'd it look like?" Link said.

"You don't know? Laid out facing east and arranged like it just lay down to rest. Like it could wake up and run away. Lines of rocks leading out from it in four directions. And the paint. Somebody painted a circle around its eye and put a handprint on the flank like an Indian pony. Nose was streaked with yellow paint of some kind."

"S'posed to be pollen," Two Nose said, coming up to the horseman and the man in the cart. He was carrying another battered enamel cup that he handed to Pasque. He offered a lump of heavy bread as well, but Pasque waved it away. Two Nose shrugged and bit into it himself.

"Reckon she didn't have no pollen in her possibles poke," he went on with his mouth half full and chewing. "But war paint shines 'bout as good. She allus carries it. It's fer th' buffler bones, y'know. It was her fixed yore cayuse to run with th' Injun ponies, comes The Risin'. Them magic circles 'round th' eyes make it so's it kin see 'em, over in th' other world. Th' Injun brand she put thar so's they'll know 'im."

"Risin'?"

"Risin'. Accordin' to her medicine, as soon as what's left o' her people get through gettin' all the butchered animals rounded up an' laid out th' sacred way, why *waugh!* Ain't *thar* gonna be a time! All us white *wasichus* are jus' gonna up an' vanish like smoke, an' the buffler an' pronghorn an' hosses an' what-not are gonna shake the whol' peraira like thunder!"

There was nothing more to say. Pasque politely sipped at the noxious dark mixture in the cup and regarded Link. Link remained sitting there, both hands around his cup.

"So what now?" Pasque said.

"Crows Woman," Link began, "she's been in the Gorre Valley before. She told Two Nose it's guarded at two passes and there's no way to get in without havin' to fight our way past a whole nest of guns. Hidden in the rocks, they are. But I'm thinking somebody could maybe *sneak* in, if Crows Woman's willing to help. The guards are sure to let her and Two Nose drive these carts into the valley. No reason to stop them. So we hide under some skins in the cart here and get past the guards, then, after it gets good and dark, we find where the main boss is and take 'im. I guess it might work."

Link said nothing of his frightening experience with the three he had already met, or of the risk of them recognizing him in his reeking buckskins and shooting him on sight. He had a feeling they might just let him into their stronghold so they could taunt him some more. But he didn't want to talk about it. He did mention the horse for sale in town.

Pasque studied his friend. Link's voice carried none of the former certainty, none of the old confidence. To be sure, he could imagine Link cleaned up and dressed in his familiar clothes. He could easily remember what he looked like clean-shaven and straight in a saddle. Yet, there was something missing in the picture, something lost about his friend. That characteristic sharp, alert look in his eye seemed gone. Pasque had seen a similar thing in the eye of a *lobo* that some of his *vaqueros* had roped and put into a cage. After a few weeks the wolf's eyes changed. It still snarled at the hands offering it food, but the snarl was without spirit, without life. Out of the cage, it displayed a bravado that made the animal seem bigger than life. But after a time in the cage. . . .

Two Nose gathered the cups and stowed them in the cart, ate the final bite of bread, kicked dirt on the small fire, and resumed his seat on the lead cart.

"I will go back and buy that horse, and then I will catch up with you again," Pasque said. "And I will leave word at Ehre's Hole, for Art and the others to wait in town until they hear from us. When I am returned, we will figure out what to do about getting into Gorre. However, I will tell you one thing now, my *amigo*. *You* may be willing to ride in that stinking *carreta*, but I am not. No matter what. I would rather try to shoot my way into the valley before I would do that."

★ ★ ★ ★ ★

It took little over an hour for Pasque to return to town and bargain for the horse, but when he returned with it, Link refused to leave his pile of bones and discard the reeking leathers and rags he wore. He had sunk back into a condition like a man in a trance, his face wearing the blank expression like Pasque had seen on the faces of the *penitentes* in the Purgatory River country. Rather than try to argue his friend out of this mood, Pasque tied the extra horse behind the cart where Link could see it—hoping it would eventually stir the old *caballero* instincts again—and then he rode on ahead of the little caravan to be sure the tracks of the outlaws did not leave the road.

The early twilight hours found the strange party on the ridgeback of a *cuesta* that stretched for miles in either direction, making a wall out in front of the foothills. The road zigzagged up the steep sage slope until it came to where there was a break in the rocks, a natural pass. From that point they could see that the road crossed two miles or more of open flat valley before coming to another slope, presumably another *cuesta* forming a barricade to another valley. Rather than risk crossing that open space, they decided to pull off and make camp. Link got out of the cart and merely stood there, looking around at the country while Crows Woman and Two Nose unloaded gear and collected firewood.

Pasque dismounted and stretched his back. "Come," he said to Link. "Let's walk up onto the rim and see what might be on the other side." And so saying, Pasque took his small brass telescope from his saddle pocket and led the way, with Link following a dozen paces behind. He had just topped the rim of the *cuestas* when Pasque stopped suddenly and raised the telescope to his eye. He waited for

Link to catch up to him.

"Look there," he said, handing him the telescope and pointing down the slope. A small figure was on foot down below, a figure wearing a skirt. She was staying parallel to the two-track road but well out into the brush as if she wanted to be ready to hide from anyone who might be coming along.

"A woman," Link said, looking through Pasque's telescope. "Carryin' a bundle of some sort. Seems like she's tryin' to avoid the road."

Pasque took another look. *"Sí,"* he agreed. "She has not seen us, but she keeps looking behind her. A runaway. Maybe from Gorre?"

Link seemed to brighten at the suggestion. Out here, away from the cart, standing next to Pasque, he could think more clearly again. "Could be," he said. "Nobody seems to be following her. Maybe she knew how to get out without being spotted. Maybe we could get in that way."

"Tell you what," Pasque said. "I will go back for my horse and ride very quiet to the other end of this outcrop. She will see the smoke of Two Nose's fire and she will try to avoid it. I will make a bet with you that she will climb that landslide place, there, instead." He pointed at the jumble of rock fallen from the cliff. "You hide near there and we will catch her between us. Once she knows who we are, she'll be all right."

Pasque was right. Halfway up the slope the woman stopped and sniffed the air. Her nose had caught the scent of a campfire. Immediately she became more wary and began to change direction, working her way north so as to go unnoticed around whoever was camped up above. Her route now took her up a steep slope of loose rock that threatened to slide out from under her feet with every step.

When finally she struggled over the top and gained the flat slab outcrop that ran along the crest of the cliffs, she found herself trapped between two men, one a shaggy, evil-smelling figure on foot and the other a young, well-dressed man of polite bearing sitting on a good horse. The shabby one frightened her, but the other was obviously a gentleman. It was he who questioned her.

Yes, she had come from the Gorre Valley. Yes, she was running away. And, yes, she knew about the Keystone Ranch. She also knew that it lay north and east of here and was many miles away. It was to the Keystone she was fleeing. However long it took, however far she had to walk, it was upon the Keystone she had fixed her hopes.

Pasque dismounted and gave her water from his canteen. He pointed to the brand on the horse and told her that both of them—yes, that one, too, even though he needed washing—were from the Keystone Ranch. Pasque then gently took her bundle from her and helped her up into his saddle. He handed up the bundle, picked up the reins to lead the horse, and through the gathering twilight they walked through scrub piñon and juniper and among the yucca and rabbitbrush back to the camp of Two Nose Thomas and Crows Woman.

# Chapter Six

And that, unknowing what he did,
He leaped amid a murderous band,
And saved from outrage worse than death
    The Lady of the Land!
  "Love"
  Samuel Taylor Coleridge

"I *have* no name," the woman replied. "Flynt Malin took care of that. To him I was only 'you!' or 'her'. Or nothing at all except just something to look at. My folks are all dead, I guess, and I never knew who they were. As for my stepfather, I won't even say his name, let alone use it as mine. He grew tired of me and gave me over to Flynt Malin without a word."

She was sitting with Link and Pasque, staying upwind of Link. All three of them kept their distance from the carts and bones.

"I was hoping Malin would marry me. But hope is a foolish thing to take into Gorre with you. I finally tricked the curse, though."

"Curse?" Pasque said.

"Yes. I figured out how to do it. I began telling myself I *wanted* to stay there forever. This idea came to me after Malin . . . after he was all through with me. You can look at me and see why. He likes his women pretty and thin, and I'm not pretty and thin any more. Anyway, after he farmed me out, I told that family and everyone else how I wanted to stay in the valley always. I told them I was planning on getting a place of my own somewhere in the valley and raise garden truck and chickens to sell. They liked that. They thought I was very ambitious."

"What do you mean, he farmed you out?"

"Whenever he or one of his gunmen gets tired of a woman, they send her to work on one of the places out in the valley. When they're done with you and don't want you around any more, that's when they want you clear out of sight. So he fixed it for me to go live with that family. I kept saying how it was so peaceful and beautiful there. I even sang, sometimes, and pretended to be very happy where I was. The curse heard me, and pretty soon all I could think about was ways to leave, to get out. The curse wanted me gone."

"And you *did* get out," Pasque said.

"But can't go back. If I went back, I'd get beaten, I know I would. Maybe locked up. That's the way they run things there."

"Will they come after you?"

"I don't think so. Just an ugly mouth to feed. Just trouble, that's all I am."

"Did you see the people he just lately brought in?"

"Only from a distance. I heard he sent the women and kids out on the farms to be watched over. He kept the pretty one and the man who was wounded."

"Where are they?" Link asked.

"In town, at his place. It's the biggest building. House, store, and storehouse all in one."

"Tell me about it," Link said.

She picked up a stick and drew a rough rectangle in the dirt. "This end is his house. There's a porch on the street, kitchen and parlor. Upstairs are four rooms. This part," she said, indicating the rectangle, "is the mercantile store and it's hooked onto the house. Malin keeps two, sometimes three women in his house and makes them work in the Mercantile. He's got peepholes everywhere, so he can spy on them. Next to the store is what used to be a kind of jail and storehouse. Has bars on the windows, thick walls. Three rooms in there. I heard he put the injured man in one and that new woman in another. I heard how she yelled at him and demanded to stay and nurse the wounded man."

"Is that so?" Pasque said. "Sounds like maybe he hasn't, you know, touched her yet."

The runaway woman laughed at that. The two men looked up in surprise at the sound of it, and their puzzled looks only made her laugh the more. She shook her head, took a bite of her food, and continued quietly chuckling.

Link's expression of puzzlement changed to a scowl. Maybe the Keystone people were strangers and meant nothing to her, but still it seemed hard of her to find such open amusement in the possibility that Malin had already had his hands on Gwen. Or one of the other women.

"That's funny," he said, "the idea of what Malin might be doin' with our women?"

"You could say so," she said. "I was there a long time and he never touched me, neither, not the way you mean. All the women who've lived in the house know how Flynt Malin can't perform. All he does is look, and he sure likes to do that. It's why he has all his peepholes. It's like some men need whiskey all the time and some men can't stay away from gambling. Malin sees a pretty figure on a woman and he has to watch her all the time. Sometimes I think it makes him crazy."

"Tell me something," Pasque said. "This, uh, problem

of his. It is part of this curse you talk about?"

"What else could it be?" she replied. "It's just like every-thing else in that damned place. What Flynt wants most he can't have. Neither can Old Malin . . . that's his father. He wants Flynt to get a wife and have kids to carry on with the place after he dies, and *he* won't get it. Nobody in Gorre gets what they want the most."

"You know we need to ride in there and get our friends out, don't you?" Pasque said. "The Keystone and other ranches are sending men. Many, many men."

"I know that. Everyone was talking about it as soon as they found out where the new strangers were from and how Flynt's gang had grabbed them. Everyone is afraid of the Keystone coming with an army of men to drive us out."

"Will any of the people stand against us?" Pasque asked. "If Flynt and his father are so bad, you would think they would welcome someone coming to deal with such men."

"Perhaps, but I don't think so. Flynt Malin has gunmen all around him, all over the valley. The people on the farms, they got guns and they'd *have* to try and stop you. If they didn't, Flynt would make it so their lives wouldn't be worth two bits. You saw the valley entrance?"

"Yeah," Link said. "That gap up there in the hogback. The Indian woman says there are stone huts, for men to shoot from."

"Yes. Off the road, up in the rocks. Three or four guards there, all the time. But," she added, "maybe they'd let you through. Maybe they'd let you ride right on past them, so you'd be in the second valley looking at an even narrower gap in a hogback. More stone guardhouses up there. If you get that far and try to go back, you'd find the gap behind you blocked by rifles, too. It's a trap. Even if you did get in, which you won't, bunches of Flynt's riders are always going up and down the roads and would catch you."

"How'd you get out, then?" Link asked her.

"I just walked past the first guards. They were too lazy to come out into the hot sun just to ask a woman where she thought she was going. They likely thought the guards at the second place would stop me anyway. When I got to the second gap, there were two men came out, men I know pretty well. I told them I didn't want to pass through there. I told them I was carrying stuff to stay out two or three days by myself, and I was going to stay in that little valley. They laughed and said I'd be running back to town as soon as it got dark and I heard the coyotes. They told me there were mountain lions and bears and snakes. Trying to scare me, you know."

"But they let you go on?"

"Yes. They thought it was funny, a woman wanting to go on her own like that. I walked on down the valley to where they couldn't see me. I didn't think it would be so easy to climb up the hill and find a way over that cliff."

"You were lucky," Link said. "What about leaders? Anybody except Malin seem to have a hand in bossing that gang?"

"Probably not. A lot of them ride for Malin just 'cause their family'd go hungry, otherwise. With him, they always seem to be lucky when it comes to stealing cattle and horses. But if he was gone . . . most of them'd probably go back to farming. Or leave Gorre altogether."

Crows Woman silently brought a kettle of stew and some spoons, which she set on the ground between them. When she was gone again, Pasque spoke to Link.

"You gotta get yourself cleaned up, *hombre*," he told his friend. "The way you smell makes me want to shoot you myself."

"Yeah," Link agreed. "I'll go look for some water here directly. But first I want to know how we're supposed to get into that valley."

The runaway put down her spoon, and she looked from one man to the other.

"You're really Keystone riders?" she asked.

"That's right," Pasque said. "I'm Art Pendragon's nephew, in fact."

"You, too?" she asked Link.

"Yep, me, too. Been riding for the Keystone for seven, maybe eight years now. Y'wouldn't know it to look at me now, I know."

"Would this Mister Pendragon take me in, if you told him to?"

"No question about it," Pasque said.

"Help me get a place to live, some way to work for wages?"

"*Sí.* Of course."

"There's others in there, too. Good people, a lot of them. But they're like prisoners and have no hopes left. They need help, too. If I tell you another way into the valley, you'll give me some kind of note to Pendragon, some kind of letter? You'll promise me he'll help us, all of us?"

"*Sí.*" Pasque said. "It will be done, if you help us."

"One more thing."

"What's that?" Link asked.

"You get Flynt Malin out of there first. Don't start a gun war in the valley. You get him to come out, then put him in jail or kill him somewhere far from here. But if you start shooting, people are so scared of him they'll have to take his side in it and you'll have to shoot them, too. Most of them aren't bad people. Just scared. If you get Malin out of there, maybe the people will be able to leave, too. If they know he won't be coming back."

"Done," Link said. "Dunno how, but we'll do it. Now how do we sneak in there?"

She moved the stew pot and swept away her dirt diagram of Flynt's compound. She drew a larger figure, a map showing the long valley as it lay between the rise of the tall mountains and the jagged *cuestas* of the foothills. She studied what she had drawn, then with meticulous care added a curving line to represent the river. Twice she erased places and re-drew them.

"I think that's right," she said finally. "This is Getaway, that's Gorre, here's End of Track." She drew a line on her map from End of Track across the river and then out into the wide valley between the *cuestas*. "That's where they built the railroad track that was never used. They put a long bridge across the gorge, across the river. It's a narrow gorge, very deep," she said. "The water is fast and powerful. People saw a man try to cross it once, when it was at its lowest, jumping from rock to rock. It knocked him down like he was a straw doll and took him. Never saw him again. But there's an old railroad trestle. They never finished building it, so it's just the rusty old rails and two what-do-you-call-'em, two sort of tower things."

"Bridge supports?" Pasque said. "Trestles?"

"Yes. Like that. Made of logs to hold up the bridge. Very high, because the gorge is so deep. Someone told me it's because it wasn't ever finished that some of the logs fell into the rapids. It still goes all the way across, though. You might be able to get over on it. Maybe."

"Sounds like maybe," Link said. "Did y'say there's another way?"

"There's a water crossing, a long, long way upstream. I

only saw it once. Man came to Gorre, long time ago, and had plans for building a mill. You know, a grain mill?"

"Yes?"

"He went 'way upstream in the mountain and built a kind of dam across the river, what do you call it?"

"Diversion?" Pasque said.

"Yes. Now the water just goes on over it, but it's not too deep."

"Cross on a horse?"

"Oh, no! No, I'm sure of that. Much too dangerous. It's all slick from being mossy, and it's narrow like a little wall. Nobody in his right mind would try to take a horse in there. Or anywhere into Gorre, except by the road."

"Which way's the shortest?" Link asked. "From here, I mean."

"The rail bridge. You could be there in a few hours. It would take you a day and a half, maybe two days to get to the watermill crossing."

The motionless air suddenly became enriched with the odor of long-dead meat and leather clothes saturated with smoke, and the three people looked up from the map to see Two Nose Thomas standing there.

Link stood up. "Still got my clothes in that cart?" he asked.

"Yup."

"You be willin' to take this lady here and git her back to Ehre's Hole? Me and my friend are goin' on into the valley."

"Iffen thet's how yore stick floats," Two Nose said. "Thet lady's ez good ez at town already. I cain't study out what fer y'wanna go inta Gorre, though. Hyar's a hoss what's rode on a avaylanch an' danced hornpipe inside a peraria twister. Snuck inta Pawnee camp atter hosses to steal, too! But he can't no-how cipher tryin' to git inta *thet* place, no! It's bein' none of my own bizness, but lessen yore medicine's a heap good, I don' figger on seein' y'ag'in this side o' ol' Nick's rendezvous, not iffen y'ride in thar. *Waugh!*"

Pasque went to his saddlebag for his pocket notebook and a pencil. After writing his note, he gave it to her.

"If Mister Pendragon is already there, you tell him all you can about Gorre. Tell him to hold off a few more days so we can sneak in. If we can catch Malin off guard, maybe . . . just maybe . . . we can take care of things without a lot of blood being shed. If he'll wait, give us time, we can do it. Maybe then he could start some kind of diversion. He'll understand. And he'll see to it that you're taken care of, too. You've got my word on it."

Link left Pasque to explain things to the woman and reassure her that everything was going to be all right. He retrieved his clothes from the cart and headed off in search of running water. Along with his clothes, Crows Woman handed him a small pouch of well-pounded root, indicating with hand gestures that he was to rub it on himself like soap. But then as he turned to go, he was surprised to feel her hand grabbing at his sleeve.

"Hah?" he asked.

Crows Woman had picked up the steel wagon rod she used for hanging pots over the fire. She held it up, as if showing it to him, as her face formed a question. She pointed to it several times with great emphasis, then she put one hand over her left eye and continued mutely to ask the same thing. Link shook his head. He didn't understand what she was asking. One eye? Close one eye? Somebody was going to try to stick a steel rod in his eye? She pointed to the center of the quillwork decoration she wore on her dress. The quills there were dyed black. Black quills. A circle design? Was she telling him something about the sacred circle the blacksmith often talked about?

She cupped her hand as if raising the black circle in her palm, carefully laying it over her left eye. Black on the eye. Steel rod. Link suddenly understood.

"Yours is the black one?" Link guessed. "Him with one eye, the one who carries the long iron bar? I heard of him, yes. Far, far north. Very far north. My people ran into him two, three summers ago. I'll tell your man about it. I'll tell Two Nose."

She stamped her foot emphatically, jabbing a finger toward his mouth, and then pointing at her own ear.

"Savvy some English, then, do you? You don't want Two Nose to listen?"

She waited.

"All right. Well, friends of mine ran into this black, yes. At a big ditch . . . you know ditch? . . . in high mountains, far north." Link gestured as if he were digging an irrigation ditch with a shovel. He spread his arms to show it was very wide. "North of the Platte. Almost to the place of stinking water. That is where the one-eye black man lives."

She shook her head. She hadn't heard of the Stinking Water River.

"Never mind," Link said, pointing at the woman who had run away from Gorre. "You and Two Nose, you take that woman to town. Find Mister Pendragon. *He* knows where the ditch is. He knows how to tell y'where to find the black man with the iron bar and one eye."

Crows Woman reached out and slapped Link firmly on the chest as if saying that his heart was in the right place, and then she let him walk off toward the creek below.

★ ★ ★ ★ ★

Link Lochlin stood at the side of the small creek. He removed the hat and set it on the ground, took off the moccasins and placed them next to the hat, then pulled off the poncho and folded it before putting it down. As he untied the leather belt and let the leggings drop to his ankles, he looked down at his white body as if he had not seen it in many years, as if it was that of a stranger. Link paused a moment, then he stepped into the shallow water and sat down slowly, feeling the chill of the water grabbing at him.

Whatever it was that Crows Woman had given him in the little pouch, it made a kind of lather and cut through the sweat and the smell. He bathed methodically, as if it were a ritual, this arm and then that arm, the chest and the legs, the feet. He made lather between his palms and spread it on his face and used Pasque's razor to scrape off the stubble. When he had rinsed, lying down in the current, he rose to his feet slowly and stepped to the bank to let the breeze dry his skin.

They felt like pieces of clothing that belonged to someone else and yet fit him perfectly. Without hurry, Link dressed himself in the summer under-drawers and skivvy shirt, the California pants and wool shirt. The broad leather belt buckled on like a piece from a suit of armor, and, once he was wearing his belt and vest and tall boots, he felt much like his old self. When at last he fastened on his gun belt and set his broad Stetson on his head, he knew he was ready to look Pasque in the eye again.

Link handed Pasque the razor, and, while Pasque was putting it away, Link stepped into his stirrup and swung his leg over the saddle. With a glance backward at where Two Nose Thomas and Crows Woman were already breaking camp, but without a word, Link reined the horse toward the north and set off. Pasque mounted and set off after him. When he caught up and rode alongside, it was the old picture again—the young rider and the one who was older, the older one leading the way again into certain danger.

Pasque and Link rode north through the brush, making good time. Almost like boys suddenly freed from their chores to go riding, they trotted in and out of groves of pine and cottonwood, pounded across gullies and hills, walked the horses easily up and down a dozen grassy draws. A fine plump cottontail bolted before them and ran perhaps ten yards before Link's bullet knocked it dead.

"Supper," he said.

And there was to be more game for supper. As they went stirrup to stirrup down into a nice green swale where a little spring reflected in the sunlight, a pair of grouse rose whirring out of the grass under the horses' hoofs. Pasque's Colt boomed twice and one of the birds came down.

"Missed one." Link smiled. "Y'need practice."

"Not true, *amigo*," Pasque laughed. "That one, it looked dangerous. So I put two bullets in it just to be sure!"

In the late afternoon, they topped a rise and could see below them the remains of the railroad track stretching out of the eastern horizon and leading into the foothills. Coming closer, they saw it was all rusted iron and rotting ties. Whatever group of hopeful investors had built it, they hadn't even come back to salvage their rails and spikes. The final work train and its crew had simply gone away one day, steaming eastward away from Gorre Valley never to return.

"Make camp up here in the trees?" Pasque said.

"Good enough. Better not get much closer. We'll cross over tomorrow, I figure. Somehow."

The horses were glad to be hobbled and let out to graze.

And Link was glad to stretch out upon his saddle blanket and let the clean breeze from the pines pour across him. He could smell the sweat of the horse in the blanket and the faint remnant of saddle soap and neat's-foot oil. His shirt still had some of the stink in it, but it wasn't bad. Better was the smell of the dirt under him, the earth smell. One of the horses dumped its load and he even smiled at the sudden tang on the air.

Pasque threw down his saddle and saddle blanket and imitated Link by stretching out on his back. Later there would be time to gather wood and make a fire. Later he would unsaddle the horses and let them have a roll in the grass. "Do you think they are all right?" he said, staring up into the cloudless sky.

"I don't know," Link said. "All I know is that they don't want to be there and we need to do something about it."

"I wish Art would show up about now."

"Yeah. Except a big bunch of riders charging in there could touch off a regular war. Besides, I don't feel like just waiting around out here for help to show up. Never did like doing things that way."

"I been thinking," Pasque said easily. "Having myself what the *vaqueros* call a *pensamiento*."

"Oh?" Link said.

"I'm thinking about these crossings into this valley. Sounds as if the only one where the horses could maybe go across is up at that water mill."

"Yeah? Well, *maybe*. She did say it couldn't be done."

"Thinking we might take a look at this railroad trestle place, then get on upriver to the other one. If there's no way to get horses across, I mean."

"Two, three days, she said. Then figure another day or two to get back down th' other side to Gorre. I don't want

111

to take that much time to do it," Link said.

"No other way to do it, is what I'm thinking," Pasque said. "It would be better to spend more time at it if it means having our horses when we get there."

"So what happens if Art charges in with that posse of ranchers while we're fooling around upriver?"

"I don't know. What if he charges in and we are lying in the bottom of that gorge like two tortillas smashed flat on the rocks?"

"Well, we'll see," Link said. "Come morning, we'll see what it looks like. Let's take care of the horses and get a fire going."

In the light gray haze of early morning they stood at the brink of the gorge and weighed their chances of getting across. Below the toes of their boots the river ripped and thundered at the rock walls. River mist rose into the morning haze, the cold damp that might have been the reason both men felt a chill prickling along their spines.

"What'd somebody call it?" Pasque asked. "Deathwater?"

"The name seems to fit," Link agreed.

Or the reason for that stiff and icy sensation under the shirt may have been the sight of the trestle. Seemingly against all odds and in defiance of the obvious power not only of the rapids but of gravity and time, two towers stood in the midst of the current. Pasque looked at it with his telescope, then let Link have a look.

"What kind of men would build such a thing?" Pasque said.

"God knows," Link answered. "I don't even see how they did it, short of turnin' this whole river outta its bed. Look how much timber they used in those towers!"

Standing by some miracle in that fast-moving river, the towers were connected by long timbers stretching from the cliff edge out to the first tower, then across to the second, braced up with diagonal supports. On top of these timbers the builders had constructed their track, but it was not built on a solid deck. They had saved lumber by leaving wide spaces.

The structure was no more than ten years old, but the elements had treated it badly. The two rails running from the edge of the gorge out to the first trestle tower had a serious dip and twist to the track where some ties and bridge timbers had given way. Even using the telescope it was impossible to tell whether the wood had rotted or had just warped and was still strong enough to bear a man's weight.

Near the center of the span, over the most violent part of the foaming river, the whole bridge was tilted over until it looked as if one rail was only hanging by its spikes to the tie, and that the tie was only hanging from the other rail. The log cribbing of the first tower leaned upriver. If it were to lean another few degrees, it would dump the ties and rails and timbers and all down into the river.

Beyond the first tower there was only one rail. One of the long timbers spanning the next gap had sagged. Several of the ties had dropped away when the missing rail plunged into the gorge. Even at this distance, Link could see other ties that were broken in half. But he figured a man just might be able to make it across if he bent over and held onto the rail to keep his balance.

The second tower leaned downriver, like the first. On the far side of that tower it was the other rail that was still there. Link turned the little brass telescope down toward the river and saw the fallen one among the rocks, sticking up out of the current like a long cavalry sword. The remaining rail went all the way from the tower to the opposite wall of the gorge, but it dipped in the center and was twisted. He couldn't tell, but Link figured that the spikes holding it were rusted and the wood was rotted.

Suddenly the telescope picked out a movement and he focused on it.

"Git down!" he shouted to Pasque over the cavernous roaring of the river. Both men dropped to their bellies behind the rocks, and Link handed Pasque the telescope.

"Riders!" Pasque said. "I make it five! Moving somewhere fast, that's for certain."

Near where the railroad met the other side of the gorge was a small square stone building, the kind a railroad might build as a place to house a watchman or a work crew. The Deathwater riders trotted up to this building as a pair of figures came out to meet them. There was some kind of exchange, but the riders never dismounted. Instead, they whipped up their horses and hurried away as if they were going from place to place putting people on guard.

"S'pose they heard y'tryin' to shoot grouse?" Link said.

"Maybe. Or maybe they smelled *you*," Pasque countered. "Well, we had our look at this so-called bridge. We'd better get started for that watermill crossing."

"*You* start," Link said. "I'm crossing right here."

"Here?"

"Yup."

"First, you're a bone picker, and now you figure yourself one of those trapeze *hombres!* Tell me, you been knocked on the head recently, somehow?"

"My head's all right. Say, look at that!"

Two small figures came out of the stone building across the gorge and in a few minutes they rode away.

"Better yet," Link said. "I guess Malin sent those riders

to call in all his men. Probably doesn't think anybody could cross here."

"He is probably damned right," Pasque replied, shaking his head in disbelief.

"Here's th' idea," Link went on. "You take both horses and git upstream and across if y'can. Maybe somewhere over there you'll find some of those nice people the woman told us about and get 'em to help us. You work your way to Malin's place, and I'll do the same."

"Just you and your Colt, huh? Just figure to take a little *pasear* over that nice footbridge and wander into town. Lemme feel that bump on your skull and see if it's gotten worse."

"Me, my Colt, my saddlebags. That's a big, big place over there. I can get lost in it easy. Sneak around, get the lay of the land, maybe even talk to some of those farmers she mentioned. But I just can't be this close and not get in there! Can't wait two more days! I'm goin' over, and y'can either come along now or meet up with me later on."

Pasque raised up on his elbows to look at the trestle and gorge once more. For an instant he thought that, in a cockeyed kind of way, Link's plan made some sense. No, it didn't make any sense at all. Crossing that long span of wobbling steel in slick boots? Pasque wrestled with it, trying to see how it would all happen. Like the blacksmith had once told him, it was time to see things as the eagle sees, high and wide. So—Malin *was* expecting a big posse to come riding into the gaps far south of here. He might even have a spy in Ehre's Hole who would report the arrival of Art and the other men. Also, there were people in Gorre Valley who didn't like Malin and would prefer to see him gone. Two riders coming in with guns on their hips would probably make people close their shutters and bolt their doors, but one man on foot might be able to approach them. So might one man riding and leading another horse.

If Link made it, there would be one man behind the enemy lines who could possibly protect Gwen and the other people. If not—nothing would change. Besides, Pasque admitted to himself, Link is going to do it no matter what I say.

"*Bueno,*" he finally said. "At least if Art decides to charge the place, anyway, we'll be in there to provide confusion and crossfire. You got enough shells?"

Link had already taken two of the four boxes of ammunition Pasque had brought from the Keystone. "Yup. And I got a little jerky and bread in the saddlebag. I'm all right."

"*Hmm.* I still have doubts about *that!* Well, you better do it while those outlaws are still gone from over there. I'll stay here until you're over, just in case you need me to provide artillery fire."

"The way *you* shoot?" Link grinned. "Well, suit yourself. But do me a favor and try to aim high."

"Link?"

"Yeah?"

"*Vaya con Dios.* May God guide your steps, *amigo.*"

"Thanks."

And with that, the Keystone rider put his saddlebag over his shoulder, put the horse's reins into his friend's hand, and stepped out onto the first railroad tie. It was solid under his boot, but between it and the next one was nothing but that long dizzying drop through the cold river mist into the rapids far below.

# Chapter Seven

I will not henceforth save myself by halves;
Lose all, or nothing.
*The Duchess of Malfi,* V, 3, 48-9
John Webster

"Is Malin gone?" Gwen Pendragon asked.

Davy Dunlap had just come running into Gwen's room, wary and breathless.

"Yes. I heard him and the old man say they were goin' out to the river to look at a building. Somethin' about a granary or somethin'. How's Mister Riley doing?"

Gwen smiled at young Davy's way of always leaping from topic to topic as if his mouth just couldn't quite move quickly enough to keep up with his ideas.

"Mister Riley's still weak, but he's a little better. You can go on in and see him."

Davy was halfway to the other room as soon as he heard "You can. . . ." Mrs. Pendragon came up behind him at the doorway. Bob Riley lay on the bed with his head swathed in a bandage and his arm in a sling. His reaction, upon seeing Davy, was to turn an apprehensive eye toward Gwen, for Davy was not supposed to leave the so-called Mercantile without permission.

"Where's Malin?" he croaked. In the fight back at The Tanks he had taken a blow across the throat and was still trying to get his voice back.

"Davy says he's gone off to look at a building. With his father."

"Oh. So, Davy, you got another plan for gettin' us outta here? Maybe you'd pour me a cup of water from the jug, there."

From the hour when Malin's bunch had locked Gwen and Bob Riley in the rooms with the steel bars on the windows, and had told Davy he was going to be the fetch-it and swamper at the Mercantile if he ever wanted to see his mother again, Davy had been making plans for escape. Whenever he got a chance, such as now, he would open the connecting door and hurry in to tell his latest scheme to Mrs. Pendragon and Mr. Riley.

"I'll leave you two to talk about it," she said. "I'll stay in the other room and watch for Malin, should he return."

She didn't bother to tell Bob not to wear himself out with talking. She had said it to him far too often the way it was. And, anyway, she was glad he could talk again, and had longer and longer periods when he was awake. She never again wanted to go through anything like those first days and nights when he lay so still it was hard to tell whether he was alive or dead. Sometimes, she would touch him to see if he was still warm, or change a bandage just to reassure herself the blood was still flowing. Had it been up to Malin, Bob Riley would be lying in some dirty room attended by one of his half dozen women who moved about the place as if in a daze, like half-wits.

She'd taken the hard tone with Flynt Malin right from the start, even before she found out that the wretched man's father lived nearby, and that *he* took a very, very dim view of his son's abduction of the Keystone group. Right from the beginning she set her chin at Flynt, planted her feet firmly, and told him she would not have Bob Riley in anyone's care but her own. Malin had glared into her gray eyes, then blinked and shifted his focus, and he knew right then he had lost the argument. When he had taken them into the two storerooms adjoining the Mercantile, it had been almost as if he were asking her approval of them. She had inspected the beds, one for Bob Riley in the farthest room, one for herself in the nearer one. The barred openings were fitted with hinged glass windows (albeit grimy with dust), so there would be fewer drafts on Bob. She had told Malin to have his *men* bring more firewood for the small stove. She had said it that way—*men*—as if to imply she held them to be little more than trash.

Later, when Malin had returned, he had told her *his* conditions. She could keep these two rooms and tend to her foreman, but only until he'd recovered enough to take care of himself. Then *he* would decide what to do with him. The other captive women and their brats were being kept on farms outside of town. The older kid was to work in the Mercantile. As for her, she was going to stay in those two rooms. There weren't to be any attempts at running away, or there'd be consequences. He had taken a stance before her, his thumbs hooked in his gun belt.

"Just to guarantee you're gonna stay put an' out of trouble," he had snarled, "you're gonna take off that dress and hand it to me. Right now!" Flynt had worn a nasty lopsided grin, and Gwen had seen his fingers fidget against his groin. "An' if y'try to run off, you'll be runnin' in your corset and drawers. I catch y', an' I'm takin' *them* away, too!"

His hard little eyes had glittered. He had been enjoying himself. But if he had been looking to have a private peep show at a woman in her corset, he would be disappointed. Gwen had decided against wearing a corset and corset cover the morning she had dressed for the picnic, thinking the excursion would be a chance to relax in more comfort. So beneath the simple shirtwaist dress she was wearing, she had on only her vest and chemise, her pantaloon drawers and stockings, and of course a cotton underskirt.

Gwen Pendragon had looked at the unconscious man on the bed, and then turned her gaze back to rest fully upon Flynt Malin's ugliness. She had neither blinked nor looked away as she unbuttoned the dress, stepped out of it, and threw it in his face. Taken by surprise, Malin had caught the garment and turned in confusion to leave the room.

Pasque lay down again behind the rocks with his telescope. In the round disk of glass the image was sharper in the center and bent toward the edges, making Link look like a hunchback balanced on a maze of curved timbers and rails. Pasque wished he could move right to the edge of the gorge where he could see better, but from this upriver vantage point he'd be more likely to spot anybody moving around that building.

Halfway to the first trestle tower, Link trusted his weight on a rotten tie and Pasque saw him tip and lose his balance. He grabbed air desperately as broken chunks of wood plummeted down into the torrent, twisted himself to grab one of the rails, got his weight onto the leg that was still wedged against the iron, and threw himself down flat on the timbers, trying to spread his weight over as many of them as he could. After a few moments he rose again and adjusted the saddlebag on his shoulder. Even at that distance, Pasque could tell that the saddlebag had been a mistake. It was a clumsy burden.

Link put one foot out ahead of him, close to the rail, and went on. He came to another rotted tie hanging from the tracks at a place where one rail sagged and drooped away from the other one. Pasque saw Link gingerly lifting first one foot, then the other over the upper rail so as to be on the outside of it. He fussed with the saddlebag again, swinging it around so it would rest on his back and stay there as he bent over. Moving in a crouch, Link slowly picked his way along, examining every spike and piece of wood as he went, keeping his hands poised to grab the rail if he should slip.

A few more yards would bring him to the first tower.

Link tested each railroad tie by gingerly pressing the tip of his boot down against it and then putting more pressure on the ball of his foot and finally trusting most of his weight to it. The worst part was putting one foot out in front of him and getting set to lift the other foot. All of his weight was on the new foothold at that point. He could feel the sweat from his hands soaking into his gloves and wondered if he could save himself by catching the rail if the tie broke away. At least the rail wasn't greasy or worn slick. Instead, it was rusty and rough. In places, chunks were broken out of the metal.

Looking down to make sure the spikes were going to hold began to make him dizzy. His eyes wouldn't quite focus. He was holding his breath at every tie. The water rushing below created the illusion that the trestle was moving upstream. At times, the rails seemed to be also rising and falling with the river. And just as he was stepping onto the last shaky tie before the trestle tower, Link got disoriented and tried to lean upstream against the hallucination and lost his balance. He went to his knees, hands clutching at the rail.

When he finally reached the tilting trestle tower, he threw himself face down on it and held on for dear life. He could feel the thrumming vibration of the river hammering at the pilings, and he couldn't shake off the conviction that the whole thing was tilting upriver and moving. But after the crossing he had just made, it felt like the safest place he had ever been.

Pasque watched almost without breathing. Minutes went by as Link just lay face down and motionless on the trestle tower. Finally Pasque saw him rise to his knees, then to his feet. He seemed to be shaking his head like a drunken cowboy coming out of a saloon, trying to get his eyes to focus. Pasque thought he caught a glimpse of movement across the river and swept the telescope over the opposite side of the gorge. He saw nothing, but *something* out of place had flicked across his peripheral vision. The stone building looked to have a window facing the railroad track; he could see only the very edge of the sash. It was no more than a vertical shadow of window frame, yet it had somehow changed appearance. He cussed himself silently for watching Link when he should have been keeping an eye on the building. Still, he couldn't resist swinging his telescope back to the bridge.

Link now had his arms out like a tightrope walker fifty or sixty feet above the rumble of the rapids. The cross timbers and beams holding the center span of the bridge had dipped and twisted so badly that the whole track, ties and rails, was canted over at a steep angle. Link had no foothold on the ties now and so he was inching his way along the side of the tipped-over track. He shuffled gingerly, keeping his arms out for balance and sliding each foot a few inches at a time along the groove. At least the rail he was on looked strong enough.

Link came to a joint in the rails and cursed under his breath. To make a splice, the hunkies had driven four spikes at the end of each rail section and then bolted the sections with a steel plate. He'd have to step over it, plates and bolts and all. He kept his eyes fixed hard on the canted-over rail, figuring whether to put his foot in the space between spikes or try for a long step over all of them while he fought the whirling in his head and the sensation of being carried upstream.

When he had the rail joint behind him, the angle of tilt grew less severe and he was able to use the ties for footholds again. Five or six yards from the second tower he could step down between the ties and use the main beams of the bridge, lifting his foot over each tie as he came to it.

The second trestle tower was not as solid as the first. He sat down on it to rest until his legs stopped trembling. But it felt like his added weight might be all it would take for it to topple over and go crashing into the gorge—with him on top of it. Like the first tower, this one felt like it was swaying and he could feel the pounding of the water through the wood. Link leaned over the edge to look down at the base and instantly wished he hadn't. This was the worst part of the rapids. Heavy-breasted waves reared up and slammed the base over and over, the water trying to climb up the logs. All of the roaring of the rapids was concentrated against that one tower. Link got to his feet and checked the saddlebag, then turned and waved to Pasque. When he turned back and saw what was waiting for him in the next section of trestle, he nearly gave up.

In the gap between tower and cliff, down where the torrent rumbled its deafening roar, one of the two rails stuck up out of the rocks and foam, twisted into a corkscrew from the force of the water.

Downstream of the twisted rail, the river flattened out into a narrow eddy. As he stared into the water and rested his body, Link imagined he saw the face of a woman, the white water flowing like long, wild hair. He rubbed his eyes and looked again and it was gone—a trick of the light—but it had been there long enough to jolt him back. The water and the fear, the swaying trestle and the constant roar had driven everything else from his mind. But now the image of Gwen was there again, and he knew she was waiting for him, somewhere on the other side. Her friends, too, although her face was the only one he could see before him. Only her.

He bent over, touched the rail for balance, then stepped out away from the safety of the tilting tower onto the trembling rail and went on.

Pasque was watching when Link's weight knocked a heavy tie loose from the one remaining rail. It dropped, turning and tumbling down through the gorge, into the river, leaving the steel rail bouncing and bucking like a bronco under Link's feet. When Link grabbed for the rail, his saddlebag slipped from his shoulder. It turned slowly in the air as it fell, following the railroad tie down and down and down to vanish in the white torrent. For a moment, Link made no move except to bend over with his fingers clamped onto rusty steel rail, hardly daring to breathe, hoping the structure would hold. After what seemed like an eternity, he carefully drew his weight forward to the next tie, tested it. Then he went on to the next one, sliding one foot at a time. There was such a sag in the rail that he had to pull himself along it with his hands, afraid to push any weight onto his feet. If another tie should decide to fall, the rail itself could start bouncing up and down until it broke. For that matter, he didn't know why it hadn't already broken.

To slip again—he imagined losing his balance and

sliding down one of the dangling ties with his gloves clawing hopelessly at the rough wood, finally dropping off the end to plummet through empty space to the rapids below.

There was another lurch and the rail gave a bounce. Link froze; when the steel finally stopped jiggling up and down, he discovered that it was not only the saddlebag he had dropped into the torrent. His holster was empty as well. He thought he had checked the hammer loop earlier, but it must have come loose.

Pasque didn't notice that Link's Colt was gone. He breathed fully again as he watched the small figure reach the opposite side of the gorge and haul itself up onto the solid rock. From this point on, Link would do what he could do. Pasque now felt an urgency to make tracks for the other crossing and find a way to get himself and the horses over into Gorre Valley.

As soon as his legs quit shaking, Link made his way down off the railroad embankment. He couldn't believe that he hadn't tied his gun down tightly before trying to cross the trestle. He should have tied the saddlebag around his back somehow, too. It wasn't like him to be so careless. He crept cautiously through the sage and cedars toward the stone building. Two upstairs windows faced the gorge, but the doorway and another window faced the tracks. It looked abandoned; indeed, it looked as though it had never been finished. But he wasn't in any position to take a chance on it being empty. His best chance, if anyone was inside, was surprise. He slid along the front wall, ducked to pass under the window opening, took a deep breath, and threw himself through the doorway with his hand on his holster as if he was about to draw his gun.

His bluff with the empty holster didn't work. The room contained a table with a chair behind it. The chair contained a man sitting in the gloom and the man's hand held a revolver pointed straight at Link. After a long silent moment, during which each man sized up the other:

"Keystone rider?" the man said.

"That's right," Link replied.

"Happened to see you gentlemen over across the river. I had a meeting here, with my son, but he got called away suddenly. I thought I'd stay and see if you would actually make it over the trestle. You're either a brave man or a stupid one. I can't remember when I've seen anything quite like that."

Link saw no reason to start a chat with this old man. As far as he was concerned, the less said the better.

"Henry Malin is my name," the older man continued. "You might know my son. Flynt?"

"Can't say I do," Link said.

"Oh? Perhaps you weren't there . . . at the Keystone Ranch, I mean . . . when he went to pay his respects. But you *do* know, I suppose, about the bit of trouble he has begun?"

"Kidnapping women and kids, murdering a Keystone hand? Yeah, I know about *that* bit of trouble. Where is the bastard?"

"I can't blame your anger," Malin said. "And I have no doubt but that you'd attack him on sight, even unarmed as you are. You strike me as that kind of man. Dangerous and determined. My son, I fear, has underestimated you."

"I told you. We never met."

"Ah. Yes, so you say. However, he had quite a laugh lately over supper, and I'm afraid it was at your expense."

Link glared around in the gloom, ready to jump Malin

the instant the man let down his guard, listening hard for anyone who might be coming. If he kept the talk going long enough, and nobody showed up, he just might have a chance to do something about getting Malin's gun.

"You see," Malin went on, "my son has several associates in the horse and cattle business and three of them went to the big North Platte Independence Day Blowout. It was you, I believe, and another Keystone rider, who humiliated and assaulted two of those men. Perhaps you recall that event."

"If it's the two who were picking on small boys and shootin' at live chickens tied to a railroad track, then they were asking for it."

"I have no doubt of it. This valley . . . something about this valley . . . makes people sluggish, uninspired, inactive, or what you will. When my son and his companions leave here to go acquire livestock, they are apt to become overly zealous and rambunctious. I had hopes . . . please don't fidget like that. This old revolver of mine *is* cocked. As I was saying, I had hopes that Flynt would apply his energies to finding a nice woman to marry and sire me some grandchildren. What he *did*, however, was to carry off the one woman he could not possibly have. Probably the one woman most likely to bring about his downfall."

"Missus Pendragon," Link said.

"The same, exactly. An impressive woman! But we are straying from the story here. The two men in question, the ones with your face burned into their memories, happened to encounter you again, and recently. But you were, apparently, much changed. As they told it to us over supper, you had fallen into deep disgrace somehow, possibly by becoming a drunk, and had taken a squaw for wife, and were now engaged in the profession of collecting old bones, trav-

127

eling in a thoroughly repulsive cart-like contraption with this same squaw."

"I figured that was them," Link replied dryly. "Now I've got even more of a score to settle with them than before."

"And they figure you to be little or no threat. I won't repeat the various terms they used for you. But they *have* seen . . . as I'm sure have you . . . a good many riders turned into hapless range bums through one cause or another. It generally involves drink, women, and gambling. In that order. Often, it also includes larceny and murder. At any rate, my son had quite a laugh at your expense. Being tied to an ugly squaw, he said, riding in a bone cart. He and his friends found it very humorous, even more so because of your reputation as the best gunman on the Keystone."

Link's jaw clenched hard and blood heat rose in his neck.

"Looks like you're goin' to give him a good chance to kill me without findin' out who the best gun is. Not that I think he'd give a damn about that. A man that kidnaps women doesn't care much what other men think of him."

"Flynt won't be coming back this way," Malin said, refusing to rise to Link's bait. "He and I were standing here, talking about how to turn this building into grain storage, when a posse of his friends came by and told him a farm woman was missing. They left in search of her. I'm sure they will make a circuit of the valley and return to Gorre."

"By missing, you mean she ran away? Got away from here?"

"Tried to, probably. A few people think about leaving here, occasionally. Some even attempt it. They are generally discovered wandering the sage flats out there, lost, bewildered, and despondent. They'll find this woman, no doubt. Or she will return of her own accord."

"Where's Missus Pendragon, and the others?" Link managed to move a few inches closer to the table.

"Safe," Malin said. "Safe enough. In time, we should be able to gather them all in and send them home without incident, provided your Mister Pendragon doesn't come charging into the valley with an army of gunmen. Although I would be surprised if he doesn't, knowing his reputation. Missus Pendragon is the key, you see. She was the object of my son's misguided attentions. The others merely happened to be with her when he let his obsession overcome his reasoning."

"She all right?"

"Oh, yes! She seems disappointed in *you*, I must say. Does it surprise you that she believed their story of your disgrace and downfall? One could see it in her face when she heard it. I don't know whether it was the intelligence that you may have taken a squaw, or the news you were seen riding in a foul-smelling bone cart that brought that look to her face. But to answer your question, she is indeed all right where she is."

"Are the other women with her, and the kids? Where's he keeping them?"

"She and your wounded foreman and one of the boys are together at Flynt's mercantile store in the village, in two spare rooms. Flynt sent a woman to watch her and to bring her whatever she needs from the store. As soon as I learned what my son had done, I hurried myself to prevent him from doing any further harm, from doing anything more to incur Art Pendragon's wrath."

"Too late for that," Link said. "You got me, but when he gets here with all the ranchers and all of our riders, they won't leave a stick standing in this place."

"I do realize the possible consequences of what Flynt has done. You see he is not a fully rational being. I'm afraid that a man needs to deal with him more diplomatically than is usually possible. His mother, God rest her soul, often had to employ sheer guile in order to control him."

"To hell with him. What about Missus Pendragon?"

"I went to the Mercantile building and found Missus Pendragon in a high state of dudgeon, herself and my son spitting demands at each other. I stepped in as arbitrator and persuaded him to allow her to have the spare room, and also to allow her to tend the wounded man. She insists that she will not leave her foreman, Riley, until he is well enough to go with her, and so, at the moment, both sides are in what you might call a stand-off. My suggestions pacified Missus Pendragon somewhat, and sent Flynt off in a huff. Since then, she and I have quietly collaborated to insure that Flynt does no more than look at her. It is a harmless occupation. It is a strange weakness of his . . . perhaps you will find this amusing, but he fancies women only as objects of visual excitement."

"But he won't . . . I mean he can't. . . ."

"No. As you will learn, if you live long enough, is that something about this valley stifles what a person wants most. In my case, I'm denied a worthy son who can give me grandchildren. In his case, he is sometimes overcome by a feverish desire to have carnal knowledge of many women, which is invariably frustrated. As for his associates, they began as young men whose dream was to build an immense livestock operation respected throughout the region. In choosing *this* place as their refuge, they only managed to become a collection of dangerous and unpredictable thieves led by an equally unpredictable impotent."

"I suppose I need to thank you for tryin' to help Missus Pendragon like you did," Link said. "What are y'going to do with me now?"

"Take you to her, of course. You and I need to work together if we are to pull the fuse from this very dangerous situation. The only way I see to do it is for all of us to come to an agreement."

Henry Malin rose from the table and waved his gun to gesture Link outside. Around the corner of the building two saddled horses were tied to a scrub pine. "If you don't mind," Malin said, pointing the gun from Link to one of the horses.

The railroad bed had neither ties nor rails but provided a straight, level, and sterile path. Link and Henry Malin rode northwest along it. The older man kept his revolver cocked and lying across his saddle, pointed at Link. They passed through a collection of shabby wooden houses huddling together along either side of the rail bed where the only thing to indicate what place it might be was a faded sign nailed to a post. End of Track it read. Link saw thin faces peering from behind faded curtains at the windows, but no door opened to welcome them and no voice was raised in greeting.

Afterward, they came to another settlement, a kind of miniature town with a small, boarded up one-room church and a false-front general store. There was a smithy that had smoke coming from the chimney, but all around it were signs that it rarely saw any business. Weeds grew up through piles of broken wheels and rusty machinery stacked against the wall. As they rode through, Link saw four narrow dirt streets lined with little frame houses. Some of the houses had picket fences, but the fences did no more than separate the dirt of the yards from the dirt of the streets.

"They called it Getaway," Henry Malin explained. "Gorre was to be the stockman's town, so someone decided another town was needed for the farmers. Many of our immigrants are farmers, or came from farms, but after they settled here, their hopes of filling railroad cars with grain came to naught. Now, each autumn, they manage to collect a few wagonloads to sell outside the valley. It brings barely enough money for them to buy more seed."

Link knew the kind of town. It would have a general store where no one bought anything, and a barbershop where men went and sat even though they couldn't pay for a haircut or shave. Sometimes, the barber would give a man a trim for free, just for something to do.

"Not all the people live in the towns, of course," Malin volunteered. "There's farms and a few trading posts scattered around."

Link had seen such people scratching dirt and cussing their way from one dismal crop to another all over the region. They seemed to go on existing in every dried-up dust pocket and forgotten corner of the West. You could find them wherever the range was poor or wherever the roads and rails had overlooked a few acres. There they scrabble away, down-and-outers, wearing themselves out waiting for a break that never comes their way.

It was a hostile place and dangerous—more dangerous, maybe, than Flynt Malin and his dozen guns. Any man foolish enough to ride in here and threaten what little these people had would be likely to find himself pulled off his horse and chopped to pieces with hoes and shovels.

He was glad when they were out of sight of Getaway. They rode along a small stream flowing sluggishly over mossy rocks, and after a half hour Malin pointed ahead to several groves of trees half hiding some low buildings.

"Gorre," he said, chuckling as if the very name of the place was some kind of joke. "Your lady awaits you, sir knight. However, I doubt that your reception will be to your liking. But with any luck at all, we may have an hour or so before Flynt arrives. I'll have to continue treating you as my prisoner, though, if only for the sake of appearances."

They halted in front of the Mercantile and dismounted. Henry Malin ordered two men, standing guard, to bind Link's hands securely, but let him go to the window of the room where Gwen was being held.

At first he saw only gloom as he looked between the bars, but, as his eyes adjusted to it, he saw there was a bed, a table against one wall serving as a washstand, a couple of chairs, and a lantern hanging from the rafters.

"Missus Pendragon," he half called, half whispered. "Gwen? You there?"

An inner door opened and she appeared in the room. He wasn't prepared for what he saw—her white underskirt and white chemise seemed to glimmer in the dimness like an apparition. Her blonde hair hung long behind her shoulders, very loosely tied with a ribbon. Her shoulders were bare except for the straps of her chemise, and her skin gleamed white in the light from the window. She came toward the window, but stopped well away from it.

"Where is Art?" she asked sharply.

"Art? I dunno. Probably back in that town we came through. Ehre's Hole. If he's there, he's probably waitin' for word from us, since Pasque and me sent word to him that we were going to sneak in here and spy out the place. I think he'll hold the other ranchers back a little while longer. Nobody wants this to blow up into a range war like that one up at Buffalo. But are you all right? Is Bob Riley here?"

"Yes, he's here. He doesn't seem to be recovering. I

think Flynt Malin might be putting something in the food. I
don't feel so well myself."

Link stared at her. He wanted to shield her, to comfort
her by holding her. More than anything at that moment, he
wanted her to be able to rush from her prison and fall into
his arms. Instead, he stood there with his wrists bound and
a barred window between them. And there she stood, proud
and very strong as if she did not need him at all. Almost as
if she wished he had not bothered to come.

"Need to figure out how to get us all out of here," Link
said, glaring around toward the guards, who were standing
near the corner of the building. He needed to make sure
they couldn't hear.

"Did you say Pasque is with you?" she whispered.

"Yes and no. I was comin' back from my trip down to
cañon country and he was on his way to look for you. We
met up just outside the valley. Now he's gone to find another way in. I came across the old railroad trestle. I figure
he'll show up in a day or two."

He remembered the sick feeling in the stomach from
clinging to the bouncing, swaying steel of the trestle. But it
was nothing compared to the empty gut he got from the
way she looked at him. There was steel in those eyes, and
haughty disgust.

"I won't leave here until I know Pasque is safe," she said
coldly, "nor will I leave without Bob Riley. And the boy,
Davy, and the others. Even if you *could* do anything to get
me out of here, I wouldn't go with you alone."

"Gwen, I. . . ." Words began to fail him. "I come a good
long ways to get here. Things will be better now."

She kept looking at him with that level, almost disinter-
ested gaze.

"It seems to me, now, that you're as much a prisoner as I

am. And where is your companion, the one Flynt's men were talking about, the Indian woman? Or did you just leave her and ride away the way you rode away from the Keystone, without so much as a fare thee well?"

Link recoiled from the window as if she had reached out and struck him. It was true he had left the ranch without saying good bye to her, but how could he tell her he had left because of what he was starting to feel for her? Before he could answer, one of the guards came and grabbed his arm and jerked him away from the window.

"The boss is comin'," the guard said. "If I was you, I'd watch what I said. Jus' stand there and don't say nuthin', that'd be the smart thing to do."

# Chapter Eight

Something was dead in each of us.
"The Ballad of Reading Gaol"
Oscar Wilde

The bone cart was only a thing of wood and metal, an ugly contrivance fit to carry the rotting, bleached remains of buffalo. It conveyed the dead to unknown destinations and was itself made of dead wood held together with dead leather and rusting spikes. It had almost nothing to do with being alive. How, then, could it have brought Link Lochlin so utterly low? It was only a thing. He had gotten into it only to help a woman who needed him.

Deep in his mind, even as he was pulled away from the window to confront Gwen Pendragon's attacker, he could not shake off the feeling that it had been some other cowboy, some other rider who defended that boy against these same bullies at North Platte all those months ago. It seemed like some other Keystone man had led the riders in that mad chase to catch up to this pack of horse thieves. Link felt the change in himself. It was as palpable as the dryness in his throat. Choosing to ride in a bone cart and reduced to rags, stripped of everything that identified him, humiliated, Link Lochlin seemed no longer the man he once had been. It didn't make sense, shouldn't make any difference, and yet he couldn't get rid of the effect. Now, on foot and with his hands tied behind him, his holster empty, he stood in the dust of the Deathwater Valley drained of his strength. The very place itself seemed evil and he did not know anything to do about it.

Three men galloped into town and dismounted at the hitching rail across the street, then walked toward him slapping dust from their clothes. A few curious people came out of the Mercantile building and away from the shade of the boardwalks to gather in the street.

The three men stopped in front of him.

"That him, Army?" Flynt Malin said.

"That's him, all right," wheezed the whiny voice of Hodge Perkins. "Ain't it, Army? Ain't he the same one?"

The man called Army came so close Link could smell his breath. Link knew him. He was the stranger Link had run off the Keystone when he found him sleeping off a pint of whiskey in one of the Keystone wagons. He was the same swaggering tough who had turned up at the North Platte Independence Day Blowout, bullying kids around and showing off with a gun. Link had taken his gun and whipped him.

"That's him," Army said. And without warning, he punched Link in the gut and followed that punch with another to the face. Link staggered backward and fell.

"Flynt!" It was Henry Malin's voice. "Don't let your man do that. It's cowardly, and I won't have it."

"You don't know nuthin' about it," Flynt sneered to his father. "But if you say he ain't to do it. . . ." He walked up and yanked Link to his feet, then chopped his forearm down across Link's neck and shoulder, and snapped: "I'll do it myself!" Again he hit Link, and then he hit him again.

With each attack the Keystone rider became more bent over, smaller. Link went to his knees. He struggled to stand up again, but Flynt knocked him down again with vicious blows across his neck and shoulders. Flynt hit at him again and again, chopping until his forearm began to tire. He paused to catch his breath and his little eyes glittered while he waited for the Keystone man to get up again. As Link struggled to stand, Flynt kicked him in the groin to send him stumbling backward into the knot of onlookers. Someone stopped his fall but then held onto him, probably uncertain whether just to hold him or to propel him back out into the open. Someone was also grabbing at his bound wrists. In his daze, Link thought it was someone forcing his arms up to dislocate his shoulders or trying to push him over. But then, through the fog of pain and blood, he realized they were holding his hands steady while they picked at the knot in the stiff pigging string.

"Flynt!" Henry Malin stepped in and put his hands on his son's shoulders. He kept his voice low, hoping the onlookers couldn't hear what he had to say. "You've got to stop this!" he half whispered. "Don't you see how bad it makes you look? These people know this man is one of the Keystone riders. Your own men know it. It's cowardly and shameful to be doing this to him. It shames you, especially in front of Missus Pendragon. Let him go. Let them *both* go!"

"Get out of my way!" Flynt snarled, twisting away as he pushed at his father's hand.

But Henry gripped him again. "I do not want to see you dead!" he said. "What you are doing to him is going to get you killed."

Suddenly a strong dust devil blew from out of nowhere, whipped sand and dirt in their faces, and passed on with no more sound to it than that of a bellows blowing on a blacksmith's forge. Both men froze for a moment, watching it whirl on down the street.

Then Flynt laughed into his father's face. *"Me?"* he said. *"He's* the one you're gonna see dead!" He pushed his father away and advanced on Link with his fists cocked to dole out more punishment.

The spectators fell back so that Link stood alone, but now there was a difference: those unseen helping hands had succeeded in working loose the pigging string and now Link held it behind his back in his right hand, one end still looped around his wrist and the other end hanging down to the ground. From somewhere deep in his instincts and with strength born more of desperation than of any hope of victory and escape, he swung the hard rope and caught Flynt fully in the face. The younger Malin staggered back, a hand on his cheek, feeling the blood from the rope's laceration. His eyes flared in surprise and pain.

Link came forward, lashing back and forth, whipping Flynt on the arms and shoulders, flailing wildly to hit him anywhere he could. Flynt clawed for his gun and managed just barely to clear his holster before Link slashed down with the stiff rope and knocked it into the dirt. Link paused, his chest heaving for breath and his arm aching. Flynt's men started forward, but Flynt raised a hand to stop them, and they dropped back.

Looking past the Keystone man, Malin had caught a glimpse of white behind the barred window. The Pendragon woman was watching the whole thing. "Leave him be," Malin panted proudly, loud enough for her to hear. "I'll take him myself. He ain't got much left in him."

Again Flynt closed on Link, dodging with a raised arm to fend off the lashing, his other fist cocked to deliver a hard punch. Link struck at him with the rope, but his arm no longer had the fury it needed. He slammed Flynt with his other hand, but Flynt came right back at him, punching at his face. Link turned with the blow, blindly groping to wrap the pigging string around Flynt's neck; suddenly, they were on the ground, rolling over and over while Flynt clawed at the rope across his throat as Link held both ends, twisting his own body desperately to get his knee into his Flynt's back. Both of them were gasping hard, choked and blinded from the dust.

Henry Malin picked up Flynt's revolver and stood over them, his usual expression of polite hopelessness over-written with a look of desperation. "Stop it!" he cried. "At this moment I *don't* particularly care which one of you I shoot. Get up from there!"

Flynt could not speak with the rope crushing his wind-pipe, but noises of defiance came gurgling out of his throat, and he kept thrashing back and forth, pulling at the rope with one hand and trying to grab Link with the other. Link got his knee into Flynt's back and kept the pressure on.

"You might as well shoot," Link panted. "I figure I'm dead either way."

Henry Malin thumbed back the hammer, aiming first at Link, and then at his son. Then he fired into the dirt next to them. He cocked the gun again, and fired again. After the third shot, they both lay still. Link let go of one end of the rope and rolled to his knees. Flynt lay there wheezing. Both men, their lungs burning from the thick gunsmoke and dust, were nearly deaf from the three shots.

"Don't either of you move!" Henry Malin's voice seemed to be coming out of a cave, an echo both close and far away that came muddling through the loud ringing in Link's ears. "Flynt, you have gone too far!" Malin continued. "As soon as you brought those people into the valley, everyone knew there would be bloodshed. I'm surprised we haven't seen an army of ranchers coming with

ropes to hang every last man of us! Hodge, go and bring
Missus Pendragon out here."

Hodge Perkins vanished into the building and came out
with Gwen. She had thrown a blanket around her shoulders. Henry Malin got the two combatants to their feet.

"One of these two men," he said to her, "will surely kill
the other. And whichever it is, it can bring only more violence and anger. I see no outcome to this that will not bring
more death. Can you?"

"Probably not," Gwen said. "Even if you let us go, my
husband and our neighbors are certain to attack this place
sooner or later."

"I thought as much," Malin said. "It is a dilemma. My
fault, of course, for hoping to start a new town here in the
first place. Most of these people . . ."—he indicated the
crowd that had gathered—"are not involved with the
stealing, yet their homes and fields would become the bat-
tleground. And I invited them to come here and settle. But
I let my own son become a leader of thieves and rustlers . . .
if your husband attacks us, I don't know which of these
people would side with him and which would side with
Flynt's men, once the gunfire began."

"I can say as much to Mister Pendragon," Gwen said
after a moment, "provided you let me and my friends leave
this place immediately. I cannot tell what my husband
might do, however. But all I can worry about at the moment is the safety of my friends. And my foreman, of
course."

"Missus Pendragon," Henry Malin said, "would you be
willing to listen to an idea of mine? It may shock you, but it
may also be the saving of lives."

"Go on," Gwen said.

"You two," he said, pointing the pistol at Link and Flynt

for emphasis, "need to decide this issue on your own. Man to man in a fair fight. But in an honorable arrangement, not a street duel. And *not* here in this accursed valley. I suggest letting the Keystone folks go, all of them. . . ."

"No!" Flynt croaked. "No. Without them there's nothin' stoppin' Pendragon from bringin' a whole damn' army in here. We couldn't set foot outta the valley again, neither! I'd rather kill 'im here and take our chances. You're talkin' crazy."

"Let me finish," his father said. "The outside people will never again see us as anyone who they could trust, that much is certain. Not now that you've turned from cattle thief to kidnapper. But if you settle this with some degree of honor, they might just give us a little respect, maybe enough respect so we can put the valley back on its feet again."

"So we let 'em go?" Flynt argued. "Pendragon brings his men and the Army and they troop us all off to prison, is that it? Those as don't get killed in the fight?"

"No. We allow these people to leave, all the people who want to. In return, you . . . *you*, Flynt . . . you agree to go to the Keystone after things have calmed down. Next spring, let us say. You go there and have your showdown with Mister Lochlin. You go alone and you give him a fair fight. I hate the thought of you . . . or anyone . . . being killed, but, even more than that, I hate the state of things to which you have brought us all. A sacrifice must be made."

"Well, that suits *me* right down to the ground, by God!" Link said. "Guns, knives, fists, you name it. If he's got the guts to come to the Keystone, we'll have it out."

"Missus Pendragon, can you offer Flynt here a fair chance? No retribution if he wins, no intimidation from your husband's men?"

"I think it's awful," she said. "It's pagan. It's *worse* than pagan! Two adult men beating and battering each other! But, yes, I'll agree to it as long as Mister Lochlin is so willing. Mind you, I would never ask him or *any* Keystone rider to agree to such a thing. It is his own decision, and I have no part in it. In fact, it sounds as though he has already decided. So . . . I promise your son safety while he's on Keystone land, so long as you return my friends to their homes. Now!" For all of her outward appearance of calm dignity, Gwen trembled inside the blanket.

Henry Malin turned to Flynt's men. "Army, Hodge, Steve, you see about getting wagons and horses to return these people to their homes. Flynt, you will ride out to the farms and tell the outside people to come into town."

"Me?"

"You need to get away and cool down. Unless you want to try to kill me right here and now." Henry Malin leveled the gun steadily at his only son.

Flynt glared at his father. A couple of dozen people stood behind him, watching. "Ah, have it your way, old man!" he snarled at his father. "I'm gettin' sick of this whole damned place anyway."

"One more thing," Gwen snapped.

Henry Malin turned back to her.

"If my foreman dies," she said, "or if any one of my friends is injured, or if my nephew is harmed on his way here, I will personally see to it that the governor, the Army, the militia, and vigilance committees descend upon this place like the wrath of God Himself." With that she turned and, drawing the blanket more tightly around her, withdrew into the gloom of the warehouse doorway.

Link wiped his forearm across his mouth and looked at the blood it left on his sleeve, but neither the blood nor the pain seemed to register with him. He looked into the space where she had been, staring at it as if trying to fill it again with her presence. He wiped again at the blood coming from his split lip. He wondered if he could find some way to clean himself up and brush his hair. Back when he was making his way across the swaying, rotted bridge, he had felt like a hero going to save his lady. But now he felt like a schoolboy who had been caught fighting behind the outhouse, dragged by his ear into the presence of the principal.

Link and Flynt Malin exchanged hostile glances and parted from each other. Link limped through the dark doorway and followed the narrow corridor to a heavy wooden door, which was open. In the room, Gwen stood wrapped in the blanket, looking out the barred window. Link tried to speak, but managed only to clear his throat. He tried again, but the words that came were not the ones he wanted to say.

"Somebody said Bob Riley was here?" he said. She did not turn to look at him and her only reaction was a very slight movement of her head toward the adjoining room.

Link found Bob lying in the bed, head bandaged and arm in a sling. The man was thin and pale. "Bob?"

He opened his eyes. "Link."

"How are you? Is that arm broke?"

"I guess I'll live," Riley said. "Question is, what the hell are *you* tryin' to do?"

"Tryin' to get you outta here! All of you. Me and Pasque found a way in."

"Where is he?" Riley asked.

"I dunno. At least not right at the moment. He rode on up north a ways to come in from a different direction.

Should be here by now, maybe tomorrow."

"They probably caught him," Riley sniffed. "I don't know, Link. Don't know what y'think you're doin', that's all. Why isn't Art here, 'stead of you?"

Link had never seen Riley like this, at least not toward him. He'd seen Riley in a foul mood before, but that was back on the Keystone when a green hand had let a range bull get away from him and it had knocked down a corncrib, or when a cowboy had come home drunk from town. But now Riley seemed irritated with him, seriously irritated. Link scowled, trying to sort it all out. There was Gwen in the other room not even looking at him, and here was Bob Riley, who should be glad to see him, just glaring at him as if he'd peed in the milk bucket.

Link drew up a stool and sat down at the bedside. "I kind of took the bit in my teeth," he began. "I figure Art and the other ranchers don't want to make a full-blown war outta this, so they're goin' to take it easy and wait until they're sure they have enough men to see it through if there *is* a war."

Riley kept looking at him like he was disgusted. "So you took it on yourself to come and rescue us, huh? You and Pasque?"

"Wait a minute. You and me better spread out our cards here," Link said. "Somethin's gallin' you . . . and Missus Pendragon out there . . . and I guess I oughta know what it is, but I don't."

Riley grimaced as he rolled onto his side so he could look at Link. "Her and me," he said, "we've been talkin' with the older Malin. On the sly, sort of. He's a good man. Just about worked out a way we could get outta here. The next time that damn' Flynt and his gunmen went out of the valley to 'purchase' more livestock, ol' man Malin was gonna get us outta here. We even worked out a way to let the other people know when to come into town so we could all leave together."

"Sounds good," Link said.

"Sure! Up until you and Pasque figger to be heroes! Now Flynt ain't gonna leave until he's got everything nailed down again around here. . . ."

"I took care of Flynt," Link interrupted. "We got us an agreement. . . ."

"You? You took care of things, huh?" Riley was getting red in the face. "Y'said yourself y'don't even know where the hell Pasque is . . . y'lost him somewhere. Then Flynt's boys spread the story of how you're out there pickin' up bones an' sleepin' with a squaw. A hag at that. Yeah, Lochlin, you done us a whole lot of good, comin' here."

"Bob, look here. I. . . ."

"I'll tell y'what, Link. And this is Art Pendragon's foreman talkin' to you now. If you've got the run of this place, you better get out there an' find Henry Malin. You tell him you need to go find Pasque. And tell him to get word to Art, somehow, that Missus Pendragon and the others are all right. Otherwise. . . ." Worn out with anger, Riley dropped back into his pillow and let his eyes find the darkness again.

Link hesitated, his head burning and his chest full of things he wanted to say in his defense, but, in the end, saw there was nothing more to do but rise and leave. Gwen was sitting on the edge of her bed in the next room and did not look at him as he walked past her.

Link did not have to look far to find Henry Malin. The older man was sitting on the edge of the horse trough, surrounded by five other men. All of them were wearing guns, Link noticed, and Malin had his son's revolver thrust under his waistband. They were in deep conversation when Link walked up to soak his kerchief in the scummy water. He began washing the dirt and blood from his face.

"How's your friend?" Henry Malin asked.

"I think he'll be all right," Link said. "Soon's we can get him back home, he'll be better, though."

"We're working on that," Malin said. "Just trying to decide the best way to go about it."

"Well, while you figure it out, I need to go find my other friend. He's prob'ly in your valley somewhere north of here. Don't suppose y'can fix me up with a horse, can you?"

"Certainly," Malin said. "There's a number of horses over behind the Mercantile. And there's tack in the shed. Theo, why don't you show him?"

The man Malin addressed as Theo stepped forward. "Sure thing," he said.

As Theo buckled the bridle and held the horse so Link could saddle it, he offered advice and directions. "If your friend made it across the river and got into the valley," he said, "the first thing he'd come to would be the mill road. There's a couple of mill buildings there, too, but nobody in them 'cept a dwarf kinda hermit and a girl. People up around there always hoped there'd be a mill for their grain, but I don't think it even got finished. Anyways, if he came across the river there, then he'd cut the road. The natural thing would be to head south on it. Pretty soon he'd see a kind of homestead off to the right. Just a couple of bachelors livin' in a dug-out. Probably he wouldn't go there, I'm thinkin'. It don't look like the kinda place you'd wanna just ride up to. But a way farther along, there's three, four families located. One's a brother, I think one's a son or else a married daughter. Anyway, it's a clean-lookin' place, and, if it was me, I'd sure stop there."

Link took hold of the saddle horn and pulled hard on it to test the cinch. "Whereabouts is this?" he said.

"All right," Theo said, "you go along this alley here behind th' store and, after y'pass the last building, you'll see a pretty good road goin' north. Takes y'toward the gorge, and there's the mill road. It pretty much follows the river. Y'might get to that place I mentioned before dark. Dunno. I ain't been there in a long while. Might find yourself out in the open, come dark."

"I'll manage," Link said. "I slept rough often enough, I guess."

There were homesteads and hide-outs along the road Link traveled, a scattering of poverty-whipped places where gloomy men swore at their bread and broke their wives as they waited to join Flynt Malin on his next livestock roundup. Almost as soon as the first punch was thrown in the fight between Flynt and Link, a weasel-faced gossip mounted on a skeletal pinto was spreading the news from one of these hovels to the next. It added to the messenger's self-importance to be the bearer of the news, so naturally he embellished the facts. For the moment, it was his only claim to any importance at all.

"Keystone rider showed up," he would wheeze. "Damn, but I'm dry. Got whiskey? Flynt whupped 'im good. Might be big doin's comin', if he was followed. Flynt wants you all to be on your guard now. Sent me ahead to warn everybody. Did y'say y'had some whiskey?"

By the time he arrived at the fifth place, a once-tidy clapboard house whose torn curtains collected dust from the road that ran less than an arm's length from the wall, the messenger's intake of raw liquor had lent plenty of color to his news. His imagination had by now conjured up an image of Flynt lying unconscious and the Keystone rider escaping.

"Big tough one," he slurred at the next dwelling he came to. "Black mustache, two guns. You hear of 'im, you get help, understand? Flynt wants him caught alive, too. Prob'ly some kinda reward for the man what gets him, I guess. I'm goin' on up to Kelly's place an' tell him, so iffen you see this here Keystone man, you get word to me. Flynt wants me to keep an eye on this thing, see?"

Link's capture took place in almost total silence and without much struggle. He had paused as the dark overtook him, seeing the lights of several houses ahead but hesitant to ride in unknown, and unsure who might be there. Instead, he found shelter under a pair of thickly branching junipers, tied the horse, huddled himself under the saddle blanket as best he could, and went to sleep.

They overpowered him at first light, wordlessly seizing his arms and tying him up. Still without speaking, they put him on the horse and tied his feet together beneath the horse's belly. Back toward the sagging clapboard house by the side of the road they went, Link wondering who they were and if they'd also caught Pasque. Maybe Pasque was sleeping in a friendly bed right there in those houses he had seen. On the other hand, maybe he was tied up in a cellar somewhere.

One of the four men who had caught Link broke from the group so he could tell the news to a pal who lived in a squalid dug-out in a gulch nearby. That specimen of semi-humanity then hitched up his coveralls and drank himself some corn breakfast and scurried away to inform others. The word spread back to the kitchen where the weasel-eyed one snapped and gobbled at his biscuit and egg.

149

"Got 'im," the latest messenger announced, looking at the food on the table and calculating his chances at some of the same. "Yeah, they got 'im all right." He withheld his news slyly, knowing that what he knew would eventually get him an invitation to the table. "Yeah," he said, "prob'ly all over now. Reckon by now Harvey and them has him all trussed up like a pig goin' to market."

"Sit," said the weasel face, although it was neither his table nor his place to issue invitations. "What's happened?"

The woman who sometimes watched Gwen and who had brought her both breakfast and her dress—at Henry Malin's insistence—also brought the story. She heard it from her husband, who never had liked Flynt much.

"I'm real sorry about your friend," she said, setting down the breakfast basket and taking the dress from her arm to spread it on the bed.

"Why, what is it?" Gwen said. "Link?"

"I don't know his name. The one with the black mustache, you know. Him as got in a fight with Flynt."

"Link," Gwen said.

"Oh. Well, anyway, last night a man come from up the valley. And he told Theo, that's my husband's friend, how that man just went crazy. He'd rode out of here perfectly sane and sober, but they say he got up into where he found a couple of those men who brought you here. You and your friends. Beat 'em real bad, took their guns, went gunnin' all over the valley for others."

"I don't believe that!" Gwen said.

"Well, that's what Theo said. He wasn't too sure what happened next, but Harvey and them . . . they're men that sometimes rides with Flynt . . . they ran him down. Theo says there's two stories. One is that they shot him right then and there. T'other's that they lynched him up there at Harvey's place."

It was a long time after the woman had closed the door behind her that Gwen broke down and began to weep. She had driven him to it, coldly insisting that he find Pasque. Everything was her fault. The stupid picnic, not telling Art about the lechery of Flynt Malin back at the Keystone. All, all her fault.

She got up and went to close the connecting door so Bob Riley could not hear her sobbing. She would have to tell him the news that Link was dead, but not now. She sat on the bed again and held the skirts of her dress to her eyes and wept.

# Chapter Nine

And what was dead was hope.
"The Ballad of Reading Gaol"
Oscar Wilde

The tight-faced woman who brought Gwen the evil rumor of Link's death lingered for a time with her ear to the door, listening with satisfaction to the anguished weeping and choked sobs inside. Then she hustled off to send the rumor racing back again in the direction whence it had come. She told a washday gathering of other equally idle tongues how "that fine woman of Flynt's" was near to hysteria. Then a rider of wandering eye heard from his cold wife that she would not be surprised if that Keystone woman threw herself into the gorge. In turn, this bowlegged Lothario gave his wife a cock-and-bull story about going to look for work, and rode away, carrying the news north to whisper into the ear of his other woman. Along the way, his imagination enlarged the tragic story considerably: now the distraught captive had plunged a hidden knife into her own breast and lay near death. Such was the effect the loss of her man could have upon a woman.

His other woman listened to him with such wide eyes that the man took the story a step further. Now Gwen Pendragon's self-inflicted knife thrust had been fatal, and what a shame for so beautiful a woman. The other woman rewarded her lover for the thrilling story by letting him grope about beneath her skirts a while, and then she was off to inform her friend, who happened to live in the house where Link was being held prisoner.

"This don't sound good," said one of the captors who overheard.

"Ol' man Malin's gonna be mighty cross about it, you bet," said another.

"Reckon we oughta take this 'un back to Gorre, then," said the third, jerking his thumb toward their inconvenient captive.

To take Link back to Gorre was not exactly a strategic decision on their part. It was more in the nature of an admission that they had involved themselves in something too large for their brains. In quick time they had Link in the saddle again, his feet bound beneath the horse and his hands bound behind him, with a noose tied around his neck and secured to the saddle horn for good measure. They took the trail to Gorre, muttering among themselves as to the meaning and importance of the Pendragon woman's suicide. They talked about other suicidal women they had known, each man besting his comrades with more and more gruesome details of women who they had seen hang themselves, poison themselves, or shoot themselves. None of them had ever seen a woman stab herself, but they sure did agree it was possible.

What stunned them and befuddled their minds even more than reports of the woman's self-slaughter, however, was the prospect of Art Pendragon's revenge. To most of them the Keystone was legendary, a place that few had seen yet that everyone knew about. Everyone in the territory could tell a story, true or not, about the Keystone riders. Some said there was a giant blacksmith who would suddenly appear; he would point his hammer at an injustice, and a band of riders dressed in black would come charging over the hill with guns blazing. Others spoke of Pendragon's granting huge tracts of land to widows and orphans, and still others knew that he had personally defeated scores of outlaws and left them hanging by their own ropes in cotton-wood groves throughout the land.

Now it was slowly dawning on the Gorre Valley men that this same Art Pendragon was soon to learn about his wife's death. In a matter of days he and his riders would come down upon the Gorre Valley like the wrath of God Himself. The men who were leading Link back to town made some very brave noises about "bein' able to hold 'em off" at the well-guarded pass, but then they began to talk about the "what ifs" of the situation. The three of them then pooled their collective intellects and agreed that the best thing to do would be to leave the Keystone man at Gorre and then find themselves some way to get the hell out of the valley.

Meanwhile, the Keystone man trailed behind, riding hat-less and his head hanging. Never had he felt so far from the Keystone, so empty of human feeling. Never before had he known this utter confusion of thoughts, thoughts that were no more than scattered, shrieking images flying about in his skull, colliding with one another, whirling here and there until he was dizzy from it. His head bobbed up and down and from side to side like that of a rag doll. The three who rode before him ignored him altogether as if he was only some burden they needed to deliver. His horse was tied by the reins to the tail of the horse ahead, and he jerked and swayed along behind, unseen, unheard, and unknown

Link's mind was numb, but by instinct his hands kept picking at the clumsy knots that bound them. It was unnat-ural to be immobile while he was riding a horse. His body kept lurching this way and that. Sometimes he humped himself to adjust his seat in the saddle. His hands kept trying to jerk free of the bonds to help him keep his balance. After a while, a loop of the rope came loose and fell over his knuckles. A little farther on, another loop twisted off his wrists, and now he could feel some slack in the rope. Link's head was still vague, so even as his hands were exploring the possibilities of the slack rope, his mind seemed oblivious to it. He did not really care what was happening to his body. His mind wanted only to wake to consciousness again, to think and see. But there was nothing but images of Gwen, her golden hair, shining eyes. All he wanted was to be with her now. All this talk of how she had died—his mind could not accept it, yet at the same time it was devastating to his spirit.

Link's groping hands examined the puzzle of the knots and his arms began trying to use the slack in order to get the rope up and over his head so he could see it and maybe work it loose with his teeth. He gripped the horse with his legs and bent and pulled one arm up until he felt great pain in the shoulder. It almost worked. The rope almost went over his head. But the squeezing pressure of his legs made the horse nervous so that it shook itself and stiffened up, its hoofs now hitting the ground with more of a jolt at each step. The trussed rider twisted his body the other way, lifted the other arm to the point of screaming pain, tried to drag the rope over his head. Ahead of him, the three horse thieves rode on, oblivious to Link's struggles. Each one had a different version of the speech he was going to make to Flynt about his own personal rôle in the capture of this Keystone man, just as each one had a grandiose plan for what he would do when they got free of the valley. Once they had escaped the avenging guns of Art Pendragon and the ire of Flynt Malin, they would go straight and get good jobs. They would live a clean life, somewhere far away.

As they told Henry Malin later, it wasn't anything like their fault. They'd just been riding, trying to do the right thing and bring him back to Gorre. They heard he'd escaped and Flynt wanted him brought back alive. So, after they caught him, they tied him up so he wouldn't hurt himself or anything, and they put him on his horse, and then it just happened. They were almost to Gorre when one of them heard the horse kind of snort and blow like the Keystone man had kicked it in the ribs or something, but none of them thought much about it, and then one of the others looked back—this was a little later on,—and damned if that cowboy hadn't gotten the rope twisted around his neck and fallen over. Rope looped on the saddle horn, too, so there he was just hanging alongside the horse, turning about as blue as your shirt.

Link was unconscious and had an ugly rope burn about his neck. They carried him into a bachelor's shack across the street from the Mercantile, and two of the thieves who had brought him in were assigned to stand guard over him. Anxiety shone in their faces, but not because they were anxious for his health. They were anxious for their own.

Henry Malin's precaution in trying to keep the news from Gwen Pendragon went for naught. Her gossiping attendant made sure she had the news immediately. The Keystone man—"your cowboy friend"—lay dying just across the street. He had tried to hang himself by putting a loop around his neck so his horse would drag him to death. Poor man. He probably heard that rumor—nobody knows how those things get started—that Mrs. Pendragon give up all hope of ever getting home and killed herself. Or threw herself in the gorge—that was one of the stories going around. It was a shame, so it was, that this accursed valley does that to folks. Just takes away any kind of reason to live at all.

This time there was no crying, no tears, no hurling of herself onto the bed. Instead, she went to the window and stood staring between the bars. On the opposite side of the dirt street, the sheds and empty stores leaned against each other. She held one hand tightly to her breast.

Two wagons stood back to back on a low hill outside Ehre's Hole, an awning stretched between them. Dark smoke rose straight upward from the forge nearby, and at the anvil Evan Thompson's heavy hammer pounded away at a cherry-red steel rod. Art Pendragon waited to speak until the metal had cooled to straw color and blue-black.

"You strike hard this evening, Thompson," Art said.

"Because the steel is stubborn. It fights against being shaped."

He pushed the rod back into the forge and signaled for the boy to pump the bellows. Art looked into the nail keg standing next to the wagon wheel, the keg in which Thompson kept the metal he forged onto his seemingly never-to-be-finished chain.

"Maybe y'ought to pick another piece of steel," he said.

"It wouldn't matter, Pendragon. Wouldn't matter at all." Thompson drank deeply from his giant cup of water. "Every piece has to go into the chain sooner or later."

"I see y'don't have many pieces left, anyway," Art observed. And, indeed, the keg was nearly empty.

"Not many. It's nearly finished. Now, what brings you to my forge?"

"Advice," Art said candidly.

"About Gorre?"

157

"Yeah. Pasque and Link said not to try any kind of frontal attack, but I haven't heard from them in days."

"Gorre Valley is still too strong," the blacksmith said. "The time is not right. I believe Missus Pendragon is there for some purpose, just as I believe she and the others are safe. Unless you start a war, that is."

"What kind of purpose?"

"I don't know. But when the time is right, you will have another message from Gorre. You will know then."

The blacksmith's boy silently pointed to the steel rod, indicating that the hot coals had brought it back to a glowing red color. Evan Thompson picked up his hammer in one hand and his tongs in the other. Seizing the glowing rod and laying it across the horn of the anvil, he smote it with all the force in his arm. Sparks shot off in all directions each time the hammer rang, and the metal grudgingly took shape. Art Pendragon shuddered involuntarily, but not because of the blacksmith's giant blows. He shuddered because he felt the chill come over him again, as if he were standing in a cold wind. But there was no wind.

In Gorre itself the slow-growing darkness of evening was bringing out the first of the house lamps when Link finished his supper. Henry Malin watched him anxiously as he wiped out his soup bowl with the last of his bread. He had told the Keystone man everything: how the lady was all right, how Bob Riley was probably good enough to go out by wagon, how he'd sent his son to bring in the other people. Nobody killed, thank God! Everybody was all right. Mrs. Pendragon's nephew—Pasque, they called him?—was still nowhere to be found, but he would be.

Flynt, he was undisciplined and wild. Something about this place had him all mixed up. Once he really got to know some decent people, out of the valley, he'd straighten up. Planning for this man-to-man fight next spring at the Keystone was probably the best thing that could happen. One way or another, it could be the saving of the boy to get himself a good thorough beating. Link said nothing, but he was thinking that the showdown was going to be with guns, not fists.

Henry Malin took up Link's supper tray and looked around the sparsely furnished room as if to see if there was anything else Link needed. The cowboy had been given a clean shirt and they'd brought him a razor and hot water. And, of course, he could go anywhere he pleased. Henry was going to send Flynt's men away to work somewhere else, anywhere. There'd be no more prisoners in Gorre. All of that was over now. Flynt had just lost his head for a while, but he'd be all right now.

Malin backed out of the door and Link followed him as far as the sagging porch where he sat watching the long evening darken. Across the street he thought he caught glimpses of white at Gwen's window. And then a small light appeared behind the glass. She had put a candle on the window ledge. Instantly he knew what it meant, that bit of yellow shaped like a teardrop glowing in the deepening gloom. He knew and his mouth went dry at the thought.

Link stood up and started across the street very slowly, wary as a thief. His eyes stayed fixed upon the flicking yellow teardrop of light. Once, then twice, he thought he saw a pale form behind it, a face at the glass. He froze, watching. The face was there, then it was not there.

Inside the room, Gwen Pendragon did not notice the cool floor on her bare feet nor the cool draft along her legs, which were bare beneath her cotton nightgown. She was

159

busy listening. Listening to nothing. She could not hear Bob Riley sleeping, for she had already closed his door. She could not hear the woman who sometimes sat in a chair in the back hallway near her own door.

Gwen's mind told her to blow out the candle and go to bed. Take the candle and set it next to her bed, blow it out, pull the covers up, and go to sleep. Her mind went over it and over it as if it was an act that required careful thought, but it was so simple a thing to do. Take the candle, go to the bed, blow out the flame, and let the night's darkness protect her from what she wanted. By morning's light they would find themselves over it, like a fever come and gone. But the candle posed a dilemma not so easily extinguished. She knew full well why she had put it in the window. She wanted him to awaken and see her light and know.

Twice, she stepped to the window and tried to look out across the street only to have the grimy panes of glass throw back images of her own face at her. The glass reflected two candle flames against an abyss of jet black.

She went to the window a third time. She reached for the latch, hesitated, drew back, rubbed her hands together for warmth, reached out and moved the candle, took firm hold of the latch, and drew the sash inward on its hinges. There was an inrushing of cold air and absolute darkness that made her gasp, but she picked up the candle again and shielded it with her hand as she shone it out through the bars to see if there was anyone in the street.

He was there. And he was coming to her! The little flame showed his face barely ten feet away. And now she had no doubt of the next few moments. Through the bars he saw her moisten two fingertips with her lips and heard the tiny hiss as she pinched out the light of the candle.

"Link," she whispered as his hand reached between the

bars to touch her. "Oh, Link."

"Yes," he said.

And for a time they could do nothing but stand there. Her hand was in his. Her breath and his breath met between the bars. There were the beginnings of a few words, but finally there was only the quiet in which they needed nothing more than the warmth of the hand and the breath.

"Shall I . . . ?" he said at last.

"Yes," she said. "But. . . ."

"I know."

"There's a woman guarding me," Gwen whispered. "She sleeps in a little room out there, like a closet almost, in the back hallway. Right by the door." She paused and then whispered again. "She'll hear you. You'd better go back and get some rest. We can talk tomorrow."

"Do we need to talk?" Link said.

"No," she admitted. "I think we both know. Now."

"I want to be with you," he said again.

In the dark she heard Link testing one of the bars with his free hand.

"I think I can work a couple of these bars loose," he whispered, letting go of her to apply both his hands to the corroded iron. "You go over and get in bed, just in case somebody comes. That way it won't look like you'd been helpin' me."

Gwen lacked the will to say no. With pounding heart she hurried to the bed and got into it, sitting there shivering in the dark. She heard him grunt with effort and heard creaking noises of iron against wood.

Link found the bars to be made of poor steel, not iron. The blacksmith who made them must not have held out much hope of them keeping anyone out of the building. Probably just used some old wagon rods he'd had lying around. Link pulled one of the bars this way and that, and finally it was bent enough to come right out of the window frame. The second one was a little stronger. As he was tugging at it, his hand slipped and he felt the rusty metal tear his palm, but he was far beyond caring about that. This bar, like the first, was soon lying on the ground. He paused and caught his breath. His fingers explored his palm in the blackness and discovered a place that felt tender and had a flap of skin torn loose. He wiped it against his pants, boosted himself into the window, dropped noiselessly to the floor, and stared through the absolute dark toward the wall where the bed would be. He crossed the room with silent stealth until his outstretched hands encountered the end of the bed. He felt his way along the bedclothes until his fingers came against her arm.

"What about Riley?" he whispered as he touched her.

"I've closed the door," she said breathlessly.

"Gwen," he said, finding her with his arms and sinking into her embrace.

She drew him to her and kissed him.

"I know," he said.

"Oh, Link."

No reply was possible because his lips were pressed against the warmth of her neck.

Long before the skies held enough morning light to wake the first bird, long before it was light enough to see anything but star-bright sky and black earth they said their fearful good byes and pulled away from each other not once but a half dozen times. Link shivered as he dressed himself in the chill of the room. More good byes, more final kisses, and he went out as he had come in, through the window like a culprit. The steel rods were easy to replace in their sockets, and, when he had bent them back into shape, it was next to impossible to tell they had been removed. Quietly he moved across the street to the shack, and, trembling, he lay down on his own cot to stare numbly at the ceiling while the morning crawled slowly toward the valley.

Link eventually fell asleep only to be awakened by sunlight coming in at the window and the sounds of commotion across the street. He peered out the door, and there seemed to be three or four people yelling at once over there. He took time to wash his face at the basin with the cold water from the ewer and slick back his hair. The torn skin on his hand was superficial. He could hardly feel it.

By the time he got across the street, the racket had subsided to just a few loud voices muffled by the walls of the building. Link opened the door and went into the short hall, then turned and entered Gwen's room where the sour-faced woman and Flynt Malin were standing with crossed arms, confronting Henry Malin and Gwen. With a shock, Link saw Bob Riley behind them, leaning weakly against the door frame.

"What's the ruckus?" Link said. Seeing the room and seeing Gwen in it made him seem to shake all over. He was surprised to see Riley standing there.

Gwen turned toward him, and he had never seen such a look in a woman's face before. It was near panic, full of fright, and her voice was tight and edgy. "Oh, Link," she managed to say, fighting to keep her voice even and formal. "This man . . ."—she pointed at Flynt. "It's really this *woman*," she said. "I want her out of my sight forever."

"What happened?"

"She came bursting in this morning as I was getting dressed. She always does that. She pretends to be looking out for me, seeing if I need water for the basin or anything, but she's really only prying and spying."

"You can't deny it!" the ugly woman screamed. "Look! Right there it is! I *knew* I heard people moaning last night. Lovemaking, that's what it was. Filthy lovemaking!" She was pointing at the bed. On the sheet where the pillow had been and on the underside of the pillow itself were spots of blood. "You *see!*" she screeched. "See! Now look at his arm!" She indicated Bob Riley. And, indeed, there were bloodstains where the wound on his arm had come open and seeped through the bandage. "Fine lady!" the hag squawked.

Flynt sneered at Link. "I guess your friend here ain't so sick that he can't sneak into bed with this fine boss lady of yours," he hissed. "You people ain't any better'n anybody else around here."

Gwen doubled up a fist and took a step toward Flynt, but Malin stopped her. She stood with the man's hand gripping her arm and glared in hatred at Flynt and at the other woman. Link tensed, ready to hit the older Malin for grabbing Gwen that way and then to batter Flynt into a pulp. When his hands closed into tight fists, Link suddenly felt the fresh cut on his palm and he held back.

"They told me this *Mister* Malin was out in the valley, seeing to the people he kidnapped," Gwen said angrily. "Yet the instant this . . . this filthy-minded woman had her gossip to tell him, he was right next door. Probably staring at me through his dirty little peepholes."

A slow, tired voice came from the doorway. "Malin," Bob Riley said, "you're worse'n a sick skunk. I'm not in shape to trade punches with you, but, get me a gun, and I'll sure as hell shoot with you. Maybe you'd be one to take advantage of a woman like that, but I ain't. You're gonna take back what y'said or else I'm comin' for you."

Flynt only laughed. "Hell, th' evidence is right there!" He turned toward his father and Link, ignoring the sick man in the doorway. "Jus' before y'came in," Flynt continued, "she's tryin' to tell us she might 'a' had a nosebleed in the night! Ain't that a good one! A nosebleed. Horseshit!"

Without warning, Link brought his hand up and whipped it alongside Flynt's face with a *crack!* that could have been heard out in the street. Flynt staggered back, touched his face, then piled into Link with both fists pounding for the midsection. Gwen screamed for it to stop, and Henry Malin yelled over the tumult, but neither Flynt nor Link would hear them.

Link pulled away from Flynt's grabbing hands only to have him come charging in and butt him in the stomach. Again they grappled, slamming into the wall, recovering their balance, grabbing with one hand, and punching with the other. Link dodged a wild haymaker blow only to have his foot slip. He fell into the small table next to the window, breaking it and sending the candle to the floor. He came up swinging and grabbing and butted into Flynt. Flynt got him by the arm, and, locked together, they twisted, slammed the wall again, twisted again, and fell out into the hallway. Flynt got up first and threw a vicious kick at Link's head, but missed. Link scrambled up and got in one solid punch that drove young Malin backward out the door. His heel caught on the sill and he fell into the street.

"You're a belly-crawlin' son-of-a-bitch," Link panted, standing over him. "Bob Riley's worth more than a hundred of your kind, an' I'd trust him from here to hell an' back. Now you tell th' lady you were wrong!"

He leaned forward and seized Flynt so he could punch his face again, but Flynt twisted and took the blow alongside the head. He pulled at Link's arm with both hands, and, when he felt the Keystone rider losing balance, he lashed out with a backhand that made Link's head reel. Link stood in the street, spraddle-legged, trying to regain his balance, and Flynt kicked first at his gut and then at his kidneys. Link went down to his knees, managed to catch the next kick with his hands and twist. He sprung up, grabbed and got hold of cloth, a shirt sleeve, vest front, it didn't matter, and he punched with all he had. His fist made solid contact. Flynt didn't seem to move away, so Link punched again.

As his vision steadied and the dust settled, Link saw that he had Flynt by the shirt front and that Flynt's arms were hanging loose. He pulled back for another punch and felt a hand stopping his arm.

Henry Malin had hold of him. "You can stop now," the old man said. "Don't need to kill him."

Link dropped his hold on Flynt.

"My boy's always thinking he's better," Malin said. "Always hoping to have his own way. Don't kill him. A man as good as you doesn't need to take it any further."

Flynt groaned and twisted out of Link's grip. "Outta th' way!" he yelled at his father. "No man does that to me. No man."

"Quit it, Flynt!" Malin commanded. "Who cares if you beat up somebody else, here in this run-down god-forsaken town? Nobody cares! They gave you a chance to go up against him at the Keystone, in front of everyone. Don't waste it here. Come on. Step away. Step away! We've avoided a full-blown war so far, let's not ruin everything now!"

Flynt continued to glare at Link as he panted for breath. He felt the puffy wounds on his face and saw with satisfaction that Link's face and hands were bleeding and bruised. "All right," he said finally. "All right. I don't care who that woman is or who she has in bed. We're bringin' in those others today, an' I want 'em all outta my valley by sundown. Just everybody get the hell out! But know this, cowboy . . . I'm comin' for you! You'd better just watch your back trail from now on, that's all."

He limped off, stopping near the door to pick up his hat. Two of his pals went with him, and they walked with their heads bent together like conspirators.

Link knew that what Flynt had said was right: nothing had been settled and nothing was over with. Still, as he left Henry and walked back to the shed where he could wash up, Link experienced a surge of something that might be called happiness. He and Gwen—nothing now seemed to matter as much as it had a day ago.

He loved her.

# Chapter Ten

Only a look and a voice; then darkness again and silence.
"Tales of a Wayside Inn", Part III
Henry Wadsworth Longfellow

Link washed away the blood and dirt, wincing as the rag touched the open wounds on his face. He peered into the cracked mirror at the reflection of his bruises. Henry Malin went to the Mercantile and brought back a new hat to replace the one Link had lost, along with some sticking plaster and witch hazel, and, while Link tended to his cuts and bruises, Malin arranged for a horse and saddle. On the saddle horn hung a small poke bag with food in it for the trail.

Henry Malin would not provide a gun for the Keystone man; from now on, he said, there would be as little gun carrying in the valley as possible.

"So, if your son's friends decide to attack me again," Link said, "you just want me to toss rocks at them, is that it?"

"I'd rather do anything than run the risk of you shooting an innocent person by accident, or by misunderstanding. You'll be safe enough, riding without a gun for a day or two."

So, without a sidearm and on another borrowed horse, Link once again set out from Gorre along the north road. The day was as bright and sunny as any he had ever known.

The horse had a good steady gait and all seemed well with the world. No one suspected the love that he and Gwen had discovered; they had not exchanged so much as a glance that would betray it. It had been hard to do. It would be a long while before they could be together again and figure out what to do next, but, in the secrecy of waiting, there was a warm, full feeling of joy.

Link had been on the road less than two hours when he met a buggy coming toward him. He recognized the people in it and smiled broadly as he waved his new hat.

"Hi! Missus Saxon! Missus Dunlap! Oliver, that you?"

The boy who was driving lifted his hand in enthusiastic salute. The small girl in the back of the buggy stood up and held onto the seat, smiling at Link for all she was worth.

"You folks all right?" Link said as they drew alongside his horse.

"Better now," Mrs. Saxon said with her homey accent. "But what on earth happened to your face, there? Somebody hit you good, I think."

Link touched the plastered laceration and the big bruise under his eye. "Had an argument with young Malin," he said. "My face hurts, but it's not as bad as it looks. So did the people up the valley let you go without any problem?"

"I think they was glad to get rid of us," Mrs. Saxon said. "That fellow came yesterday, the one from Gorre. He told them we were wanted in town, and, by golly, first thing this morning they had the buggy all ready to go. Didn't waste no time getting us out of there."

"Have you seen my Davy?" Mrs. Dunlap asked. "I been so worried!"

"He's fine." Link smiled. "He's been a big help to Missus Pendragon. And Bob Riley, too. He's just fine. You'll see him soon."

169

"Praise God!" she said. "If anything happened to that boy. . . ."

"Well," Link said, "Davy's all right. He's with Missus Pendragon, waitin' for you in town. As soon as the others get there, you'll be on your way home."

"We sure are curious to know how you did it, Mister Link. We been talking about nothing else all the way here. Mister Pendragon and the men, they catch that evil man, did they? I hope you shot him."

"Ah," Link said. "Didn't shoot anybody, but Flynt Malin got a pretty good beating for what he did. Art Pendragon's probably goin' to meet you folks just outside the valley, at Ehre's Hole. He should have your husbands with him. When everybody's together, then we'll tell everybody everything. There's lots to talk about, that's for sure."

"What about Bob Riley? He got shot, you know!"

"He's gettin' along fine, now. Missus Pendragon took good care of him. He's right there in Gorre, so you'll see him real soon."

"Are you going to get whoever shot the other young man, Oliver Keaton?"

"I spoke with Old Man Malin about that," Link said, "and he's goin' to find out which one of those rustlers did that. Mister Malin will hand him over to the law for trial. He wants to take it kinda careful and do things right from now on. Personally I expect whoever shot Keaton is goin' to be sneakin' out of this valley real soon. But we'll catch up with him."

"And so where you going now?" Mrs. Dunlap asked.

"I need to find Pasque. You remember him, I guess? Didn't happen to see him anywhere, did you?"

"No, I guess not," said Mrs. Dunlap. "I think we'd know

him if we did. He's that nice young fellow from New Mexico, isn't he?"

"Yah, didn't see him," added Mrs. Saxon. "Now, we *did* see that man of Flynt's go past us. Heading north he was. That was . . . oh, I suppose that was near two hours ago, maybe less. He had the horse in a fair lather, I can tell you. He's the one, you know, with the bent nose. The blue scarf. That one. Oh, he was hurrying some place!"

A fast rider, racing north? That didn't sound too good. He'd bet anything that Flynt knew all along where Pasque was, and he had probably sent Banks, the one they called Slick, to tell somebody he was coming. No, it didn't sound good. Then again, maybe Banks was Keaton's murderer and was just hightailing it north to get away.

Link rode on with less of a good feeling than before, but the warm sun and the open road, and especially the night memories rising fully inside his chest soon put a very slight softness of smile across his lips again.

Slick Banks pulled up in front of the dwarf's low, log house, dug back into the side of a wooded hill. The place always made him shudder. Rumor was that the dwarf did more than just grow vegetables and pigs, that he had a gold mine tunneled into the earth behind that dug-out. But gold or no gold, there was nothing about the house that would make you want to enter it. With its low doorway and dark windows, lying in the perpetual gloom of the north slope, it was the kind of place to make you shudder and turn away.

Banks kept his distance and hollered. The dwarf appeared, followed by a gawky, homely girl of about sixteen.

"What you want?" the dwarf shrilled.

Banks got down and led the horse to the water trough. He took a drink himself before answering. "Came from

Flynt Malin," he said. "You seen anythin' of a Keystone rider up here, probably come across the old mill dam?"

The dwarf and the skinny girl looked at each other as if confirming a conspiracy of silence. They both looked back dumbly at Banks.

"Two of 'em come into the valley lookin' for those outsider people," Banks went on. "Henry decided they oughta be let go again, but Flynt wants those two Keystone men kept here a while longer. So, you seen 'im?"

"Hah!" the dwarf nearly shrieked. "How we to know? A fool. Sure we saw him. Sure! Trying to cross over here. Leading two horses. We saw him all right. Stones all slick from moss, a foot of water coming across the wall, and him trying to walk it and lead two horses. A fool."

"Where's he at?" Banks asked.

"I'm trying to tell!" the dwarf shouted back. "Went under. Fell off into the rocks and went under. One of his horses swam to us and we got him, the other went down over the rapids and falls. It's still lying down there dead if y'want to see it."

"What about the rider?" Banks demanded.

"Him!? *I* said he deserved what he got. But *she* . . ."—he stabbed a short thick finger at the girl—"she up and hauls him out. Lay there on the bank most of the day. I figured he'd die, but he didn't. Soon's he can crawl, she ups and helps him into the shack over there and starts to feed him."

"He still there?"

"You don't *see* him, do you? *We* didn't know he was anybody. He asked about those outsider people so she"—there went the stabbing finger again—"she told him where some were! And he went off to find them, and that's all we seen of him. Tell Flynt if he wants us to be his guards up here, he'd better tell us who we're looking for. Fool."

"All right," Banks said. "But now listen. There's another one comin' this way . . . sort of tall with a thick black mustache. Flynt wants him kept up here, but secret. Wants him kept for a long time. He figured you could get 'im the way you got that one called Hansen, back four, five years ago. Flynt says what y'need to do is. . . ."

"I know what to do, I *know* what to do!" the dwarf screeched. "Tell Flynt he owes me. For the last one and for this one, too. You tell him to bring grocery food when he comes, and plenty of it. Plenty! Hear me?"

"Whole damn' valley hears you," Banks said, climbing back into the saddle and pulling away. "Now I'm gonna ride on over to Harrison's, then I'm comin' back through here tomorrow. You just keep Mister Keystone here if y'see 'im, and Flynt'll deal with him later."

"Fool!" the dwarf yelled after him. "I know what to do!"

By following the river Link came to the place of the wide rapids. He dismounted and held the reins while the horse drank and was about to drink himself when he saw the dead animal out in the rocks. It looked to be a horse the color of the one Pasque had been riding, but it was so wet and bloated it was hard to tell for sure. It was far away, but Link thought he could see a saddle that the bloating had forced up around the front legs. No sign of a rider anywhere around, living or dead.

Link walked his horse on up along the run of rapids with their deafening roar in his ears and spray hitting his face. Then he saw the mill dam up ahead. He had been expecting a wide smooth stretch of river with a little diversion wall across it, but this was much more than that. The dam rose out of the rapids, anchored at its base on huge boulders, twice the height of a man. The water poured over it in a single unbroken sheet, beneath which he could see waving shadows of moss.

By now the gorge down which the river hurled itself had deepened considerably and Link began searching for a way up out of it. It was clear they weren't going to get any farther by sticking to the side of the river. Finally he found it, a faint track such as animals might make in going down to drink. He was panting with the exertion when he reached the top, dragging the horse along behind. And there on the top he saw the mill itself.

The stone building was square and heavily built. A dry millrace ran along the river side of it and the wheel looked like it hadn't turned in years. Not surprising, since everything in this damned place seemed to be abandoned and hopeless. A trail led through the dry grass toward a hill where he thought he saw a kind of cabin, or half of a cabin, shoved into the ground. He checked the saddle girth and rebuckled a cheek strap and stepped into the stirrup. Something told him he'd find news of his friend here. He had a feeling it would be good news, too. Despite seeing the drowned horse, Link was certain he would find Pasque alive and well.

With the thick, low door of his dug-out cabin opened just a tiny crack the dwarf watched the tall man approach. He didn't answer the rider's shout. He waited and watched until he was certain there was no gun and then waited again until Link had turned to leave. Then the dwarf pulled open the door and sprang outside. Link's horse reared and snorted.

"Don't shoot, Keystone man! Don't shoot!" the dwarf shrieked.

"Quiet down," Link said, trying to bring his horse under control. "Nobody's gonna hurt you."

"Where's the others, where's the others?" the dwarf shrilled, wide eyes darting all about.

"What others?" Link said.

"Keystone men. Oh! They'll kill us all! Come to kill us all! But that's Flynt's fault, not ours. No need to kill us! There's none of your people here at all! None! Please! Please!"

It was a good act. The dwarf played the part of the cringing, whining coward to perfection.

From the height of his saddle, Link looked down on the small man with curiosity and some degree of pity. If he could get him to calm down, maybe he'd find out about Pasque's whereabouts.

"I'm all alone," Link said. "No need for y'to worry. Look, I won't even get down."

"Get down, get down! Get down!" the dwarf cried.

Smiling to himself, Link swung his leg over and stepped to the ground. It seemed to make the dwarf happier now that he was on more of an equal footing.

"What do you want?" the little man said in his shrill voice. "I have food. Have food. Nothing else. No money. No people here."

"I don't want anything from you," Link said. "I'd just like to ask about that horse out in the river, the dead one. You see a cowboy come through here, some days back? Maybe he was ridin' that horse, or leadin' it?"

"We didn't *kill* that horse! No! Afraid!"

"Whose is it?"

"The cowboy. You said. You said! He tried to cross the river there. There on the mill dam. He led horses across the mill dam! A fool! So much water!"

"What happened?"

"One horse slid off and swam and got over to this side.

The other slipped down the wall! That horse pulled him over, both down together. Both down!"

Link scowled at the dwarf impatiently. "Get to it," he growled with menace. "What th' hell *happened?*"

"That horse pulled him over. *I* said he was drowned, the girl said not. *She* dragged him to the bank. Went into the water herself and dragged him."

"So he's alive?"

"He left here. He's not here! Nobody's here! Three days ago or maybe not. Hard to remember. She got so scared, caring for him. He took that other horse and he left. She gave him food to take. You want some food?"

"No. Where was he headin' then?"

"Don't know, don't know. Other people! He said he looked for other people! Not us. Other outsider people! No people here, but over there, maybe!"

The dwarf swung one of his stubby arms widely, taking in all the area west of the river. Link sighed and reached to straighten his stirrup. He was going to have to go search farther for Pasque, after all.

"Wait, wait!" The dwarf danced up to the horse to stop Link from mounting.

"Yeah?"

"The girl!"

"What about a girl?"

"You help her. You come from that place, that Keystone. She's afraid, afraid. Flynt's men when they find out, they'll hurt her. You know. Afraid of them. You know what they do with girls!"

"He won't hurt her. That stuff's about over with. Everything's gonna be all right. My friends will see to it. Tell her it'll be all right."

"Where are the Keystone men?" The dwarf clutched at

the horse's breast strap to keep Link from leaving.

"Probably across the river. Down at Ehre's Hole, most likely. We'll protect her."

"She won't come out. Too afraid."

"Come outta where? Where is she?"

"Sometimes, she hides in the mill. Down there, down there!" The dwarf pointed away toward the stone building on the edge of the gorge.

"So you're wantin' me to go tell her it's all right?"

"No! No!" he shrilled. "No! She'll jump in the river! Kill herself! Doesn't know you!"

"Well, you just tell her then."

"Would she listen? No!"

"Then I guess I can't help her," Link said.

The dwarf appeared to be turning an idea over in his head. "A note," he said after a moment. His voice took on a pleading tone. "A note. She can read. Can read good as me."

"I oughta write her a note? Sounds like somethin' school kids'd do."

"Wait here! Wait!" The dwarf plunged back into his dark cave of a house and returned with a pencil stub and a piece of paper torn from a book. "I know what to do," he said. "I *always* know what to do! We'll save her. You write."

"Write what?" Link said, taking the pencil and paper the dwarf was thrusting toward him.

"*I* know. Write this. Write this." The small man looked skyward as if mentally composing some monumental message. "Write . . . 'Everything's all right. No danger.' Then write . . . 'Keystone men just across the river.' What's the name, what's the name? The big man? Boss?"

"Boss? You mean Art Pendragon?"

"Yes, yes! I know! I know! Write . . . 'Meet with Art Pendragon.' "

"Why say that?" Link said.

"She must leave here. Leave here, anyway. Too afraid." His shrill voice dropped to a confidential whisper. "There *is* a way, another way. Another way to cross the river. You write for her to go across and find your Art Pendragon. Tell her to find him. A note with his name, it's like one of those. . . .in the war? Men had notes to get through the lines?"

"Safe passage? That what you mean?" Link said, scribbling the words as he spoke.

"Safe passage. I'll tell her that. Yes, so she'll be safe with that name on it. So write . . . 'Meet with Art Pendragon on other side of river. Go ahead to town. Or go on to Keystone place.' Now put your name. Make your mark so she'll know. That's good. She'll do it, that's good. Nothing for her here."

"She your daughter, then?" Link asked, folding the note and handing it to him.

"No. No. Flynt gave her to me. A long time since. He got tired of her, didn't want to look at her any more, not any more. Now she can go because Keystone men came. You come with me."

The dwarf hurried toward the mill house with Link leading his horse but following at a safe distance so as not to alarm the girl. He signaled Link to wait as he vanished into the gloomy interior, only to reëmerge with consternation all over his small face.

"Not here!" he shrieked. "Oh, not here!"

"Settle down," Link said. "She's bound to be somewhere. What's in that other place over there?" He was looking at a round building fifty yards from the mill. It was built solidly of stone and had no windows. The doorway stood open.

"That?" the dwarf said. "Store grain there. When the mill ran. Very dark. She does not like dark. Not like it."

Link wrapped the reins around a sapling and went toward the round stone building. "I'll just take a look," he said. He took his time going into the round stone building, moving slowly to let his eyes adjust to the blackness within and so as not to frighten the girl. *If* she was in there. "Hello?" he said. "Hello?" He took three steps into the room. At his fourth step he heard a metallic *click!* like a door latch, and the floor gave way beneath his feet.

The trap door swung downward violently, and for one breathless second Link was falling and falling through utter darkness. At the bottom of the pit, he landed on his back with a jolt that knocked the wind from his body. His head cracked against something. He lay stunned, unable to get any breath into his lungs. It felt like his whole chest had collapsed. When the red blindness cleared from his eyes, he saw a dim rectangle of light far above. He thought he saw the dwarf looking down at him, but before he could get any air into his lungs to call out, the face vanished and the trap door swung closed. He swallowed enough air to make one feeble cry, then all was lost in unconsciousness.

# Chapter Eleven

Something lost behind the Ranges. Lost and waiting
for you. Go!

"The Explorer"
Rudyard Kipling

All "those Keystone people" had gone from the various
farms and homesteads throughout the Deathwater Valley.
Relieved of responsibility for them and thus no longer as
afraid of Malin and his bunch, the valley people again
began to pay visits to their neighbors, some on the excuse of
returning a borrowed tool, others carrying a cloth-covered
basket of freshly baked bread. They were watchful of what
they said to one another, not venturing any opinions until
determining which way the wind blew. Farmers met at
fence lines to crumble soil between their fingers and bend
stalks of grass while speculating about moisture and crops.
Women asked each other about their children and exchanged recipes again. But these were only formalities to
the real topic of conversation. Eventually two questions always arose.

"Are yours gone, too?"

And:

"Have you seen Flynt since?"

Gradually it became clear and common knowledge "the
outsider people" had indeed left. And Flynt Malin was not
going to start a war over it. Nobody was going to attack

them. It was as though a kind of curse had been lifted from their lives.

In the town of Gorre, the reunited Keystone outsiders took over an empty house behind the Mercantile—there was no lack of abandoned houses in Gorre—and soon found themselves amply furnished with loaned mattresses, bedding, pots and pans, and crockery. Hardly an hour went by without one of the Keystone party visiting Mrs. Pendragon "just to check in," and to see "how things are going." Mrs. Pendragon met them with a self-assurance the likes of which none of them remembered having seen in her before.

Mrs. Pendragon, as they called her, ordered Bob Riley's bed moved across the street into the other building, the one Link had used. She commandeered a disused chair and table from the Mercantile to be put in Bob's former room, and she rummaged the Mercantile for pen, ink and paper. Her first letter was for Art, telling him to wait at Ehre's Hole, and to do his utmost to forestall any vigilante or military assault against Gorre. She handpicked a man from among the townspeople to deliver her letter, and he went without protest.

Gwen next wrote a carefully worded agreement for Henry Malin, saying that she, as representative of the Keystone Ranch, would hold him and his employees blameless in the kidnapping, *provided* that the killer of Oliver Keaton be brought to justice *and* that Flynt Malin appear at the Keystone within the year either to make public apology or defend himself in a fair fight. Two copies she made and took to Henry Malin to sign.

He agreed it seemed to be a workable compromise, but Gwen still shuddered when she thought that she was actually participating in such a barbaric medieval notion as this "affair of honor". But it seemed the only way to pacify the young hothead and prevent him doing further atrocities on innocent people. Somewhere in her most secret thoughts she may have also thrilled a little at the idea of watching her own Link thrash the ruffian right before her eyes. It would serve him right.

The last members of her picnic party came into Gorre, and in the space of two days she had all of them accounted for and settled into temporary accommodations within ear-shot of the Mercantile. The older boys she sent along with one of Henry Malin's employees to collect the Keystone mud wagon and get it ready for travel. The Keystone team was nowhere to be found, so she accosted Malin again and gave him until noon the next day to produce a pair of wagon horses of equal value.

The woman who had been the sentry outside her door vanished from town altogether. Gwen Pendragon led Mrs. Dunlap and Mrs. Saxon into the store where she ordered the clerk to get out his ledger and open an account for each of them, all bills to be sent to the Keystone Ranch.

"They are to have free rein to purchase whatever is needed," she told the man.

Through all of this activity, Henry Malin contented himself with sitting in a chair on the porch of his building. He did not want to leave town and felt it was unseemly to engage Mrs. Pendragon in friendly conversation, so he only sat. He observed the changes that were occurring. He saw children playing with other children. He saw women standing in the sunshine chatting, women he had never before seen talking together. Men, too. Men who hardly grumbled "good day" to other men could now be found lounging with neighbors at the livery or sharing tobacco in the shade of the buildings.

Something had indeed changed. This was the town he had in mind from the beginning. Up the street where the old trapper's cabin had once stood, the sluggish, discolored stream coming from the spring had diminished to less than half its previous size.

There was no more talk about Flynt's accusation of Bob Riley, nor any discussion of the bloodstains on Mrs. Pendragon's sheet. Maybe it was true that she'd had a nosebleed in the night, or maybe it *was* his blood, but got there in some innocent way. Wasn't none of their business, now that a way of settling it had been worked out. The hour of reckoning had been agreed upon, but it was so far into the future that it hardly seemed likely to happen. No more needed saying for now; in fact, most people were glad not to have to talk about it any longer. Things had changed and there was no doubt of it. Mrs. Pendragon was running things now.

As she sat at the table composing letters to the husbands and wives who had suffered through the ordeal, Gwen frequently found herself pausing to stare out the window in a sort of warm and pleasant daydream. She shook herself out of each of these absent-minded moods and scowled because she had let her quill dry out and now had to wet it and wipe it again. But before she had written two more lines, she was again sitting with the pen suspended in mid-air, looking through the window at nothing. She *did* believe in the destiny of love. She believed that Art would understand and forgive and let her go with Link. She knew they had not simply given in to desire but had mutually consummated their inevitable union. It was almost as if fate had caused it to happen here, here in this remote and dangerous place. Absently she stroked her lip with the tip of the feather.

"Gwen?"

She could scarcely believe she had heard that familiar voice at her door, and she turned with open surprise all over her face.

"Pasque!" she exclaimed. "Oh! Pasque!"

The quill pen fell unnoticed to the floor as she jumped up and flew to embrace him. She wrapped her arms around his waist and held him until it began to embarrass him, and then held him some more, laughing and crying against his vest, looking up into his face with glad tears in her eyes, hugging him tightly once more. At last, she was able to separate herself and look at him, and he looked wonderful.

"Oh! You've come, and you're well!" she said.

"*¿Como no?*" Pasque said nonchalantly. "Just took myself on a little *pasear* around this pretty valley."

"Pretty? Oh, I see! You're just being humorous. Well, where have you been? What *happened* to you?"

"A little." He smiled. "A little. Let's see. I nearly drowned in that creek of theirs, except a spooky young *señorita* saved my bacon. She lives with a dwarf. Then, after I dried out, I made a reconnoiter, looking for Link while I spied on people. Found three different places . . . homesteads, I guess they are . . . where people looked safe. So I had conversation with them, stayed for meals, slept in the barns. Just before those men showed up to tell all your friends to get goin' back to town, I had several folks lined up to help us get them back. I guess now we don't have to."

"I'm *so* glad you're safe." She smiled, holding onto his vest with both hands as if she were about to lecture him on being more careful. "Did you come with Link? Where is he?"

"No. He's not with me! I was about to ask you where he is. He's not here?"

"No!"

184

"One of those lyin' *hombres* said he was. Something about him and Flynt Malin having a fight, and Malin leaving town for a while, but Link was waiting for the people to get there, and then he was going to take them out of the valley."

"All I know is that he went to look for *you*," she said, concerned.

There was a light knock on the door frame and Pasque and Gwen turned to see Bob Riley standing there, fully dressed and wearing his hat and gun. He was grinning from ear to ear.

"Riley!" Gwen said. "Are you all right?"

"Fit as a fiddle," he said, touching his bruised face and the sling holding his broken arm. "Hullo, Pasque."

His handshake was not as firm as it could be, but the Riley standing there was certainly not the same one who had been lying in bed almost unable to take nourishment.

"I don't believe it!" Gwen said. "A few days ago you could barely stand up!"

"Well, as soon as you started to take charge, they started to feed me. Stolen beef, I imagine, but lots of it. I'm a little shaky yet, but lots better'n I was."

"Wonderful!" Gwen said. "You had me so worried there for a time."

"Sorry I was such a bother to you," Riley replied. "What's this about Link?"

"Seems he went off looking for me," Pasque explained. "I expect he headed north along the river. That's where we saw each other last. That's where I'd go if I was him."

Gwen's brow was creased in concern as she bent down to pick up her pen. She avoided making eye contact with the two men, busying herself by arranging the papers on the table to give herself time to think. Finally she turned to them. "I'm sure he's safe," she began. "And so are we. I've sent Art a letter to let him know."

"So what do you want us to do?" Riley asked.

"You?" Pasque said. "You sure you're up to doin' anything?"

"You get me a horse, *amigo,* and you'll see."

Gwen resumed control of the conversation. "We need to do something. Now our people will be fine staying here another day or two while you go up the river, like you said, and try to find Link."

"What if we don't find him right away?" Riley asked.

"If you *don't* find him," Gwen said, "for whatever reason, I want you to come back here and help us get to Ehre's Hole. Once there, we can round up a bigger group of men to come back and look for him."

"Sounds like a good sensible plan," Riley said. "Let's get me a horse and get goin'."

Gwen went to the porch with them to see them off. As she was in the middle of her final cautions about taking care of themselves, they saw one of Flynt's men come riding into town. He tied up his horse and came across the street toward them.

"Got a letter for you," he growled. He nodded at the two Keystone riders but it was not a friendly gesture.

Gwen opened the piece of paper. It seemed to be in Link's handwriting:

> Everything's all right. No danger. Keystone men just across the river. Meet with Art Pendragon on other side of river. Go ahead to town. Or go on to Keystone place.
>
> Link

She handed it to Pasque, who held it so Bob could read it at the same time.

"Looks like his lettering," Bob said.

"Where did you see him?" Gwen asked the messenger.

"I didn't see him," he snarled. "Somebody give it to me to bring here. Reckon he's some place."

"And where do you think that might be?" she said.

"How the hell would I know? They just told me to give y'that note, that's all." Flynt's man slouched off down the street, presumably looking for his boss. Or a drink.

"What's it mean?" Riley said.

"Seems to say everything's all right," Pasque volunteered.

"I'm pretty sure he's telling us that he saw Art," Gwen said, studying Link's note again. " 'Meet with Art Pendragon on other side of river.' Does he mean for *us* to look for Art, or that *he* was going to meet up with him?"

"That's how I read it, that he saw Art across the river and was going to cross over," Pasque agreed. "I'll bet Art and some of the boys rode up the river, just like Link and me did. They would come to that mill dam, and Link was probably there trying to find me. So he saw Art and some of the men and sent that note back to let us know he was going across the river."

"Then how did he get this note back across the river?" Riley asked.

"My guess is he wrote it before he went," Pasque answered. "Probably left it with that little dwarf *hombre* at the mill. You want us to ride up there and make sure, Aunt Gwen? Maybe we ought to catch up to him, the one who brought the note. Ask him some more questions."

Gwen frowned again. "No," she said. "No, I'm sure

that's what happened. What's clear is that he wants us to leave and go to Ehre's Hole. And the sooner the better, as far as I'm concerned. If it turns out for some reason he and Art aren't there, we'll go on to the Keystone, just as it says here."

"All right," Riley said. "You're the boss."

"Boss's *wife*," Pasque corrected him.

"You think so?" Riley countered with a grin. "You just ain't been around here the last couple days, *amigo!*"

Gwen rewarded each of them with a sweet and separate smile. "Get going," she said. "First, make sure the wagon is ready and we have enough horses. And find everyone and tell them we need to be prepared to leave tomorrow at first light."

"Yes, ma'am," Riley said.

There was the metallic sound of the latch opening again, then a rectangle of light appeared high above him. A blurry shadow, like a bat, came slowly spiraling downward. It turned out to be a blanket, floating into the pit. Link seized it and thrust it aside to keep staring upward at the dim opening. He thought he saw a thin face looking back down at him before something else began to drop slowly through the dark. When it reached his outstretched fingers, he found it was a basket on a string. It held something wrapped in a cloth. Maybe it was food. He felt something that felt like bread, and a piece of meat. His fingers encountered something else, something thick and greasy. It was a candle, wrapped up together with a block of oiled paper. Inside the paper was a brick of lucifer matches.

When he had taken these things, the basket was pulled back up the long black shaft. He shouted, asked who was up there, asked why they had thrown him down here, asked where he was, demanded his freedom, but the latch only clicked again and all was dark. He had to fumble for a stone on which to strike a match.

Now he could see that his prison was a dry well, lined with quarried stone, about twenty feet across. The guttering candlelight also showed that he had a cellmate, but it was a companion who would be of little comfort. The skeleton was dressed in Levi's, a vest, boots, and a homespun shirt. It lay in a repose that looked almost peaceful and relaxed, as if the man had curled up there on his side to rest and had never gotten up. His gun belt held a few cartridges, but the holster was empty. Link bent closer; the holster was branded with a thick letter L. Near the finger bones of what used to be the man's right hand, a puddle of hardened tallow and a bit of stub was all that was left of a thick candle.

"Got you, too, did they?" Link said. "Don't suppose you got another gun on you anywhere?"

He gingerly lifted the edge of the vest, in case the skeleton might have a hideaway gun. Some men carried such things in shoulder holsters. But there was no gun, no knife, nothing.

Shielding his candle with his hand, Link explored this dungeon turned charnel house and found a rusted tin cup. At the base of the wall he found a hole that turned out to be a drain for the water that seeped down a long slimy line of moss. So he had water and food, although the bread was coarse and the piece of meat was so old and dry he could not tell whether it had been roasted or jerked. They had given him a blanket, too. Someone hoped to keep him alive. Or Flynt Malin had given orders to keep him alive.

He squatted at the wall and held the cup under the dripping tendrils of slimy moss, for his throat was parched. As he sipped, he remembered the legend about the water in this valley, how it destroyed hope in all men who drank it. He wondered if this underground water had the same property. In a place like this, maybe a man shouldn't have too much hope, anyway.

He slept and woke and slept and woke and he did not know the dark of night from the light of day. The trap door opened again and more bread and dry meat came down in the basket. He shouted until he was hoarse. He threatened, he tried to reason with the door that was invisible even with the candle's light, he yelled for attention.

He tried all the stones of the wall but found none of them loose. By stretching to hold the candle as high above his head as possible he thought he could see where the rock was less smooth, less regular, where a man might climb up. But it was six, maybe eight feet higher than he could possibly reach. He lay down again and let sleep overtake him, for there was nothing else to do.

*The Keystone rider was awakened by a sudden chill and a blinding white light pouring down from above, a light so intense and brilliant it blinded him. He could only lie on his back staring into it. Then he saw the face. Crows Woman! It was the face of Crows Woman!*

*He laughed. He laughed at his own fear and laughed at his joy until he felt tears threatening the corners of his eyes. She had come to help him get out of here. The last person he expected, and she had come for him. Her hair had turned from streaked gray into a dazzling cascade of pure white, sending off the blinding streams of light. Her face glowed. The rider sat up and wiped his eyes. Her hand and arm were extended, pointing downward.*

*"Who's with you?" he called out. "Is Two Nose with you?"*

*She only pointed, down into the pit.*

*He looked.*

*"Is Two Nose there?" he called again. "I need help!"*

*Again her only reply was the outstretched phantom finger.*

*It pointed at the skeleton, and suddenly Link understood. She was not real. She was a dream, a vision, a ghost. She couldn't release him from the pit. His fate was to end up like that poor cowpoke, lying there, turning to dust. That's what she was telling him.*

*Or was she telling him something else?*

*Two Nose said she had the power to make buffalo bones rise up and walk. Even if she were a ghost, maybe she could bring this man back, make him live. Make him walk. Together the two of them could figure a way to climb out of this well.*

*"Go ahead!" he called. "Wake him up! Make him walk. He can help me!"*

*The pointing finger withdrew into the blinding white light. Then the face withdrew until it was only a small glow against the blackness of the closed trap door.*

*"Help me!"*

*And all went dark, and all was quiet except for the echo of his cry.*

Gwen Pendragon managed the withdrawal from Gorre with efficiency, keeping the party moving at a steady pace to save the horses. Once they were through the two passes and out onto the sage hills again, she sent Pasque and Riley out ahead of the two wagons to scout as far as the horizon, and then sent them back along the road as a rear guard. When it was time to stop, so the women could rest and stretch their legs, she again sent Pasque and Riley forward to check the road, and then to the rear. As the party jolted along in the wagon, she encouraged the women—and the older children—to tell her all about their experiences in the Gorre Valley so she would have a good grasp of everything that had happened when she reported to Art.

It was after suppertime and getting on toward dark when they finally reached Ehre's Hole. Just outside of town, they came to the Keystone encampment where a half dozen white canvas roundup tents were pitched in a row with a rope corral behind. The cowboys, who had been gathered around the fire for grub, left their tin plates of food and tin mugs of coffee cooling on the ground and rushed to tip their hats to Mrs. Pendragon and shake hands with Pasque and Riley. Hearing the commotion, Art came out of the hotel. At first he could only stand there on the porch, amazed. There were Pasque and Riley, the Keystone mud wagon with Gwen holding the lines, another wagon behind that, and his men walking alongside, everybody talking all at once.

When the team was tethered to a hitch rail, a happy chaos took over. Husbands came running from the hotel dining room, napkins still flying from shirt fronts. Children hugged legs, men hugged wives, and men with neither wives nor children slapped backs at random and shook whatever hands they could reach.

Gwen and Art joined hands silently, and it was not until they were on the porch and away from the happy mêlée that they embraced and kissed. He had not seen her so happy, so poised. She smiled on him as though he was her greatest friend and held the keys to a great treasure. He asked about the dangerous journey through the *cuestas* and she asked about the Keystone. He told her of his pride in her, and she exclaimed how wonderful it was to see him waiting here. He asked how she had managed it all, and she asked him how surprised he had been to get her note.

Over the next few hours, she told him everything she could.

"Dammit!" he said more than once. "I feel like charging into that damn' valley, anyway, and just ridding the territory of Flynt and his men. They're nothin' but damn' cattle thieves and horse thieves and murderers."

"I gave Mister Malin my word," Gwen said. "He wants Oliver's killer to see justice just as much as we do. Whatever happens, there are too many innocent people in there to start a range war. As for Flynt Malin, he'll either show up for his ridiculous duel at the ranch or . . . more than likely . . . put his tail between his legs and head out for somewhere much farther west."

"You won't mind if some of the boys go after him? That is, if he lights out for parts unknown? Link, for instance?"

Gwen pulled back a little. "I suppose that would be up to whoever wants to hunt him down. But I haven't seen Link yet! What have you done with him?"

"I haven't seen him, either," Art said. "Was he supposed to be here?"

"I think so! He sent a note," she said. "Look, I have it here." Gwen's voice trembled a little when she said Link's name.

Art read the note and scowled. He read it again, his lips moving as he soundlessly mouthed the words. He'd seen Link's lettering enough to be pretty sure it was his, but he couldn't make out what he meant by "meet with Art Pendragon other side of river."

"I dunno," he said, handing the note back to her. "Sounds almost like he wrote it for somebody that doesn't know any of us. 'Keystone place' and like that. I bet he was in a hurry. That's it! Sure! Link must've spotted a few of the boys on the other side of the river and was in a hurry to make sure he caught 'em. Before they rode off, you see? I *had* sent Lem and Jess and two others up the river to scout for a crossing. Then I got your note, and I told Mac to ride up there an' find 'em. They were supposed to go on back to the Keystone from there. Heck, that must be it! Link met up with Lem and Jess and Mac, and they all rode home together. They figured we were on our way back, too, and it'd be a waste of time to ride clear back here to Ehre's Hole. Everything's fine. We'll find 'em at the ranch."

"Well, I hope so," Gwen said. "I'm anxious to be there myself."

"Say," Art said, almost as an afterthought. "We owe somethin' to that young woman that came out of Gorre to tell us what the boys were doing. Without her, I guess, we'd've charged in and got a lot of people killed."

"Where is she?" Gwen asked. "I should meet her."

"Oh, she's around, somewhere. She'll be comin' back to the Keystone with us. Thanks to her . . . and you . . . things are all right now. Well, they *will* be, once I get my hands on whoever killed Oliver Keaton, and once Link settles his score with Flynt Malin."

# Chapter Twelve

There is a chamber far away
Where sleep the good and brave.
"The Execution of Montrose"
William Edmoundstone Aytoun

Art Pendragon turned in his saddle to look back at the line of travelers. What a proud picture they made, this Keystone pilgrimage! Himself in the lead on his tall buckskin, Gwen next to him, riding Link's black, Messenger, Riley and Pasque flanking them, four more riders behind, and behind them the string of wagons. Four, altogether: the mud wagon with its six seats, then the roundup wagons carrying tents and bedrolls and food and gear. In the rear rode a vanguard of four more Keystone men.

"Looks like a wagon train bound for Oregon!" Art laughed.

"Except Oregon's *that* way!" Gwen chuckled, pointing northwest.

"How's that horse of Link's behaving for you?" he asked.

"Wonderfully." She smiled, leaning to pat Messenger's thick neck. "He needs exercising, though. Look how eager he is!"

The trip out to Ehre's Hole to bring the people home had given Art plenty of chances to see Messenger's high spirits. When the boys had let him out of the corral, the big black had tossed his head and chopped the ground with his

195

hoofs and ran like a stallion in rut. When he finally had come trotting back to the cavvy, there had been a sheen of sweat on him and his nostrils had been blowing hard. *Just like Link,* Art had thought. *Always has to be off and running somewhere.*

Riley saw the same connection between horse and rider, but said nothing. It bothered him, the way Gwen was managing Messenger, the way she kept talking softly to the horse and stroking him with her glove. Sometimes, she would drop back along the line of horses and wagons to ask how the ladies and kids were getting along, and, when she urged the black horse forward to catch up with Art again, there was something about it that Riley didn't much like. He didn't even much like to see her on Link's horse. It just didn't seem right, somehow. Well, he didn't really know why it troubled him. It was best just to forget it.

"Yeah," Art was saying, speaking to the group of four who rode in the lead, "our good lady, here, did just the right thing, I think. I think we can trust Henry Malin to round up Oliver Keaton's killer and turn him over to the court. And nobody got shot . . . well, except for you, Riley . . . and we didn't have to charge in and try to deal with all those farmers. God knows, they got enough trouble already. Never heard of a worse place to try and raise stuff in than that valley of theirs."

"Pasque called it a pretty valley!" Gwen laughed. In her mind she asked herself, as she had uncountable times: *But where is Link?*

"*Con permiso,* Uncle," Pasque replied, "but what will you do when young Malin comes to the Keystone? I wish I could be there to see it!"

"Hah! Well, Gwen, here, she gave them her word, so he'll get fair treatment. And I'm sure that Link is goin' to be more than willing to deal with him. Give him a good thrashing, like his old man should have done when he was a colt."

Art turned so that he could speak to the group of ranchers who rode with them. "I have to tell you, though . . . there's a chance it could turn into a shoot-out. Flynt Malin's *that* bad. I don't trust him not to come in carryin' a gun. But I'm still not worried about Link. Back in the early days before most of you came into the territory, it was just me and men like Link Lochlin, taking care of rustlers like Malin with our guns. That's the way it always was. I remember the time when young Pasque, here, went after Tallak Hochland! Riley, you really missed something *that* time! This little *hombre,* scarcely dry behind the ears, he ups and says . . . 'Uncle Art, let me shoot the big . . . never mind . . . if that's what he wants so bad.' Nowadays, I guess we'd have to call a meeting about it, and ask a lawyer what he thinks, and then end up not doing anything at all."

"When are you leaving for New Mexico?" Gwen asked Pasque, changing the subject. She had seen this often in Art, this quick tendency to want to settle trouble with violence. At times it was admirable to see him take up his Winchester and go to help a neighbor. But the image of a battle between Link and Flynt Malin. . . . She knew she had agreed to it in order to gain their safety, but she hadn't actually believed that it would come down to a deadly gunfight. If only she knew where Link was. . . .

"I'll probably hit the trail as soon as I see you and Art home." Pasque smiled. "I've been gone too long as it is. The *Señora* Elena will have forgotten me. I miss the little ones, too."

"I know," Gwen said. She beamed a warm smile at him, a smile that warmed him all the way down to the bottom *conchas* of his fancy riding chaps. He felt instantly that here was a beautiful woman who understood love and longing very well, very well, indeed, and he felt his uncle was one of the world's most fortunate *caballeros*.

Two weeks passed, and then three, and there was still no word of Link. Reluctantly Art Pendragon ordered that the big black horse be taken from the main corrals and put on pasture with the Keystone herd, for it looked as though his owner was not coming soon.

A delegation of the kidnapped ladies came one day with their husbands, bearing all manner of baked goods. Soon the table in the kitchen was virtually buried under baskets lined in calico, redolent with fresh bread, muffins, pie, and buns. It was their way of thanking Gwen for all she had done in the Gorre Valley incident. One couple had said to another couple how they should really pay a call and thank her, and, as the word spread, it became a reunion, an impromptu celebration of their freedom and of their escape from harm. But beneath the folksy cheer and gossip, it was evident what the people had come to see.

"Link isn't back yet," Art told them. "Malin hasn't decided to show his face, either."

"Art," John Robinson said, "there's something else. Some of us were talking. We were thinking how the Keystone always ends up at the middle of these things. Doesn't seem right, you having to always put up the money and men whenever there's rustling going on."

"It's all right," Art said. "There isn't a man on this whole place who wouldn't go to war for you folks whether he ever got paid or not. That's the kind of men I got here. And besides that . . . I've been such a lucky cuss over the years that I sure don't mind sharing when it's called for."

"Still and all," Robinson went on, "we had this idea. We thought we'd form ourselves into a livestock association that could take up some of that load. A big group to police the range and help folks out. Like the one they have down in Cheyenne. We thought maybe we could meet here at your place, maybe twice a year. Plan for the fall roundup, talk about prices and feed and such, and maybe agree on how many head of cattle we should have on the range. Things such as that."

"I'm with John," Frank Saxon said. "A cattleman's association could do a lot to help people. You saved us more'n once, and you ain't never lorded it over us. We'd oughta come to the Keystone a couple times a year jus' to pay respects, anyway. And we don't come empty-handed, do we boys?"

Saxon nodded around the circle at his neighbors, and they applauded. This had been a bad business, this kidnapping, but Robinson and Saxon were right. Art could see that some real good was set to come of the incident even though Link was missing and it was still uncertain whether Flynt Malin would keep his word and show up.

"So where is that Link Lochlin, do you suppose?" Halptmann asked, as if he had read the question on Art's face. "I hope he didn't run into trouble back there."

Sitting in a shadow toward one corner of the room, Gwen was glad that her quick hot flush of concern went unnoticed.

"Maybe we oughta go look for him," Bob Riley said. "Somebody oughta."

"Give it another few days," Art said. "I know him pretty well, and I wouldn't be too surprised if he decided to go back into Gorre for some reason. He was going somewhere when Pasque ran into him, you know, 'way back before all the trouble started. Pasque wasn't even right sure Link *was* heading back here. He may have some unfinished business he's taking care of."

Gwen winced inwardly. Surely he could not have just ridden off to finish some kind of business. Surely not. Not after what had happened that night.

"So, let's figure he did go back for something or other," Art continued. "You'd have to allow him a couple of days, at least, more like a week. Then I'd add two, no, make it three days maybe to get back onto Keystone range."

Art's calculations were working against him. Even figuring that Link's business kept him an extra week, he should have been back by now. But the question was, where was he?

"That water you talk about," Frank Saxon said. "Maybe he drank that and it made him forget to come home. Yes?"

Uneasy laughter followed, for while they had all felt the drab hopelessness of the Gorre Valley, a gray dispirited atmosphere that lay like poison in the dry air, never had they forgotten their homes. Two of the women, the two who had felt most deeply that homesickness, were startled at how quickly Mrs. Pendragon left her chair and rushed from the room.


At the bottom of the black pit, Link sat, slumped and wretched, against the cold dampness of the stones. He stared through the gloom at the skeleton of the other cowboy. He spoke to it. "Why don't you get up," he rasped. "Get th' hell up and let's get out of here."

There was no answer. Link scratched at his beard. His voice sounded hoarse and strange to him. He was weakening, losing strength by the hour. His head felt oddly vacant, too. He tried to think of Gwen and the night they had spent together, but even that memory seemed to come only in fragments.

"Get up," he repeated, his voice a whisper.

There was no answer. There never was.

"Got it figured out," he went on. "You get up and stand on my shoulders, see. Or I stand on yours. Makes no difference. There's a rim up there. Kind of a ledge. We can reach it an' be halfway there."

No answer from the skeleton who lay in the dark.

"Listen," Link lowered his voice even more, like a conspirator. "Listen here. I still got my Barlow knife. We help each other get up to that trap door, and I'll get at it with my knife. I'll whittle our way outta here. Get up."

He listened for an answer. He leaned back against the wall and let his head drop to his knees. He closed his eyes—trying to stare through the darkness was too painful. He'd just rest them a little, just take a little rest. Then he needed to talk to the other prisoner about getting themselves out of this hole. . . .

*A cold light roused him, filling the pit with such brilliance that there were no shadows. He raised his face toward the source and the whole roof of the hole had been removed. The building and its roof had disappeared, leaving dazzling sky. He blinked hard against the glare and slowly there came into focus a figure standing at the very edge of the opening, so close that the tips of his boots stuck out over the void.*

*It was a huge figure, a massive man in leather apron, looking down at him.*

*"Thompson," the bearded captive croaked. "Help me!" His voice was a dry rattle, bouncing off the unconcerned stones.*

*Thompson, the blacksmith, began to lower a chain, link by link, so slowly that the chain seemed to be growing out of his hands. He seemed to be pulling it out of the sky. Down and down it came, past the narrow ledge Link had seen with his candle's light, down and down, link by link. They were strong links, each as big as a man's forearm.*

*Link found he was standing up. He called out to rouse his companion.*

*"Wake up!" he said to the skeleton. "The blacksmith! He's here! We got us a way out of here! Wake up!"*

*Link stood to grasp the end of the chain, but, even standing and stretching from his toes and reaching as high as he could, he could not quite touch it.*

*"Need more," he rasped through his dry throat. "Need more."*

*"There is no more," the blacksmith said. "Not yet."*

*"I don't get it," came Link's rough whisper. "Don't understand. Don't understand."*

Then all went dark, and he collapsed on the dank floor.

Sounds awakened him. He turned over and sat up with a moan. The sounds meant that the basket would be coming down on its string, bringing him more meat and bread and another short stub of candle, maybe. There was never so much as a hint of a human voice from the person doing the lowering, never. The only thing he'd figured out was that it was a female, probably the girl the dwarf had talked about. The girl and the dwarf were in this thing together.

He had begun to learn how to hear her coming. Unless he had fallen asleep, he would make out the sound of the outer door opening up there, and then the soft padding of her feet on the heavy wood floor just before she raised the trap. He listened to the creaking noises and figured out she was using a block and tackle to raise the heavy trap door.

The pulley probably hung right above the trap, up in the rafters somewhere.

He told himself he needed to think. What was he going to do when he got out? Make a clean breast of things with Art and then run off with Gwen? Or do what he knew was best for Art and just disappear? He wanted to be with her so very, very much. It was natural. It was meant to be. But all such questions finally depended upon his getting out of this foul, cold prison. He couldn't think about the future until he found some way to believe there would *be* one. In the end, all he could do was to listen for her to come. His whole and total hope of a future was simply that the trap door would open one more time.

He ate and he slept. He collected water from the seep and drank. He listened and waited. He conversed with his bony companion and the sound of his own voice made him realize that he needed to talk with the girl the next time she came. But it would be no use. No use at all, unless he could overcome his certainty that there was no use talking to her. Two or three times he had summoned up all his mind's strength and got himself to his feet, and took a drink from his cup so his voice would be clear, and then he waited for her. As the basket came down, he waited for just the right time, just the right moment, but each time he only waited and nothing more.

But this time, he heard her coming and barely had time to realize it. There was the sound of the door, then the footsteps, then the squeaking of rope running across pulley blocks, the *click* of the latch, then the dull rectangle of light appearing, and the basket being swung over the hole.

"Hey!" he managed to croak. "Wait! Let me talk to you! Who are you? Just tell me that, won't you? No harm in your telling me who's feedin' me."

He trembled for the answer and waited. She hadn't dropped the trap door yet. She was waiting by the opening.

"It's me," she said. The girl looked over the edge of the hole.

"Can I get you to help me out of here?"

"He'd kill me. Or worse."

"The little guy?"

"He's strange. He knows everything I do."

"Can't you just get me a ladder, or leave a rope hangin' down or something?"

"No. He'd know. He'd kill me."

"I gotta do something," Link said. "Can't stay here. If I got out, I could help you."

"Kill him?"

"Maybe. You oughta just get away."

"Can't."

She began to pull the basket back up and he knew she would then close the trap door and leave him in the black again.

"Wait!" he said. "Just get me a tool! A pry bar, or even a shovel . . . something. Then you don't have to do anything. I'll get myself out, and he'll never know how I did it. I'll get to my friends and come back for you."

"You'll come back?"

"Yes."

"You swear?"

"Yes. I swear."

"Maybe," she said.

It seemed like weeks before she returned. Link ate and slept many times. He lit the candle many times and studied his prison for gaps or cracks into which he could put a pry bar or a shovel. Sometimes he put a candle next to the skeleton and squatted there for hours, carrying on a conversation with the dead man.

The trap door finally opened. The small face looked down at him.

"Still there?" she whispered.

"Yes." He scratched a match and lit the candle so she could see him.

"Who's the Indian?" the girl asked.

"Who?"

"The Indian woman. Last night she was in my room, standin' next to the window. I saw her kinda floatin' there, but I wasn't feared. She was all made outta nothing but light, somehow. You ever see foxfire? She shined like that. Like foxfire. Only white. Who you think she was?"

"Not sure. Maybe someone I knew."

"She didn't say nothing."

"I know."

"She pointed outta my window, out to where there's that big junk pile. Be a dump heap. Mostly stuff from when they built the mill."

"Yeah?"

"I went an' dug around in it this morning afore he waked. I found this. I reckon it's what she was pointing at. Lige don't know about it, so he won't miss it. Look out, now. I gotta drop it down."

Link didn't realize what she was talking about until he saw she was holding something heavy over the opening. It looked as if it took all her strength to keep it from falling. He stepped back against the wall just as she let it go. It ripped down through the dark to *thud* into the dirt, and, when he looked up again, she was already lowering the trap door.

A pick. She had found the head of an old longhorn pick,

like the kind they use building railroads. It was just the steel head without a handle, and the two long points were rusty and chipped. It wasn't very sharp, but it would do.

"Look here!" he said, holding the pick in the candlelight so the skeleton could see it. "We'll take turns diggin' some of these stones loose, and pretty soon we'll have us a way out."

The skeleton seemed to grin back at him.

The evening was chilly. Gwen placed a chair by the fireplace and put a kerosene lamp on the mantle so she could stay warm while she did her sewing. Since Art was in his study, writing figures in the leather ledgers, the great room was quiet except for the popping and murmur of the burning logs. Quiet, and chill. She put down her needle and put out a hand to touch the stones of the massive fireplace. They were cold. A little heat from the fire radiated out to warm her feet, but there was coldness emanating from the rock.

The private inward happiness that had at first kept a constant glow in her face had now subsided. For a time there had been a continual undercurrent of memory for her, but now even those had dwindled until there were only memories of small moments. She could even plan for them to come to her. Often, she would conjure up memories while brushing her hair or lying in bed or strolling slowly back and forth along the porch. This evening she had been sitting with Art in the study, but after a while she rose and told him she had decided to go into the great room and sit by the fire. The truth was that she wanted to sort through her memories there, much the way she sorted through her sewing basket to find something to work on, and she would bring out a moment of memory to think about.

Her hand shrank back from the cold stone. She thought about Link's warmth. Especially afterward. Before it happened, when he had held her in his arms, she had felt warm and excited. Afterward, lying together with the heat of their bodies all around them, she knew it was meant to be. Afterward, in that delicious warmth, she was certain she and Link were fated to be together.

She picked up her needle and embroidery. Link's long absence worried her greatly, but it did nothing to remove her faith in him and her faith in their future together. Possibly he had gone to prepare a home for them. Possibly he was rounding up his own livestock and moving them to their own place. He would come riding up the road one day and all would somehow be well.

Inside her thoughts, Gwen gently folded her memories of that night, and put them away. As she bent to her embroidery again, there came a tiny errant draft of chilled air across the cold fireplace stones and she shuddered.

# Chapter Thirteen

"Lady, for this day's deed I shall do you service if
ever it lie in my power."

> *King Arthur and His Knights,*
> "The Knight of the Cart"
> Sir Thomas Malory

The listener lay down on the dusty planks, and put an ear to
the trap door. From down in the pit below there came the
sounds of *tap, tap, ching!* and then the scrape of metal on
stone. Next came a heavy *thump!* of some object striking
earth. This was followed by cursing, then a scuffling of
boots against rock and the *uh!* of someone landing hard on
their feet after falling. A hoarse voice could also be heard
faintly through the crack around the edge of the trap door.

"It'd go faster if you'd jus' help some," the voice slurred.

*The skeleton's head was turned to watch the man trying to
climb the wall, and he only grinned his hideous gaping grin.*

"At least brace my leg so's I don't fall, can't you," the
listener heard the voice say. "It's hard enough diggin' with
one hand without worryin' about my foot slippin'."

A long silence followed.

"Aw, y'may as well jus' lay there."

*The skeleton's arm was cocked to one side, as if he were about
to raise himself to a sitting position.*

"God dammit, neither of us is goin' anywhere this way. I
jus' don't know why that little sawed-off runt or else that

damn' Flynt Malin don't come back an' finish me off with a bullet. Wish he would, that's what I wish."

Up above, the listener listened with interest as the voice went on and on.

*The skeleton listened, his grinning line of teeth reflecting the candle flame.*

"Y'know what's happened, don't you?" the voice from the dark hole said. "Yeah, you know. Gwen . . . the lady I told y'about . . . she got out of the valley, got to Art and the rest of them. Then she told Art about that night, about me. So that's why nobody's come looking for us and never will. 'Ol' Link?' they'll say. 'Him?' Why, he's just one more good hand that went to range. 'Happens all the time,' they'll say. Or they'll say . . . 'I bet he messed with the boss's wife and can't show his face around the territory any more.' They figured I'm so shamed I rode off and won't be back. Either that, or I'm dead somewheres. Either way, I might as well be. Nobody's comin' for us. An' I ain't makin' any headway on that damn' wall. If I had a gun, I'd probably just blow my own brains out."

On the other side of the trap door, the listener frowned. There was no one else talking down there, nobody replying to the prisoner's mumblings and mutterings. He was down there alone and talking to himself. The listener had no idea what all the rambling words meant, but the voice coming from the pit probably proved that the rumor was true. People out in the valley said that a Keystone rider *had* ridden this far into the Gorre Valley. And no one had seen him ride back out again. He was still in the valley, they said, somewhere.

Three times the listener had watched from hiding when the frail girl with her basket went into the deserted granary, and three times there had come the sound of creaking pulleys and rusty hinges before the girl came out again and hurried back to the dwarf's ugly little dug-out of a house. One day, the listener figured, one day the dwarf would have to go away on some errand.

All that was needed was the patience to wait.

Link Lochlin stacked the three stone blocks against the wall, then took them down and stacked them another way. It was no use. They made only a single step no matter how he arranged them, even standing them on end. He had managed to pick and pry them out of the wall, and then used the pick to gouge back the sand behind them so as to make footholds. The third hole in the wall took him a body's length away from the floor of his prison, but it was a precarious foothold. His left hand clawed at the stones for support and he had to keep his body tight against the wall while he reached up with the pick head to hack away at the rock. Sometimes he got in two, sometimes a half dozen pathetic little pick blows before losing his balance and falling back to the floor.

He cursed each time he fell. He cursed and muttered at the skeleton for not rising up to help him. Each time he slipped and crashed painfully to the dirt, he nearly gave up the whole damned idea; each time it took even longer to summon up the will to go back up the wall.

*As the prisoner slept, the skeleton scrambled up the wall like a spider and vanished through an unseen opening. Then came the echo of footsteps on the planking, up there in the darkness, and from far, far away came the sounds of a hammer striking a ghostly anvil. In the long darkness following, the man of bones silently returned and lay down again, just as before.*

The listener, who now made furtive visits every day, could tell from the sounds that the prisoner was digging his way higher and higher, ever closer and closer to the trap door. Then on the fourth day, or perhaps the fifth, the dwarf came out of the dug-out in the early morning hours. He mounted his small mule and rode away with a sack of provisions swinging from the saddle horn.

It was time for the listener's patience to be repaid.

It happened later that morning. The frail girl brought her basket of bread and meat to the granary as usual, but, instead of entering an empty building, she found the listener there, waiting for her. The visitor had dragged a wooden crate just to the edge of the shaft of sunlight coming through the door and was sitting on it. In her arms, she cradled a double-barreled shotgun.

Link did not know whether it was time for his food or not, for in his dungeon there was not enough of day or night to mean anything. All he knew about time was that there was either a sliver of light along one side of the trap door, or there was total blackness. Day or night, it had no meaning to him. Making footholds in the wall by prying the stones out had no meaning, either, except as something to do while he waited to die. He figured he'd either fall and hit his head on one of his own rocks and kill himself, or fall and break a leg or arm and get gangrene and die, or, if things went really swell, the trap would open and the dwarf would just end his misery with a gunshot. The dwarf or Malin. With a resigned sigh he jammed the pick point into another crack and pried at the rock. It fell unexpectedly, lots easier than the others. He wondered how close it came to hitting the cowboy who was still lying on the floor down below. Serve the son-of-a-bitch right for not helping.

Link had by now managed to dig out four big stones near the top of the pit, gaining himself a good wide place to stand, and a good handhold, too. He was so close to the trap door that he could reach out and touch it. He felt the thick iron hinges and explored the latch. Somehow, the thing could be raised and somehow it could be made to swing downward, too. Twisting his neck way over, Link peered up through the crack. If he heard the girl coming, should he stay where he was, or quickly climb back down? He deliberated the problem. Well, sure: the answer was simple. Better to stay right there. His brain slowly forced itself through the probable scenario. First, she'd raise the trap door. Then, as soon as she had the rope tied off good so the door wouldn't fall back down, but before she could turn back toward the opening, he would climb out quickly and grab her.

He heard footsteps and held his breath. They were heavier. It was not the girl. The steps moved across the floor above, and then came a little scratching sound, like something being dragged across the floor. Link flattened himself against the stones and waited, even though his legs were starting to cramp and his fingers felt like they were paralyzing into hard hooks.

After a little while, there were more footsteps, more familiar ones. He thought he heard a whisper of surprise, then there was more whispering. Before he had time to figure out who could be up there whispering with the girl, the steel hook went *clink* into the iron eyebolt of the trap door. The thick rope creaked between the wooden sheaves as it took up the strain. He shrank into the wall, hugging it hard and trying to stay invisible. His eyes hurt from the sudden glare of light. He hadn't figured on that intense glare, of not being able to see, but it was too late to matter now. He swung the hand holding the pick up over the edge of the hole, then let go of it and brought his other hand up. Then he dragged his foot up to the last hole he'd made, flopped out onto the planks and grabbed up the pick head as he stumbled awkwardly to his feet. He glared around wildly, this filthy, bearded apparition from the depths, already convinced the next thing he'd feel would be hot lead ramming through his gut and smashing him back down into the dark pit forever.

But what he saw instead was the thin homely girl gagged with a kerchief and hog-tied with rope, probably the same cord she used to lower the basket. She was sitting against the wall, staring with wide eyes over the edge of the kerchief.

The woman who stood there, holding the shotgun, was tall and had a strong look to her. She was neither old nor young, neither attractive nor unattractive. Just a woman, dressed in sheepskin coat and men's overalls as if she had been herding sheep or rounding up cattle. What made her distinctive was the double-bore shotgun she had aimed at Link's mid-section.

"You from the Keystone Ranch?" she inquired.

"Yeah," he answered. "Link Lochlin."

"You got a gun?" she asked.

"No."

"Anybody else down that hole there?"

"One, but he's dead. There's just his bones down there, and his clothes."

"What kind of clothes?"

"I don't know. Vest, boots . . . shirt. Empty holster."

"Was the holster branded?"

"Yeah. Thick letter L on it."

She looked sad for a moment and her eyes searched the darkness as if trying to see clear to the bottom of the pit.

"That's not an L," she said. "That's the Running Iron brand."

"So, you know him?" Link asked.

"I expect it's my husband," she said. "Is that who it is, girl?"

The girl nodded and began to weep.

The woman took him outside to the crude corral and helped him find a saddle to put on one of Lige's starved mules. It was a broken saddle, but it would work.

Before they rode off, the woman went back into the stone building to release the girl. "Nothing happened, girl," she said. "It's best if you get rid of that pick before Lige gets back, and then just go on bringing your basket out here every day. If Lige finds out there's nobody alive down there, you tell him you don't know anything. You just lowered the basket and nobody took the food. Maybe you oughta throw the food down anyway. Tell Lige you did that, if he finds out the cowboy isn't there. It's real important for you to just go on like before. If you get in trouble, head for my place, and I'll take care of you. Understand?"

The thin girl nodded miserably. Sniffling, she lifted up the pick head and slouched out the door.

"Thanks!" Link called. "Thanks for helpin' me. Probably saved my life."

There was a slight, one-sided smile for a moment, and then she was around the corner of the building and gone.

"Where we headed now?" Link asked.

"My place."

Once again the Keystone rider was in rags, surrounded by his own foul stink, riding on a mule that no self-respecting hand would even look at. The mule had a jolting, jerky gait. The broken saddle kept shifting and chafing at him.

The woman's place turned out to be a three-room stone hut with goat pens surrounding it on three sides and a fenced sheep pasture stretching off across the hill. It was built like a fort and had narrow windows. Burned into the heavy shutters was the same Running Iron brand he had seen on the dead man's holster. She put the mule and horse in the goat pen and went into the house. When she came back to Link, she handed him a bar of soap and a towel. She pointed down toward a willow thicket.

"Stream's down there," she said. "I'll bring you some clean clothes."

When she showed up with the clothes, Link was sitting in the stream, naked as the day he was born, but clean.

"There's drawers," she said, tossing them to the bank. "And a pair of California pants, a good shirt. Brought this coat, too. Hope the boots fit."

"They look like they will," Link said. "This is a pretty chilly stream you got here," he added.

"It's good water," she said. "Awful good."

She showed no sign of leaving or looking away, so Link took a deep breath and stood up. While he toweled and dressed, she watched with mild interest.

"Sorry if that poor soul in the pit is your husband," he said.

"I imagine it's him, all right," she said. "Went missing the better part of two years back. No, three years. 'Cause I had to spend a whole winter with that damn' Malin. Three years it was. I looked for him everywhere. That lyin' snake Malin, he said Dan told him he was leaving the valley. I should have known better. No man that's worth a damn ever went away without telling his wife. Malin said Dan went to look for some sheep to breed, or some such lie. Then, when Dan didn't come back, Malin said he'd heard from him and that I was to stay with him until he came back."

"With Malin?"

"Yeah. I finally figured out Dan was dead. But I had no way of knowin' for sure, so I couldn't go anywhere, just in case he came back. I got away from Malin and his damn' peepholes, anyway. Came back here. I looked from one end of this valley to the other for some sign of Dan, and never found anything. Not even his horse. Then about a week ago, Lige came by, the sneaking little midget. He'd come for a couple of lambs I sold him, and he asked if I'd ever found Dan and he kinda laughed real nasty-like. Couple days later, I rode down to his place to ask him about what he'd meant by sayin' that. Well, he wasn't there, but I saw that girl taking a basket out to that old abandoned granary. So I waited and watched."

"So you hoped I was him, then," Link said as he tugged on the boots.

"No, not really. Didn't have any hope of that. They wouldn't have kept him alive all that time. No, I heard a rumor about you. Folks said there was a Keystone rider in the valley . . . two of them, in fact. Rumor was that they'd come into Gorre and were raising all kinds of hell. People leaving the farms, the old man taking over and reining in that damn' Flynt, even people being let out of the valley. Anyway, I knew they had Lige keepin' *somebody* down that hole, and it seemed likely maybe it was one of you from Pendragon's place."

"Dan, that's your husband?"

"Dan Hansen," she said. "My name's Charity."

"Howdy," Link said. "I thank you for the help and the

216

clothes and all. I'll find a way to pay y'back."

"Oh, we aren't quits with each other yet," she said. "Not by a long chalk. Let's get you something to eat."

Over a big bowl of the best lamb stew Link had ever tasted she filled him in on her plan for him.

"This'll sound funny to you, coming from a woman," she said, "but I want to change things around here. The Malins both figure I'll either go away or just live here with my goats, until I end up talking to myself. But they're wrong. I got good water here, and a couple of good neighbors. But Malin treats the whole place like he owned it, him and his riders. You wouldn't believe what he made me do that winter I had to spend at his house. God Almighty, it makes me see red just to think of it. Damn' lecherous son-of-a-snake."

"So you want me to do what, kill him for you?"

"That'd be nice, but no. There's old Henry to think about, and I don't want to start a new settlement up here by murdering people. That's Malin's way, not mine. No, I heard from one of his riders that he's either gone or he's going to go. They say he's headed for the Keystone Ranch, mostly so he can stir up trouble. He'll be looking for a chance to steal some more livestock, too. You can bet on that."

"So what's your idea?" Link asked.

"What I want us to do is fix you up with a horse and then get you out of here, so you can get to your friends and catch Flynt Malin somewhere outside the valley. You can get him sent to prison, is what I'm hopin', and he just won't be comin' back here . . . or goin' anywhere else. I've heard about Pendragon. I know he can do it."

"We've taken care of our share of outlaws, that's for certain," Link said. He was starting to see, maybe, what Flynt was up to. Flynt was sure he was either dead or at least wouldn't get out of that pit, so he could ride into the Keystone and make big talk about wanting to have their showdown. He'd be able to brag that *he* had been the one to keep the agreement. "And where's *your* man?" he would sneer.

Charity Hansen didn't know about his appointment with Flynt Malin, but she was right about one thing: Malin was still out to stir up trouble, trouble that would make the Keystone look bad in the eyes of the rest of the territory.

"Getting out of this valley's going to be a problem," Link went on. "I can't say I care much for the way I came *in*. My friend, he just about drowned at the mill crossing. An' we were told about the guards at the pass."

"I thought about that while we were riding over here," she said. "You're going to use the midget, Lige."

"I'm gonna what?"

"Flynt uses Lige. Lige helps him make up his schemes when he goes out to raid livestock, then helps him get rid of what they steal. He's a shrewd one. Flynt's tough and vicious, but it's Lige that gives him ideas. He's kind of afraid of the little guy, too. All the Gorre riders are. He scares them, but he's under Flynt's protection. That's the whole point. The riders do whatever Lige says."

"So if I get him and take him along with me, they won't do anything, is that it?"

"That's it. That's what I want you to do. But you don't have to do nothing if you don't want to. I'm not going to put you back in that hole or anything. I'd just like it if you were to catch him, take him as your safe conduct, then see to it neither him or Flynt Malin ever comes back here. Take that girl with you, too. If you want to."

"And you?"

"I'll be fine. Me and the neighbors, we'll start up the

mill again and build some decent roads and make something out of this place. Something besides a hide-out for stolen stock."

Link watched her face as he used his bread to wipe up the last of the gravy from his bowl. This was a woman to respect. Even with her husband dead, she was loyal to his dream and ready to go on with it. She could probably find a husband somewhere and start over, but it was Dan Hansen she'd chosen and it was his dream of a new settlement that she was going to see come true. He thought about Gwen, who was never far from his thoughts, and wondered if she would carry on with the Keystone if she ever lost Art. He wondered: *Would she?*

He shouldn't have started thinking about her. Now he found himself so anxious to be gone that he was about ready to forget the dwarf and take his chances shooting his way out, instead.

"You got a gun you could loan me?" he said.

"Yes," she said. "But you're not leaving until we get some meat on those bones. I don't know how long you were down that hole, but, the shape you're in, you couldn't even stomp a snake to death, let alone fight anybody. I'm getting you another bowl of stew, then I'll show you where you're going to sleep."

There wasn't a single person in the territory, Flynt Malin included, who would deny that Gwen Pendragon had shown grit, backbone, poise, and determination during the Gorre episode. And although it was not in any conscious and deliberate way, she herself had become aware of a new feeling of purpose, of strength. Link's confession of his love may have been the trigger, filling her heart with a deeper consciousness of her own potential. Ever since bringing her to the Keystone, Art had given her responsibilities, mostly the running of the main house, and always praised her as being smart and level-headed. But after the Gorre incident there was a feeling that she was capable of much, much more. She felt as though she were equal to any situation.

Any situation, that is, but the one now facing her. Back in school, one of her teachers had made the students write papers about moral dilemmas; now she truly knew what moral dilemma was all about.

Day by slow day it threatened to wear her down. Outwardly there wasn't much change. People treated her with respect and she smiled in return. But each morning as she woke to fresh sunlight and washed in warm, clear water and dressed herself, the sinking feeling began. Even before the last button was hooked, she felt the erosion of spirit. Every day, she had to put on an expression for Art to see, whether he was there with her when she awoke or whether she found him in the kitchen at breakfast. The face she showed him needed to say that all was well, while at the same time hiding the inevitable moment when he would have to be told about her night with Link.

Each morning, she stiffened her spine and gave the household orders of the day, and each morning her spine slumped when she stepped out onto the porch, for in the near distance was the camp of Flynt Malin and his men. She had told Art about the blood on the linen she couldn't explain, of course, and the accusation that it was left there by Bob Riley, about the challenge and the pact of free passage she had entered into.

"It just goes to show you," Art said. "Malin's mind is so poisoned that he always thinks up the worst thing he can. He oughta just know from seeing you that nobody would ever suspect you of any such a thing. But, no. Instead of letting it go, he's got to think of the worst possible thing. Why, you'd no more share your bed with Riley . . . or anybody . . . than you'd . . . well, I don't know what. Almost makes you feel sorry for a man like that."

Gwen's heart was trembling inside her. She wanted to seize this chance to tell him, to tell him *now* that the blood spots had not come from a midnight nosebleed. But this was not the time, not yet. She knew he would understand. He *had* to understand. But this was not the time.

And so each morning she arose with the same worry. Would this be the day she told him? Would Link return today? She would awaken into a newly sun-washed world, always to find her mind filled with the same worries as the day before. The presence of Malin's camp, sitting down there beyond the barns, oppressed her. She felt like fleeing, like packing her luggage and going to town or even taking the train back East, just to be free of that evil man. Just knowing that he was on the Keystone made her clench her teeth. The answer to it all seemed to be just to escape, to run. What was happening to her new resolve, anyway?

Malin's camp lay like a dirty stain on the fields of the Keystone. As he strutted around joking with his men or spying on Pendragon's men, Malin congratulated himself over and over. He had played the situation like a four-ace poker hand. It was one of his best moves ever, he thought, showing up at the Keystone Ranch with eight men and 100 head of prime cattle. He was out to do some selling and trading while he waited for Link to show up and settle their differences, he said, and surely Art Pendragon wouldn't mind pasturing these animals while he and some of the boys rode around to various ranchers looking for a buyer? And while we're at it, how about loaning a fellow stockman some roundup tents and a cook wagon so they could be a little more comfortable? His move not only threw Pendragon off guard, but was also the perfect excuse to have his whole gang with him. The way he exploited Pendragon's hospitality amused them no end.

Soon it was a little self-contained encampment with four wagons and a half-dozen tents, two cookfires, and a string of horses. Malin's men loitered around the Keystone corrals and bunkhouses, and, as they mingled with the Keystone hands, they spread the story of how Malin had found out "something". None of them came right out and said that Riley had been in bed with Mrs. Pendragon, but they hinted that Malin knew something that was "pretty bad". Then they told stories about Link. Turned into a squaw man, they said. That fancy Keystone rider was nothing but another range bum, they said. After Flynt beat him up, he tried to commit suicide.

The Keystone men put up with Malin's blow-hards for a few days, mostly because those were Art's instructions, but inevitably a couple of fights broke out. The Malin hands retreated to their tents to take care of black eyes and busted lips while the Keystone riders gathered in the bunkhouse to take turns with the bottle of witch hazel and box of gauze. When Malin's men set up a shooting range and started taking target practice, the Keystone boys broke out their own armament and perforated a few lard cans themselves.

Between the guns going off all afternoon and the frequent fistfights, Gwen was rapidly becoming a nervous wreck. Then, one evening, as she and Art were in the middle of having supper with Bob Riley and Will Jensen, Flynt Malin and two of his men suddenly entered the big dining room uninvited. None of them bothered to remove his hat. The two cowhands dropped into chairs near the door while Malin strolled over to the table, his spur rowels dragging on the polished floor.

"Looks good," he said, reaching out a hand that was none too clean and taking a slice of the roast from the serving plate.

"Need something?" Art asked coolly.

"Nah," Malin said as he chewed the meat and wiped his fingers on his vest. "Jus' wonderin' when that ramrod of yours is comin' back, that's all. The boys and me are getting a little anxious to be home."

"No way to tell when he'll be here," Art said. "But don't let it keep you, if you need to be getting back to Gorre. I expect he'll come looking for you if he doesn't find y'here."

"Yeah? Well. It's startin' to look like he's all talk and no fight. I come here in good faith to settle this thing, expectin' he'd maybe like to give me the lie about what happened back there at Gorre."

He grinned at Gwen, but she refused to acknowledge or even look at him.

" 'Course, if y'already tipped him off and he's gone to range, I guess that right there shows y'who's lyin' and who ain't. Some of the boys are sayin' that he knows I'm here and he's afraid to show up. Maybe I'll just finish sellin' my stock and mosey home, and, if he wants me, he'll know where I am."

Bob Riley folded his napkin with elaborate care and began to speak. "Talking of your stock," he said. "Me and some boys were down at the calvin' barn the other night late an' just happened to see your hands bringin' in some more steers. Noticed how your herd seems to be growin, and *not* because you got 'em on Mister Pendragon's free grass."

Malin snitched another slice of beef and folded it into

his mouth, then turned toward Riley. "So you're sayin' we're a bunch of rustlers, that it?"

"I'm sayin' you came to sell cattle and y'seem to be pickin' 'em up instead. I'd sure admire to check your bills of sale against some of those brands."

"Now, that just ain't very hospitable. . . ." He started to raid the meat platter again, but found it had been moved beyond his reach. He turned his back on Riley and spoke directly in Art's face. "Your man here thinks he's some kinda stock inspector, don't he? Trouble is, I don't see no badge on the s.o.b., and I ain't gonna. . . ."

Malin's sentence never got finished, because before anyone even saw Riley start to stand, the foreman yanked him around and slammed his fist into Malin's mouth. Malin staggered backwards across the room into the arms of his two accomplices. He shook his head and blinked to clear the red fog away, and Riley was there again, his left-handed punch going straight for the nose. Gwen saw thick red drops falling on the floor. Malin cocked his fists and shook off his men, then stopped and wiped his bleeding nose with his shirt sleeve.

"Not here, Riley," he said. "Not now. But you can bet we'll finish this one of these days, and on *my* ground. That is, unless y'decide to run away so you and your pal, Link, kin hide out together in the brush till I go away."

Wiping his sleeve across his face once more, Malin turned and stalked out. His men followed him and didn't bother to close the door.

"Sorry, Mister Pendragon," Riley said, "I shouldn't've done that in your house. But that skunk has just about rubbed me raw, and I couldn't help myself."

"It's all right," Art said. "If you hadn't hit him, I probably would have done it myself. Don't let it worry you."

"Well, I wish him and his men would leave, that's all. I'm afraid the word's going to get out into the territory that the Keystone's been used to hold stolen cattle. And if that ain't bad enough, we haven't done much to find poor Keaton's murderer, either. I'm just scared we're startin' to look bad."

"I know," Art said. "I've had the same thoughts myself. I don't know how things could get worse, but I wish Malin and his men would pull stakes and get outta here before they do."

# Chapter Fourteen

"We leave behind a bit of ourselves
Wherever we have been."

> "Rondel de l'Adieu"
> Edmond Haraucourt

In the days following her discovery of the imprisoned Keystone rider, Charity Hansen kept to her regular routine as though nothing had happened. Two neighbors dropped in to visit one day, but, while they sat in her kitchen and drank her coffee, they saw nothing odd in the fact that the door to the sleeping room was closed.

"I guess all those people Flynt kidnapped have gone home to their families by now," she said.

"That's what I heard," one neighbor agreed. "And what a load off the mind it is, too! We were expecting to see the militia and the Army come charging in with guns blazing. I didn't dare even let the kids get out of sight of the house!"

"They're gone, all right," the other neighbor said. "Flynt Malin's gone, too. Naturally he left some men to guard the pass, just like before. I expect him and his gang will come back with more stolen livestock, also like before."

Another neighbor, riding past her place as she was feeding her animals, waved to her and she waved back. As far as he could tell, she was just minding her sheep and goats as she always did. If anyone heard gunshots coming from the direction of her house, they probably thought she was just shooting at varmints or maybe picking off a rabbit for the stew pot. No one suspected she was harboring the missing Keystone cowboy, feeding him with almost aggressive enthusiasm, and putting him to work with axe and shovel so as to get his muscles back in shape.

Link co-operated, working to near exhaustion two and three times each day and eating to the point where he thought he would founder. He cleaned Dan Hansen's .44 Colt and oiled it, then fired six shots through it to be certain it worked. That left twenty rounds in the box, which ought to be plenty. At night he rode the horse around and around the enclosure to strengthen his legs for the saddle. One evening, Charity finally said he seemed ready to do what they were going to do. She was not a woman who wasted much time on strategy and planning.

"It's time I go to get Dan," she said as she cleared away the supper dishes. "And catch Lige at the same time. We'll leave early and grab him as soon as he gets up."

Early the next morning, they were on the way to the dwarf's dug-out.

"I'm sure Lige hasn't tumbled to the fact that you got out of his hole," she said. "We'd have heard something about it by now, you can bet. The girl probably kept telling him you were still alive and eating. Lige is the kind who'd be content to let her feed you and keep tabs on you. He'd keep himself clear until he knew Flynt was coming back. Then he'd take all the credit."

"Y'suppose Flynt would tell Lige to just kill me?" Link asked. "Or let me starve down there? Is he that bad?"

"Darn' right he is! I'm guessing that's how they done for Dan," she said. "Tricked him into falling into that hole, probably, then either shot him or let him starve. Guess we'll never know for sure."

"How'd you get his gun back?" Link asked, patting the Colt stuck in his belt.

"Found it in a drawer at Malin's place. I asked him about it and he claimed it hadn't been working right for Dan. Flynt said Dan borrowed one of his guns, instead, and left that one behind. When I told him it seemed to me to work all right, he said he'd gotten it fixed, and I should keep it for Dan to have when he came back. Damn' lyin' snake! All right, now, let's ease up and ride quiet-like. There's the dug-out."

They left the horse and mule and carefully crept up to the dug-out on foot. The latch string wasn't out for guests at that hour of the morning, but Charity quickly took care of that by sliding the blade of her hunting knife between the jamb and the door. When the latch fell and the door suddenly swung open, a small figure bolted upright from his blankets, blinking into the dark. It was still gloomy in the place, but not so dark that he couldn't see the Colt .44 and the double-bore shotgun pointed at his face.

"You get outta that bed and get your clothes on," Charity said in an even voice. "I come to get my Dan's remains. *Then* you and this here gent are taking a little ride together down to Ehre's Hole."

"Where's the girl?" Link said.

Lige glared and kept his mouth clamped shut.

"She sleeps back in the root cellar, I imagine," Charity said, using the shotgun to point into the darkness. "She won't come out till we're gone."

There was no protest from the little man, no indignation, no attempt to flee. One thing the dwarf had learned from years of being small was when to yell defiance at people and when it was better just to shut up and comply. Except for muttering—"Fool, fool."—under his breath as he put on his clothes, he was quiet. Charity and Link wrapped him in a blanket, then trussed him up in it like he was a Christmas turkey and carried him between them to the granary building.

"I'll keep an eye on him," Charity said. "You go back and find somethin' to put Dan into."

On his way back to the dug-out, Link spotted the girl hiding in a thicket of chokecherry and wild rose. He called out to her and waved, but she only ducked out of sight. Deciding she'd come out when she wanted to, he went on into Lige's cave-like house where he scrounged around until he found a decent-size trunk full of old clothes. He dumped its contents on the floor and brought it back to the granary. Meanwhile, Charity had found the long ladder that had been stored high up under the gable ends of the building. With the trap propped open and the ladder in place, Link descended into the pit once more, carrying a lamp with him. Charity lowered the trunk and Link placed the skeleton into it gently, apologizing to the dead man under his breath because he had to dislocate the arms and legs. These he laid carefully beside the torso. With Charity hauling on the rope and Link working his way up the ladder to steady the trunk as it rose, the first prisoner of the pit was returned to daylight at last.

Link caught up one of Lige's mules and found a pack saddle for it. After lashing the trunk to it, they threw a saddle on another mule for Lige. They were not gentle with him, as they had been with Dan's remains. However, they freed his legs but left him wrapped and trussed in the blanket, his feet tied under the horse with a rope and his hands bound to the saddle horn.

"Back to my place," Charity said.

After the trunk was stowed safely away to wait until she

could get a proper coffin, Charity fixed a poke bag of food for Link.

"I'm obliged for the loan of the horse, and the gun," Link said as he put a foot into the stirrup and swung himself up.

"You're welcome," she said, patting the horse's shoulder. "He's a pretty good one. And you'll be back this way, someday, and maybe you'll bring him back."

"I'll sure try," Link said. "But I still say we got time to hunt around for the one I borrowed from Henry Malin."

"*I'll* do that," she said. "You need to get out of Gorre before Flynt comes back."

"You saved my life," Link said. "You and that girl of his. If ever you need anything. . . ."

"I know," Charity said. "Well, you come back someday. I'm going to go find her, first thing I do, and give her a decent place to live. Then get some folks together who knew Dan and give him a proper burial service. After that, we're going to make something out of this place. You come on back in a year or so, and you'll be surprised."

"I'll try," Link said. "I'll sure try."

Riding away, Link looked back to see her standing with a hand raised in farewell and he knew in his heart that she would make good on her dream. This small corner of the Deathwater Valley had lots of potential, and a woman such as that was just the one to make it come to something, something good. He returned Charity Hansen's wave, then looked to the south to face the guards who watched over the entrance to the valley.

Link rode behind the mule to which the dwarf was tied, keeping Dan Hansen's gun ready. He knew that the way to the two gaps through the *cuestas* would take him right through the edge of town, but he saw no way of avoiding it. He'd have to try and bluff his way through Gorre. Probably no one in town would care or even notice him riding past the town with his hostage. It was Flynt Malin's guards at the gaps who worried him.

However, Link had not counted on the Gorre Valley gossip web. One of Charity's neighbors had already spotted the two of them taking the well-wrapped Lige toward her cabin, and the news had gone racing along ahead of Link even before he set out from her place. By the time he rode out from behind the last building in town, there were more than a dozen men standing at the end of the street. Behind them stood a crowd of curious women and kids. Some of the men carried rifles or shotguns. One of them stepped forward and raised his hand, his other hand resting on the butt of a revolver he carried on his belt.

"Might ask where you're heading," the man said to Link. "I see you got somebody with you."

"I'm headed out of this valley," Link answered. "This little son-of-a-bee coyoted me into his granary pit, and I'd've starved to death down there if Missus Hansen hadn't come along. This worthless midget was fixed to let me stay there. Him and me, we're taking a little ride together, right on out of this place. I plan to let him loose, once we get to Ehre's Hole."

"I see," the man said. "You probably know about the guards at the pass, don't you?"

"Yep," Link said. "I don't see Henry Malin among you. He around?"

"Henry's gone up the valley for a few days."

"Oh. Well, I can't wait around for him. Tell him thanks for all he tried to do."

"That fella you got there, Lige," the spokesman said, "he's not going to be much of a safe passage for you. He's one of Flynt Malin's men, all right. But Malin's other guns don't care all that much for the little sneak. They'd rather shoot him than let you ride out. Flynt sounded *real* determined to keep you from leaving."

"I appreciate the advice," Link said. "Even though he knew I was in that pit and couldn't get out." He paused and adjusted his seat in the saddle. As yet he had not made a move toward the gun he carried in his belt.

"And what about you folks?" he asked. "You willing to let me go on my way without any trouble?"

"Nope," the man answered. "We have another idea."

Two other men, the two with the shotguns, stepped up beside their fellow townsman. Link's gun hand tensed and his eyes narrowed as he began to measure the distance and pick his targets.

"We aim to go with you," the spokesman said. "You won't make it on your own, Lige or no Lige."

"What do you mean, go with me?" Link asked.

"We're in this with you. We want to see that murderer caught just as bad as you do. We're tired of listening to Flynt Malin, tired of his gang, tired of owing everything to his store. We want that pass opened up so we can come and go from now on. So we're goin' with you."

At the speaker's invitation, Link dismounted and took his two animals to the watering trough while the dozen citizens of Gorre got their horses saddled and collected extra ammunition. A youngster from the crowd eagerly ran forward to pump water for him.

"I thought old man Malin told me there was a pipe from a spring, feedin' all the horse troughs in this town," Link said to the boy.

"No, sir, not any more. That pipe come from up by old Mister Malin's house. Been near a month ago it started to dry up."

232

He went after the long pump handle with a will, and Link saw that the gushing water was clear and sparkled in the sun.

Within a half hour, Link was on the road again, with the trussed-up dwarf riding ahead of him and a posse of armed men at his back. The spokesman rode alongside.

"Jack Buchanan," he said, extending his hand.

"Lochlin," Link said. "Friends call me Link. Short for Lincoln. You related to the circuit preacher Buchanan?"

"Not that I know of."

"I appreciate your comin' along on this deal," Link said.

"*We* appreciate what your Keystone folks did in Gorre," Buchanan answered. "I'm sorry as hell your man got killed. Not to mention the one that got shot so bad. It's a damn' shame, Flynt tryin' that stupid stunt of kidnapping folks. But on the good side, it sure stirred things up. It put a spur to the old man, for one thing. Made people start to talk about what Flynt and his gang were doing to the valley, too. People started thinking maybe we could be more than just a hide-out for rustlers." There was a little space of quiet, then Buchanan chuckled and spoke again. "Funny thing about it," he said. "About the water. That superstition, I mean. Everybody always kinda went along with Flynt mostly because nobody got hurt and nobody had any real hope that they'd ever do any better."

"And that's supposed to be funny?" Link said.

"No, that's not what I mean. What's funny is what we're doin' now. Men without much to hope for ain't got much to live for, see? So why not go up against those guards at the pass? Nothing to lose. I guess it's more of a puzzle than a joke. Might even call it ironic."

"I guess that's what I'd call it, all right," Link said. "Ironic."

When they had ridden far enough to see the first *cuesta* gap ahead of them, Buchanan called for a volunteer to go and scout the situation. Meanwhile, they rested the horses, the posse men talking softly among themselves. Link had a chat with Lige—a one-sided chat, considering the gag in the dwarf's mouth.

"Don't suppose you'd care to just go up there and tell Flynt's men to let us through, would you?"

Lige shook his head and tried to kick at Link, mumbling curses into the gag.

"I didn't think so. Well, you won't mind, when the time comes, if I use you for a shield, then. I don't figure to stop any bullets I don't have to."

The dwarf just glared at him.

"My word's good, though," Link said. "Soon as we get to Ehre's Hole, the ropes come off and you're free as a bird. 'Course, if you're all shot up, it won't be all that nice for you. You could still tell those shooters of Flynt's to let you and me pass on through. No trouble for anybody. You want to try it that way?"

Again the dwarf tried to kick Link, mumbling a curse.

"It's your call then," Link said. "If y'behave yourself, I might take that gag off later on, so you can tell your pals not to shoot."

The spokesman, Buchanan, returned to Link's side after dispatching the volunteer scout.

"What's the layout here?" Link asked.

"Well," Buchanan said, pointing toward the gap in the *cuesta* ahead of them, "there's two cliffs . . . this one and one farther on. The next one has a gap in it where the road goes, just like this one. So we've got two passes to go through. As soon as we're into this first one, just over the rise before the road starts down again, you'll see two blockhouses on your left. They're fifty, maybe eighty yards apart. All they are is square stone buildings with windows to shoot out of. Their field of fire covers the next pass and the valley in between, so, if you rode in through that first pass, you'd find yourself facing 'em."

Link saw the scout coming back, moving quickly for a man running across broken rocks and through sage and cactus.

"Then," Buchanan continued, "just this side of that second set of cliffs, there's a third blockhouse guarding that gap. The way they built it, anybody in it can see out the valley in that direction, and can see into the valley between the cliffs, too."

"So if you rode in from the east, you'd be caught in a box between that one and the two that are nearest to us."

"Right." Buchanan turned to the young man who had just returned. "So, what's goin' on out there?" he asked.

"It looks pretty good," the young man said. "I sneaked in close enough that I could hear their voices. Couldn't tell what they were sayin', though."

"Probably doesn't matter," Buchanan said. "How many are they?"

"I figure there's three or four in the first hut. Heard 'em arguing over a card game. And guess what?"

"What?"

"Somebody tore down the back wall of the second hut. Or else it fell down. I could see three men, with rifles, in there. Plain as day."

"They probably needed ventilation and figured they'd never be attacked from this side, especially with the other blockhouse defending that side. *Hmmm!* Their mistake!"

"I didn't try to cross all that open ground, so I never got to where I could see the third one," the scout explained.

"That's all right," Buchanan said. "We'll take these two and then figure out what to do about the third one when we get to it. Probably no more than four men in it, anyway."

As the group started moving up the slope leading into the pass, still out of sight of the blockhouses, Link made a suggestion. "Maybe I'd better ride ahead, with my little friend," he said, "and see if they'll dicker at all. Could be we won't have any trouble, once they see him."

"*Could* be they serve cold lemonade in hell, too," Buchanan replied, "but I wouldn't count on it. No, those boys would just as soon shoot that dwarf as let you go! Like I said, Flynt gave orders you aren't to leave no matter what. That's what he was saying in town before he left. Nobody was to let you leave. Of course, he was probably saying it 'cause he was trying to make us think you were riding loose somewhere, instead of locked down in his own little dungeon."

Buchanan's plan was straightforward and simple. They stopped short of the crest of the hill, still out of sight of the first blockhouse. Buchanan took off his holster and stuck his revolver in the back of his belt where it wouldn't be seen, then he rode over the rise and down the other side all alone. When he was close enough, he shouted: "Hey! Anybody home?"

The guard knew him.

"That you, Buchanan? Tryin' to run away, are you?"

"Naw," he said, climbing off his horse, careful to keep his back where the guard couldn't see the gun.

"Got any water?" Buchanan said pleasantly. "I'm plumb parched."

"Sure. C'mon in."

There were only three men on watch. The other two guards looked up from their card game, mumbled something, and resumed staring at the cards in front of them. The first one, glad to have something to do other than play endless games of three-card monte, turned his back on Buchanan and stooped forward to fill a dipper from the water barrel. The barrel of Buchanan's gun applied with zeal to the little knob just behind the ear took care of him for the rest of the day, and, when he leveled it at the other two, they merely placed their hands, palms down, on the table.

Link and the others came up quietly, doing all they could to stay out of sight of the second guard station farther down the slope.

"That went pretty slick," Link said, as the posse tied and gagged the guards. "You suppose we can sneak up on that next one?"

"I don't guess we can," Buchanan said. "If I walked up on them, they'd be suspicious that I came past this one without a challenge. Let's see if we can come up with a different plan. This situation kinda reminds me of a time back durin' the war when my detail located some Reb sentries holed up in a cabin."

"What did you do?"

"We had some open ground to cross . . . like here . . . and, if they spotted us, we were bound to lose some men. But like here, we had more firepower. So we just poured it into 'em. Those guards of Flynt's, they're in a small hut with one side open toward us. No place to go when the lead starts to fly. Sure, they're gonna shoot back. But pretty soon that hut's gonna be full of their own gunsmoke, they're gonna be half deaf from the racket of their own guns, and they won't even know for sure where we're shooting from."

"What about the third blockhouse, over at the next pass?"

"Where are they goin' to go? They'd never charge at us, and they sure as hell can't send to town for reinforcements! We can take our time with them."

Buchanan held the two shotgun bearers in reserve and to act as a rear guard. The captured rifles and ammunition were handed out among the Gorre posse, Link getting a .45-70 Winchester and a pouch full of extra cartridges. Then they fanned out into the rocks, each man finding himself some good cover that would afford a clear shot at the rear of the stone building down the hill.

"They might try to come at us, I s'pose," Buchanan observed, "but they'll have an awful lot of open ground to cross. Well, looks like the boys are ready. Mister Link, I can't tell y'how good this is going to be! Feels like old times again!"

Buchanan gave his signal. Ten rifles opened fire, pouring lead through the wide gap in the stone wall of the blockhouse. At first there was no response at all, as if the place was abandoned. But then Flynt's men began to shoot back from behind the remains of the wall. After their first volley, they could see nothing through the smoke drifting in front of them. When it cleared a little, they saw puffs of smoke coming from the other blockhouse as well as from the rocks and brush on the hillside. Hot lead came whining through the gap to spatter and ricochet inside the stone hut, adding dust and the smell of hot metal on rock to the acrid stink of burned gunpowder. On and on it came, a steady whiz and smack of bullets, like hail hitting a roof.

Soon the defenders only crouched under the meager protection of the broken wall, afraid to rise up enough to shoot back. Seeing this, several of Buchanan's men rose to their feet to fire offhand, taking their time for the smoke to clear so they could place their shots inside the opening. In less than two minutes, they saw a hat and a handkerchief being waved.

"Quit shootin,' dammit!" The voice called out from behind the wall. "We had enough!"

"OK, boys!" Buchanan yelled. "Cease fire now!"

The men from Gorre stood ready, rifles trained on the three shaken outlaws as they came out of the building with their hands in the air.

"Flynt ain't gonna like this, Buchanan!" one of them shouted as he recognized who was leading the posse.

"You come along peaceful and maybe . . . just maybe . . . you'll live long enough to find out how he likes it! Get up here!"

The posse took the captives back to the first blockhouse and tied them up with the others, along with the dwarf. Two men with two shotguns stood guard. Once again, the captured rifles and revolvers were distributed among the posse.

"Feels like old times!" Buchanan repeated.

The men standing around him grinned and nodded. Most of them were holding two rifles now, and each man had a couple of pistols stuck in his belt. Ammunition was in good supply.

To begin the assault on the remaining blockhouse, which had undoubtedly been alarmed by the gunfire, Buchanan sent Link and half the men to ride in a wide circle north, cross the open valley, and come in behind it. He and the remaining men would ride south and do the same thing. Within the hour, both groups had crept close enough, along the boulder-strewn hillsides beneath the cliffs, to pour volley after volley of rifle and pistol fire into the other stone building.

Buchanan's strategy paid off in less time than anyone

could imagine. Once the defenders realized they were being fired upon from two directions, that they had no way out, and that their small stuffy fortress was choked with smoke and dust, they elected to throw their guns out and follow them with hands raised. The posse called them by name as they tied them up and led them away, even joking with them about taking them by surprise.

"Haven't seen my neighbors in this good a mood for years," Buchanan told Link. "Goes to show what a little fighting can do for a man."

"There's something to be said for that," Link agreed. "I s'pose I've never seen cowboys as happy with life as when they're fightin', whether it be rustlers or just a rowdy bunch of steers. Found one of our men in town one afternoon getting beat up by four other fellows and I'd swear he was grinning like a pig knee-deep in slop."

"Yep. Well, Link Lochlin, looks like you won't be having much fighting from here on. Not until you get home to your Keystone Ranch, anyways. Rumor is that Malin went to meet you there."

"I'm looking forward to it." Link smiled under his thick mustache. "Nothin' I'd like better than to find him waiting for me."

"You got enough for the trip?" Buchanan asked. "Grub, money?"

"I'll be all right," Link said. "I just want to ask you if you're all right with me setting that little piss ant, Lige, loose as soon as I get him to town? I did promise him I'd do it."

"Seems kind of like letting a rabid dog go loose, but go ahead and do it. He might even find his way back to his dug-out."

"Well, if he does, I guess Charity Hansen can keep an eye on him, then."

"If I was as mean as him, I don't believe I'd *want* Charity anywhere near me."

Link chuckled. "Me neither," he agreed. "Matter of fact, that woman's carryin' such a grudge that I expect she might hunt him down."

Buchanan held out his hand. Link leaned out from the saddle to grip it.

"*Vaya con Dios,*" Buchanan said. "See y'again some time, maybe."

"*Adiós,*" Link replied. "Y'never know."

And with a wave to the posse the Keystone rider rode out through the now unguarded pass, his hat brim level to the horizon. His eyes were already turned toward the green pastures and friendly faces of the Keystone and the woman with the angel hair who awaited his coming.

"*Vaya con Dios,*" he repeated with a smile. The same words he'd heard before, back when all this began.

# Chapter Fifteen

Where'er I roam, whatever realms to see,
My heart untravel'd fondly turns to thee;
Still to my brother turns with ceaseless pain,
And drags at each remove a lengthening chain.

"The Traveller"
Oliver Goldsmith

Link rode at a steady pace, making good time. Out of
Ehre's Hole he retraced the route of the bone cart up the
long switchbacks and out onto the high sage plains, back to
the arroyo where he had first met Two Nose Thomas and
Crows Woman. He paused at the remains of the horse that
had died there, now reduced to bones. Traces of yellow
were left on the stiff scraps of hide that stuck to the skull.
The circle of stones Crows Woman had arranged brought to
mind Evan Thompson and a conversation they had had two
years ago.

"Sometimes," the blacksmith had said, "a man stands
outside his own medicine circle. So say the Cheyenne
people."

"And what does that mean?" Link had asked.

"It means"—Thompson had smiled—"there are times
when a man knows a great experience is waiting for him. It
will be a learning for him."

"So he just needs to go ahead and do it. Take the bit in
his teeth."

"Yes. A man standing outside the circle always wants to wait until he finds the best way in, not knowing that the way is always right in front of him. It may be the way of wisdom, or the way of innocence, or the way of the eagle that has the greatest perspective on everything when he soars to great heights. Or, of course, the bear way, the way of insight. What they call the looking-within way."

"Makes it sound pretty simple," Link said to himself, staring down at the bones. From nowhere came an echo of the blacksmith's booming voice.

*To be whole, you must walk your circle in all four ways. Beware of believing you have finished your circle before it is done. Beware of believing that you have arrived at the center. You have* not *arrived at the center until you understand how you got there!*

Link looked around him. He wondered where the Indian woman was by now. Possibly she was already on her way into the mountains far to the north, in search of a one-eyed black man who carried an iron bar.

With a couple of hours of daylight remaining, Link made his way up out of the arroyo and headed north by east through the sage and yucca flats. By the time he decided to camp for the night, he was in a region where the absolutely flat, featureless landscape stretched out to the encircling horizon in all directions. On his horse he was the highest thing for miles around and felt as though he was at the hub of an infinite wheel of empty space.

He got down, looking around for a stout bush to picket the horse, and nearly stepped on the skull. It was a very old skull, a buffalo skull, lying among the sage at the very place he'd decided to stop for the night. Respectfully he led the horse to another open space a few yards away, and there he made his small fire and spread his blanket. Almost before it was dark enough for all the stars to appear, he was in a deep sleep.

*Crows Woman came walking through the brush, was young again and beautiful. Her doeskin dress clung to her breasts and hips; the long fringe swayed as she walked. A line of women followed in her path, all wearing beaded dresses of pale doeskin. In silent moccasins they walked toward him; his camping place suddenly became a wide round clearing and he heard a drum begin the steady rhythm of a circle dance.*

*The women dancing in the vast circle were joined by many men who materialized out of nothing. They were also dancing a circle, moving in the opposite direction, a male circle and a female circle rotating against each other. The women held green branches in their hands, fresh green sprigs of evergreen to show that the life they held in their bodies went on forever green, forever reborn. They stood for fertility and new life coming. Some of the men carried buffalo skulls, others held buffalo bones or rattles made from dried gut, but Link didn't know their significance. Possibly the men didn't know, either, but there was no doubting that the women knew.*

*The drums beat the rhythm for the dance, and the ghosts went on and on, steadily dancing, but they were not dancing for him, or because of him. Link understood. They were dancing the old ways back again, dancing back the buffalo herds, dancing back a time before there were cattle and ranchers and guns.*

He awoke at dawn, with a few stars still faintly visible, and the dream had not left him. He rose from his blanket, expecting to see the Indians camped with him. But except for Charity Hansen's horse and himself, the sage plains flowed away in all directions around him, toward the endless, empty, and unbroken horizon.

He rode all day, and in the afternoon he came to a road and knew what road it was. It led north to the Keystone. He rode on, and in the evening he came to a crossroads. He had been there before, many times. From this meeting of roads a man might turn and ride west into the mountains and on to the Grand River region, from there on into the Utah and California country. Or he could turn and ride east toward Kansas, toward the cities and towns of the Platte. But north lay the Keystone. He got down and picketed the horse, gathered firewood, spread his blanket, and built his cooking fire. As he worked, he thought about all the directions he might go when morning came. Each road seemed to lead away from some problem and toward some place of promise. But even as he weighed all the possibilities, all the places he might end up, he felt the tug of a long tether drawing him toward the Keystone. By nightfall of the next day he'd be home, back home at the place where it had all started, and where it all must end.

Gwen did not mean to be eavesdropping, but she was. When Bob Riley and Will Jensen were summoned to Art's office, she happened to be sitting on the porch with her knitting. The office window was open far enough that she heard every word.

"Something wrong, boss?" Riley asked. "The Kid said you wanted to see us."

"Yeah," Art said. "It's that *damn'* Malin." He looked around quickly to make sure Gwen wasn't in the room to hear him swearing.

"Hah?" Will said, surprised. The boss almost never swore in the house.

"Yeah, *damn!* I've just been down at the wagon sheds and ran into him. He started right in on that old story of his, about how Link's afraid to come back and face him. 'He the best you got?' he said. Asked if I'd talked to my wife about her and Riley. The boys say he does it all the time, hanging around where they're working, that damn' sneer on his face, droppin' hints about her, makin' fun of Link. Jesus, he made me mad!"

"And you didn't shoot him?" Will asked in disgust. "Wouldn't be any different than shootin' a skunk."

"There for a minute, I had my hand on my gun. Wanted to blast that look right off his face, and his face along with it."

"So what finally happened?" Will said.

"That's why I called you boys in. He made me so mad I lost my temper and told him we'd settle it ourselves, him and me, and not wait for Link to get back. I shoved that son-of-a-bitch back into the wall there, pretty hard, and said it right in his face. 'Get yourself ready,' I told him. 'You just shut your filthy mouth and get ready, 'cause tomorrow I'm comin' for you.' If he'd only gone for his gun. . . . Well, he just went too damn' far, talking about my wife that way! We're gonna have it out. Tomorrow."

"Nope," Riley said flatly.

"Nope?" Art echoed. "What do y'mean, nope?"

"I mean it ain't you that's gonna get him first. He's the reason *I* got shot. I'm the one in the dirty lie he keeps spreadin'. Besides that, I'm *pretty* sure he gave somebody orders to feed me bad food so I'd be sicker and maybe die, instead of getting better. Oh, no, Art, it's *me* that gets to go up against him! Not you!"

"Now you listen here," Art said. "*I'm* the one he riled up. And he's standin' on *my* land doin' it!"

"Yeah, but I still say I got first rights to him! He tried to kill me, maybe more'n once. I can't let that go. What'd people think if I let you settle a score for me? You never did refuse a man anythin' he wanted this bad, you know that."

246

"This is different," Art said. "I can't forget the lies he's tellin', either. Will, what do you say?"

"You can leave me out of it! But I'll tell you *one* thing. Whichever of you it is, I'll go along."

The debate went back and forth as Gwen listened in secret. She could hardly breathe. It was as if a hand squeezed the air from her lungs. Two men arguing over which one would risk a beating and risk death, and all on her account. Almost as awful was the idea that both were ready to beat or kill another man over something he said about her.

"I don't guess I need to remind you," Riley was saying, "how you gave Pasque a chance to go after that big strange *hombre* who rode into the dinin' room a few years ago, or how you told Link he could go after those North Platte outlaws. This ain't no different."

"All right," he said. "All right. I guess you deserve first crack at 'im. I hate it, but you got a point. Well, I told Malin I'd pick a place to do this, and told him we'll tell him tomorrow where it is. That way he won't have time to plant his gunmen for any kind of ambush. We'll alert Emil and Dick and some of the boys to keep an eye on his men and be sure they don't try anything. I told him he could bring one man with him, just one. And that I'd bring one, too."

"You mean *I'll* take a man along with *me*," Riley corrected him.

"Right," Art said. "Well, then, I'm going with you and carry a rifle to back you up. Will, don't you even *start* to argue which one of us is going!"

"Good," Riley said. "Where's it gonna be?"

"I gave that some thought. Best I can think of is that place over beyond the creek where the big pine is . . . that meadow with the cedars all around it and that great big ponderosa in the middle. It's real private, plenty of good cover, far enough from here that none of his boys could get there in a hurry."

Now Gwen felt the world turn beneath her like a carousel slowly starting to revolve. This was not going to be another fistfight. There was going to be shooting and probably killing. And to choose *that* place . . . ! She dropped her knitting and clutched the arms of the rocking chair to keep her balance. The lawn and fence beyond the porch became a blur of green and white. A dull red color seemed to be descending from the porch roof. She and Art had made love there shortly after he brought her to live at the Keystone. They had run, laughing, in the grass, and he had caught her near that giant ponderosa and carried her back to the picnic blanket where they kissed and embraced and surrendered to a happy passion. Now, with her hand gripping her throat, she heard Art planning to use it for a duel, a showdown. It was like something from the primitive frontier days, when gangs of lawless, uncivilized ruffians settled arguments with brutal violence. And all because. . . .

"I guess that's it, then," Art said.

His words came out through the window and across her mind like distant thunder heard through fog. "Will, I'm puttin' you in charge of the other boys until this is over. I want you all to keep an eye on Malin's men, all of 'em. We don't need any back-shooters showin' up at the meadow. If you need more men to help you, ride out and pull 'em off the job. Bob, you'd better make sure you're ready. You know what I mean."

"I know. I guess I'll see if Garth will loan me that short saddle carbine of his. I'll be ready."

The sound of their voices faded as Art walked the other two men through the house toward the front door. Gwen sat paralyzed. This wasn't the way it was to be, not the way at all. It was *Link* who was to settle things with Flynt Malin, *Link* who would defend her honor. But now. . . . What did it mean if Bob Riley defended her? What if *he* were killed? What if Art should be wounded? Or what if *Art* were the one to be killed? Gwen's fingers clutched her dress just above her heart, her knuckles as white as her face. She felt like a prisoner again, helpless to do anything.

The road went up a small rise and Link already knew what lay on the other side. There was a good barb-wire fence that he had helped build. There was a stone post, one which he had helped set in the ground, with the Keystone brand carved on it. And a well-made gate, tight and strong but easy to open from horseback.

After he passed through the gate and was once again on Keystone range, Link turned the horse out of the road and took to the open country. He didn't really know why he wanted to take this longer and trackless way, except that he had been on the road all day, jogging along, kicking up dust, heading north, seeing only the road going on ahead of him up one hill and down another. At times he almost dozed in the saddle. Getting off the road it would be more like the old days, the simple times when a man could just spend his day chousing cattle out of pine breaks and cedar thickets, picking his way through draws and gullies. Riding cross-country wouldn't save him any time or distance, but it was what he wanted to do.

After two hours he stopped in a draw to let the horse out on its picket rope to graze a little and drink from the creek. He took the last of his jerky and bread and walked up the next rise to work out some of the kinks from riding.

When he got to the crest of the hill and looked down the other side, he again recognized where he was. It was the west edge of the Keystone's west horse pasture. From here he could count maybe 100 horses, some close, some far away. It was a sight to make a horseman smile! Some lay in the grass, sleeping in the sunshine. Some would suddenly stop cropping the grass to kick up their heels and race around their comrades until others joined them in an exuberant dash across the meadow. Here and there a horse lifted its head and whinnied, and there was usually a whinny in return. Most of the horses, though, simply and silently grazed.

Link suddenly thought he saw a familiar shape. He squinted and shaded his eyes to look harder. A couple of colts were frisking around a majestic black horse. They had interrupted his grazing and now he playfully feinted at them with his hoofs, rearing and arching his neck in mock savagery as if they were full-grown stallions who had challenged him over some mares.

It was Messenger. Messenger! They had put the big black out to pasture. Link was glad. The first familiar face he saw upon returning to the Keystone after all those months, none other than Messenger. It seemed like a good sign, a very good sign. Now he had come full circle and knew where he was.

*"Never believe you are in the center,"* the blacksmith said, *"until you understand how you came there."*

Link almost ran as he went back down toward the creek to get Charity's horse. It took only a few minutes to ride back to the fence surrounding the Keystone pasture, but, since he didn't have any cutters or pliers with him, he had to ride almost a half mile down the fence to find a gate, and then ride back again to where the horses were. Most of them ignored the stranger riding up to them. Some threw their heads up and cocked their ears forward like self-appointed sentries for the herd. A few trotted away, casting apprehensive glances back over their shoulders.

Messenger stood his ground. When Link whistled and called to him, Messenger pretended at first not to notice, as if he had forgotten this man who had left him for so long. When he did finally deign to approach, it was with his eyes wide and ears cocked forward, coming toward the saddle horse and man in a sideways trot. Messenger was putting on quite a show, playing the part of a powerful male coming to challenge an intruder. Link had to laugh. He swung down from the saddle and waited, holding out his hand for the big black stallion to nuzzle.

"So *here* you are," he said. "Me out there fightin' outlaws and getting thrown into dungeons and starving and you just playing in a big ol' meadow with the colts. Here I am, ridin' a borrowed horse, and all the time you're getting fat! We need to put you to work chasin' steers again!"

Link transferred saddle and bridle to the black and turned Charity's horse loose to graze. As soon as he was through with Malin, if he was here, he'd see that her horse got back to her.

The moment Link swung his leg over Messenger's back and settled down into the seat, he felt himself stronger, more erect than before, holding the reins in a hand that felt firm and confident. They left the grazing herd and rode away through meadows and draws, across low hills, and around gullies where birds rose from the thickets, and finally they came to the east gate of the horse pasture. From there, a double track led them down over the wooded hills until it came at last to the creek that ran behind the Keystone stables and wagon sheds and bunkhouse. They were coming in the back way, out of sight of the main house, but it wasn't long before they were spotted by a cowhand out

251

behind the stables emptying a wheelbarrow into the muck pile.

"Holy Moses!" Sam yelled. "Link! It's about time! Welcome back!"

Tim came around the corner of the buildings, pushing another wheelbarrow. Link grinned. The first two Keystone cowboys he came to, and both of them youngsters doing the honey detail, hauling manure from the stables. But manure and wheelbarrows were quickly tossed aside as they reached up to shake the rider's hand and pound him on the leg.

"Excuse the smell," Sam said, jerking off his soiled glove to extend his hand.

"Believe me, I've smelled worse." Link smiled.

"I see you found your horse," Sam said. "Mister Pendragon felt sorry for him, bein' penned up."

"Good t' see you!" Tim repeated, wiping his hand on his dungarees, which were less than laundry-fresh themselves, and reaching up for a handshake.

"Listen, I'm gonna run on ahead and tell the boys," Tim said.

Link followed on Messenger, young Sam walking beside him like a squire accompanying a knight into the lists.

"There's something up," Sam told him. "The word just came that Riley wants all of us to finish up what we're doin' and get back to the main building."

Bob Moore came out of the bunkhouse, the man who had been Link's partner in Kansas and who had come with him the first time they rode to the Keystone. He grinned from ear to ear as they shook hands, but his grip wasn't as strong as Link remembered.

"You all right, Moore?" Link asked.

"Had a touch of flu, I guess." Moore smiled. "Kinda had me down this past week."

The Pinto Kid emerged next, his spurs jangling and his silver *conchas* flashing in the late afternoon sun. And Garth Cochran followed soon after, then old Pat came stumping out from the wagon shop wiping his ebony brow with a big kerchief, and in no time at all Link was surrounded by Keystone men.

Link wanted to ask about Gwen, his first thought upon seeing the big house again, but didn't know how.

"Looks like this place is nothin' but men," he joked. "None of the ladies about?"

"Sure!" The Pinto Kid replied. "Even that nice young woman you and Pasque helped out, she's around somewhere. You and Pasque promised her we'd look after her, and we sure have, you bet! It looks like Missus McCarthy's gonna take her in, down at her place."

Link left it at that. If there was anything wrong where Gwen was concerned, somebody would have said something by now. He'd just have to be patient and wait to find out where she was.

At the stair landing between the first floor and the second floor, Gwen halted to look out the west-facing window. For many days, she had found herself pausing like this at nearly every window in the house to look toward the main gate of the ranch for the first glimpse of Link. She always imagined him riding in that way. Now, however, all of that had changed. Art had told her about the arrangement with Flynt Malin and had told her not to worry. It wasn't just worry that she was feeling now, however. It was a tight, chilling panic.

The top of the window had been lowered so cool air could come in, and through the opening she heard distant shouting and excited voices coming from the direction of the wagon barns. Her first thought was the hope that Malin and his crew had packed up and pulled out and the Keystone men were celebrating—as, indeed, they should. Then she thought there might have been a big fight and the Keystone men were cheering the victor. More likely somebody was showing off by riding a wild bronco in some impromptu display of manly horsemanship. Oddly enough, it never crossed her mind that the commotion was because Link had returned. She turned to the small settle on the landing and deposited the folded linens she'd been carrying. If the commotion were important, someone would soon let her know what was going on. If it did turn out to be because Flynt Malin and his men were leaving, there would be a general celebration. Gwen breathed a silent prayer that it would be so.

At the center of the group gathered next to the corral, Link was explaining how he was so late in returning from Gorre.

". . . so finally I got tired of sitting in that pit, waitin' for you all to show up, you see," he was saying. "Oh, I guess that hole was about a thousand foot deep. So I takes out my Barlow knife and I dig m'way out of there. And then, since none of you boys was there to help me, I went ahead and shot m'way out of the valley, all alone."

It was a lie, and he knew it, but seeing the main house again had put him in such a good mood that he couldn't do otherwise. Later on, after things got quieter, he'd tell them the real story. He turned to take care of Messenger, but eager hands seized the reins and led the stallion away. And it was then that Link noticed Bob Riley was wearing a gun. A revolver is about the most awkward thing you can wear while doing chores; guns were generally kept in the bunkhouse, unless a man was going somewhere where he might need one. Bob was not only wearing his Colt, tightly tied down, but was wearing his heavy sheath knife as well.

Link now noticed that Garth was carrying his short saddle carbine. "I see you boys got your guns out," he said as they shut the gate and latched it.

"Yeah," Bob said as nonchalantly as he could. "Garth here is goin' to loan me his carbine. She's a honey, ain't she?"

Garth handed the weapon to Link, who dutifully examined it, shucked the lever to open the breach, and then put it to his shoulder and aimed at a cloud.

"Real nice," he agreed, handing it back. "Coyote problems?"

"Y'could say so," Bob said. "One coyote, at least."

"Ah. So what's been goin' on since I been gone, besides coyotes?" Link asked the question as though he had been gone only a few days instead of as long as he had.

"Not much," Garth said.

"Pasque around?" Link asked.

"He's come and gone. After we got outta Gorre and heard you were all right, he had to head on back home."

"How'd you hear that? How'd you hear I was all right, I mean. Fact is I was pretty much in trouble."

"It was that note you wrote."

Link looked puzzled. "Seems like we got some straightenin' out to do, once I get cleaned up a little and report to Art. What else has been goin' on? Anythin' interestin' at all?" He was eager to hear Gwen's name, even some little thing about her.

"No, most interesting thing lately was that little trip we had to take 'way out to Ehre's Hole looking for you! 'Cept for that there hasn't been much . . . well. . . . Ah, hell, Link!

There *is* pretty much of a problem you've come home to. Things are real serious, I'm afraid."

Will Jensen stepped into the conversation and pointed off across the little rise. Link could see the tops of roundup tents and two covered wagons.

All was suddenly quiet. The horses in the corral shuffled their feet and snorted softly at the feed bin. Water dripped into the water trough. A couple of steers in the meat herd, penned up some distance away, were bawling. But the men were quiet. All faces were turned toward Malin's camp.

"What's all that?" Link said. "Is that what the trouble is?"

"Flynt Malin. That's his camp."

"Malin?" Link looked at Riley, then back at Will.

"Been here quite a while," Will said. "Brought a bunch of steers and men with him. Claims he's here to buy and sell some stock while he waits for you, so him and you can settle things like was agreed to. I guess you shamed him pretty bad back there."

"I told the boys," Riley said. "I told them all about what happened at Gorre. I thought Malin agreed to it just to get rid of us, get us outta his town because his old man was so upset. I didn't figure it would really happen. Nobody did. We figured after we were gone, he'd get out of Gorre for a while, and everybody would go back to their lives and forget about it."

"So that's why you're packin' your Colt and borrowin' Garth's carbine?" Link said. "You figure to get even with Malin, Riley? What's Art got to say about all this?" Link asked.

"He's the one that was gonna do it. It was Art that got tired of Malin sayin' you weren't never goin' to show up, and they had a little shovin' and shoutin' contest. Art got so mad he told him he'd meet him, man to man."

"What about you, then?" Link asked.

"I'm gonna meet him, instead. Me and Art, we talked it out an' come to the agreement that I deserve first crack at the s.o.b. It'll just be Malin and me, with Art backing me up in case Malin has a back-shooter out there. Art figured the place to do it would be that opening where the big ponderosa is. You know the place."

"I know the place. So what kind of fight is this going to be?"

"Who knows? Fists, knives, just words . . . I guess we'll find out when we get there. Won't be surprised if there's some shootin'."

"And this is gonna happen today?"

"Yeah. Just about now, as a matter of fact."

"Where's Art?"

"I s'pose he's up at the house to tell Missus Pendragon good bye. Said he'd meet me here, anyway."

"She can't be any too happy about all this," Link said. "She already came near to losing you at Gorre, and here you go, headin' toward maybe another gunfight."

"I guess she wouldn't like it much. But Malin's been saying things, and about her, too. Link, I got to shut him up, one way or another."

There was silence. Then Link spoke again. "Now that I'm here, you and me need to have us a little debate about who's goin'. You know that, don't you?"

"Yeah. I figured so, soon's I saw you coming."

"Want to do it here with the men, or somewhere in private?"

"Here's all right. Either way."

"Let me tell you about this, then," Link said. "I took a power of abuse from Malin's men, too, and all because I was comin' to help you and the others. You know what happened. You were there when him and his friends were beatin' on me. Well, after you left, Malin fixed it so I'd get trapped in a pit to starve. Him and a damn' dwarf, they left me to die, Bob."

"Yeah, but it's me he said had been. . . ."

"No! That was Missus Pendragon he insulted. Let's don't forget that."

"I still want to get first crack at him," Bob Riley said.

"Seems like we both do."

"We could go together."

"No, I don't want it that way. Bad as he is, we don't want anyone sayin' there was two of us against one."

"Here comes Art. I imagine he's goin' to be the one who decides."

Art fairly jumped from the saddle, tossing the reins to the nearest man and rushing to grip Link's hand in his. He clutched Link's forearm with his other hand and shook him vigorously. "Link, you son-of-a-gun! Where the hell you been? I told you, you could leave for a month or two to look around for some land, but didn't figure you'd make a vacation out of it!"

"Took a little detour is all." Link grinned. "Nuthin' important. I'm back now."

"Where the hell *were* you? You had everybody around here worried. What happened?"

Link withdrew his hand, grinning. "Long to tell everything that happened to me, Art," Link said. "She's a two-smoke story, at least. A whiskey story, even. But everything's OK here, everybody all right?"

"Yeah, fine. People still worked up over Oliver Keaton getting killed and his killer not bein' hung yet. But Henry

Malin promised us he'd find the one that did that. If he doesn't, *we* will."

"The boys were telling me about young Malin bein' here at the ranch. Lookin' for me, they say. Stirring things up."

"That's right," Art said. "But Riley and me are just about to ride over and take care of that little problem. Why don't you go ahead and put your gear in the bunkhouse and clean up. After I've done what I need to do, you can take supper with us. Gwen'll be glad to see you."

Link looked at him steadily. This talk about Keaton's killer and the showdown with Flynt Malin had all but pushed thoughts of Gwen from Link's mind. But at the sound of her name, the image of her face and remembrance of their night together came surging back. He felt hot blood rushing into his face as he hurried to cover his nervous guilt with a forced smile.

"Pendragon," Link said lightly, "I'd *never* buy a horse from you, you know that? I don't know how y'can stand right there, flat-footed, with your blank face hangin' out an' pretend I don't have any stake in this. It's *me* that owes Malin a whipping, or worse. Me. And I'm the one that oughta go. No, let me say it different than that. It's me that's *gonna* go meet him."

For a moment, the two men looked at each other. Link could not know what Gwen might have revealed to Art in all that time she had been waiting. Art could not know Link's dreams of a new place and a new life, with her, far away from the Keystone. Each man's eyes were fixed on the other's and a world of pain and anger spun just beyond their recognition. If Link were to die in the imminent encounter with Malin. . . . Or if Art were to die. . . .

It was another crossroads.

Art stepped away. He took the reins from the cowboy

holding his horse and led the animal to the corral, where he tied it to the rail. He walked back again, serious and thoughtful. "All right," he said at last. "We go together. Like always, right? That's it, then. You better get yourself a gun you can depend on."

"I guess I'll stick with this one," Link said, patting the old Colt thrust into his belt. "I'll just step over to the bunkhouse and get my extra holster and some cartridges, though, and my knife."

"Here," Bob said, unbuckling his belt and slipping his Bowie knife off of it. "Take mine. It's a good one."

"No offense, Bob," Link said, "but I'd like something lighter, something quick. I would admire to borrow that little Winchester, though."

Garth stepped up and handed Link the saddle carbine. "All loaded up," he said.

Bob dug in his pocket and brought out a handful of .30-30 cartridges. "Extras," he said, giving them to Link.

Two of the boys caught Messenger and wordlessly began saddling him again. They made it a solemn business, a fitting and possibly final service. Without a word, Link and Art mounted up, rode to the bunkhouse for the holster, then set their hats down hard and headed for Malin's camp. There they would tell Malin where to find the clearing in the cedar grove where their rendezvous would take place.

Gwen Pendragon opened the front door and went out onto the front porch with as much nonchalance as she could manage so that anyone watching her would think that she was only stepping out to watch the late afternoon unfold against the western horizon. When she reached the lip of the porch and raised her hand to shield her eyes against the late afternoon sun, she saw two horsemen leaving the stables and barns, but they were not coming toward the house. They were unmistakable even at that distance, the big shining black with the proud neck and Art's big pale buckskin. Both riders sat straight and serious in the saddle, riding stirrup to stirrup, up and across the hill leading to the camp of Flynt Malin.

# Chapter Sixteen

Mine honor is my life; both grow in one;
Take honor from me, and my life is done.
*King Richard the Second*, Ii, 182
William Shakespeare

Art Pendragon and Link Lochlin rode past groups of Keystone men, past the corrals and horse barns, past the sheds and cattle pens and toward Malin's camp. Link looked to one side, off beyond the haystack enclosure, where he recognized two familiar wagons parked in the big meadow. He could smell the burning coal and saw the yellowish smudge floating into the late afternoon sky.

"Looks like Thompson's outfit," he remarked.

"It is," Art said. "He's been here, been gone, been back. He's fixin' up a big plow and scraper for us, so we can get that old north ditch back in shape. An' he's makin' a nice iron fence for the graveyard over against the pines, too."

"Where that young woman, Elaine . . . ?"

"Yeah. There'll be other people buried there, as the years go by."

"No doubt," Link said. "I want to pay him a visit, after we finish with Malin. Tell him about a dream I had."

At Malin's camp, they were greeted at first with silence, but it didn't last any longer than it took a man in long johns to dash from tent to tent. A tent flap opened and another of Malin's men stepped out. Link recognized him as one of those who had taunted him and Crows Woman, back at Ehre's Hole. The tent flap moved again, and the man was joined by his partner. They'd both been at Gorre. There wasn't much doubt but that they'd helped Flynt kidnap the women and kids. They recognized Link as soon as they saw him.

"Well, well!" one of them said. "Lookee here, Slick! Ain't that our ol' pal, the squaw man?"

"I believe it is, at that," Slick said with a sneer, touching his hat brim in a mocking salute. "Howdy, there, *Mister* Keystone. I see y'done takin' to ridin' horses again! Last time we seen you, y'favored ridin' in a Injun cart full of. . . . What was it, Steve?"

"Bones," Slick said. "Old rotten bones. Don'tcha 'member the awful stink?"

"Oh, yeah," Steve returned. "Now y'mention it. A top hand wearin' rags and livin' with a squaw, ridin' around in a bone cart. . . ."

Slick did not get to finish his description. With surprising speed, Link swung Messenger around and struck out with his foot, planting the heel of his right boot into Slick's chest. Slick went stumbling backward into the side of the tent. He scrambled up, reaching toward a pile of clothes for his gun, but, when he saw the look in Link's eyes—and Art's hand on his Colt—he thought better of it.

"I'd sure like to go on talkin' old times with you boys," Link said calmly, "but I got a message for your boss. Where is he?"

The question was unnecessary. Flynt Malin heard his visitors and was already on his way, walking insolently down the passage between the roundup tents, followed by four swaggering toughs wearing guns.

"Lookin' for me?" Malin asked.

Link turned and saw him. On foot, and right in front of him, was the man he wanted, the man who had kidnapped Gwen, shot Riley, gave him a beating, lied and schemed and murdered. Link looked steadily into Malin's eyes, remembering all those hours of darkness in the pit. Now the low-life stock stealer stood right where Link could shoot him down. Most people would say he had it coming, that killing him was no more serious than shooting a rabid dog.

"I see my boys remembered their little run-in with your squaw man," Malin said to Art. "If he's a sample of what you're hirin' for top hands 'round here, your big Keystone ranch can't amount to much any more."

Art leaned on his saddle horn and met Malin's eyes with a look that was cold as a blue December's dawning. "I guess you don't know why we come," Art said. "Missus Pendragon promised you a fair fight, and, by God, the time is *now*."

"Is that right?" Malin said. "Well, let me tell you somethin' about your Missus Pendragon. . . ."

"*You* shut your damn' mouth!" Art ordered. "The next time you so much as say her name, I'm going to put a bullet through your head! I'm goin' to tell *you* something . . . when this battle of ours is over, whatever happens, your whole bunch of cattle thieves is gonna leave here for good. After this is over with, my wife's promise is taken care of and all bets are off. Come mid-morning tomorrow there'll be twenty Keystone men ridin' into this field, and, if we see even one of your bastards still here, they're gonna start shooting. And you can bet your whole poke they're gonna shoot to hurt."

The four men backing Malin said nothing, but, along the row of tents, there were nervous glances exchanged. A couple of the less loyal outlaws immediately made plans to start packing up as soon as Malin left camp. Art had planted the seeds of a surreptitious mutiny.

Malin was unruffled. "Big talk," he said. "But have it your way. How y'want to do it?"

"It's gonna be you and me," Link said. "And Mister Pendragon and one of your men, just to make sure everythin's on the up-and-up. That's all. My friend, Riley, and the Keystone riders, they'll see nobody else gets involved, just in case you had something else in mind. Over east of the creek and then over that hill there with the big rock on it, the one that looks like a haystack, you'll see a big ol' ponderosa stickin' up above a bunch of cedars. There's a clearing there. You and one man. I'm givin' you an hour to show up and finish all this. If you don't show up, then you won't even have until tomorrow to clear out. One hour, and then we're comin' back here and stomp this whole nest of snakes."

Malin looked from one man to the other. "Purty brave talk," he said. "Tell me something, Pendragon. Where *is* that other ramrod of yours, that one called Riley? He's the one I said was sleepin' with your wife, not this one. . . ." Malin looked steadily at Link and some kind of recognition, some kind of realization seemed to creep into his glassy rodent eyes. "But I guess maybe I was wrong! You kin bet somebody was playin' rabbits under the quilts, though. All the signs was there. Just might even of been your boy, here."

"One hour," was Art's reply. "*Be* there."

The two Keystone men turned their backs on a half dozen outlaw guns to ride slowly away, headed for the meadow hidden in the distant cedars.

It should have been like old days, Art was thinking, like the times before Link had arrived at the Keystone, like the times before he had met Gwen. In those days, it was just him and the boys and the building of the Keystone. Weeks in the saddle, faces set against cold rain or blistering sun, moving herds up into all that rich, open grassland of Wyoming. Sleeping on the ground, keeping watch for marauders, human as well as animal. And taking what time he could, and any men who could be spared, to cut and haul logs for the big house and the first barns.

All kinds of men had been there, men who had since drifted off to chase their own dreams. But before they did, they shared the great adventure of toiling together and fighting together to build something worthwhile. It should have been like that now, but now it was only two men riding to a fight over something you couldn't quite put your finger on. Oh, he knew it was called honor and reputation and justice and all that, but it was no longer tangible. And it was no longer just plain old Art Pendragon, either. A dozen or more ranchers in this newly founded stockmen's association were looking to Art for their own peace of mind. People on the ranch itself who had little to do with livestock—the Pendragon's cook, the old man who tended gardens and fences, the girl who helped out around the house—they looked at Art as a kind of combination businessman, judge, and boss, not just a man riding out to protect his good name with six cylinders loaded.

He had sometimes sensed there was something more than friendship between his wife and Link, of course. How could he avoid feeling it? They seemed to be pulled toward one another in the living room of an evening when they shared coffee and talk. There was an extra lilt in her voice when Gwen opened the front door and found Link there. She seemed almost to cling to him when she brought him into the study.

More than once Art had thought about the day when he might get killed, and he felt that Link would maybe be the first to show up at his widow's doorstep, carrying pansies and candy. Sure he would. As for Malin's remark that they'd already tried part of being man and wife . . . well . . . nothing to that, he was sure.

Link rode quietly with hard realizations sinking in. Maybe he should have let Riley have first chance at Malin. Then again, if Art really believed anything of Malin's story about bloodstains on sheets and all, Riley would have been in a tough spot. For all Link knew, Gwen had already told Art all about him and her. It didn't seem like it, though, not the way Art was acting, but it could be. Like a tumbleweed rolling across a road, a stray thought went across Link's mind: what if Art knew, and what if he'd already planned on riding home alone? He'd be busy with Malin. Maybe Art could sit it out and wait for the outcome, then pick up his long gun and make sure Gwen's honor was safe. Or maybe Malin or his partner would get a bead on him and maybe Art's gun would pick that particular moment to jam. Or something. But that was crazy thinking. Such ideas would never even enter the mind of a man like Art Pendragon. He had honor.

The thought went rolling on and faded to nothingness, and Link felt shame at having had it. He thought of his own sense of honor, and set his mind to remembering the insults, the beating, the capture, and the pit. He wanted to fill his head with anger and revenge the way it had been back at Gorre. He wanted to be good and angry when Malin showed up. But, without invitation, another wandering idea intervened. Art could get killed in this fracas. What if Art and Malin were both killed? Link didn't want it to be so, but if Art *didn't* make it. . . . There could be a stray shot. Or a ricochet. Gunfights went fast and confusing, smoke and noise and movement. Art catching a bullet meant for somebody else was the most natural thing in the world to happen. Link didn't want it to happen, or did he? He couldn't help thinking what it would mean for him and Gwen. He damned himself for the thought, and self-anger burned in him as he jerked Hansen's Colt from the holster and checked the cylinder load for the third time that day. If he was angry enough to kill Malin on sight, he was even angrier with himself.

"How y'want to do this?" Art asked Link.

They had come to the clearing in the cedars and stopped just inside the perimeter. The place was several acres of open grass, good grass watered by a little spring. From side to side it was the length of a pistol shot, but to make that pistol shot count for anything, a man would need to be about halfway to the middle, where the giant ponderosa stood. From end to end it was more like the range of a good rifle shot, that is, a man who was pretty good with a long rifle could hit something—a deer, for instance—at the other end. In between, there was only that one lonely big tree and the squat rock where the spring water seeped.

"If I was you," Link said, "I'd stay on this side so as to have the light at your back. The shadows are gonna be deep over here, too. Let's tell Malin's man to stay over there on the other side of the clearing, where we can see him. Me, I'll ride down to the south end and find a good place, one where I can keep an eye on both of them."

And so it was.

When Malin and his sidekick, Army, got to the clearing, they found Art Pendragon waiting in the shadows of the cedars. Art pointed to his left with his Winchester, but Malin had already spotted Link away down there, sitting on his big black horse.

"You can stay here," Art told Army, "or else y'can go across to the other side. Either way, you're gonna stay where I can see you. You try to drop out of sight, or even raise your gun, and you'll be goin' home tied across your saddle."

Army said nothing but rode across the expanse of grass and tied up his horse on the other side, kneeling on the ground with his Henry rifle held upright. Art left his horse back in the cedars and reëmerged to stand in the shade, cradling his long Winchester in the crook of his arm. Out on the meadow, Malin had begun riding in a wide cautious circle, staying close to the cedars. Link merely sat on his horse and watched him.

Malin had played this game before, and he knew some good tricks. He began by doubling back on himself, turning his horse with apparent carelessness, keeping Link's attention by shouting insults at him. His maneuver put him between Art and Link, so neither one of them could take a shot without first wondering if he would hit the other one. Malin rode a little farther, then doubled back once more, putting himself closer to Link, farther from Art.

"Surprised to see y'show up, squaw man!" he yelled. "How many shooters y'got hid back in the trees, anyway? Half a dozen?"

It didn't bother him that Link only sat still and listened, waiting for him to make his play. What the Keystone cowpuncher didn't realize was that Malin had already started making it. When next he turned his horse to double back again, now even closer to Link and farther from Art, he yelled back at Art, who was still standing in the shadows.

"Where's that purty wife of yours, Pendragon? I figgered

she'd be sure to come see how brave you boys are! Why don't you jus' run home an' fetch her while we wait? 'Course, she might be busy with one of your boys, if y'catch my drift!"

"Shut up, Malin!" Link yelled at him.

"Oh, the big bad ramrod don't like that idea, eh?"

"You're a foul-mouthed, low-crawlin' skunk, Malin."

Malin laughed. He had made another doubling of his tracks and he was now well within range. He was also directly between the two Keystone men. It was time. Malin gave Link an ingratiating smile and carefully held his gun hand up in the air to show it was empty. "All right, all right!" he said. "Now, jus' let me check my gun!" He gingerly lowered his hand and slid his revolver from its holster. It was a long heavy gun, one of the old Scofield conversions that fired black powder cartridges. With exaggerated, almost theatrical movements he opened the gun and looked at the six cartridges in the cylinder, then eased it shut again. "Seems all right!" he said, sneaking it to full cock as he pretended that he was about to holster it again.

And without warning, he threw a shot at Link, then a quick second shot. He kicked his horse into a dead run, almost before the second bullet cleared the muzzle.

One of the shots caught Link's sleeve and burned a scratch along his arm. Messenger shied and tried to rear up on him, and Link hoped the other bullet hadn't hit him. "Damn it!" Link swore. He knew he'd been caught off guard. He drew Hansen's Colt, afraid that Art was pretty close to being in the line of fire. All he could see was the cloud of gunsmoke, but he saw a shadow moving in it and fired. As his shot boomed out, Malin's horse came running out of the smoke, headed up the clearing.

From his place at the end of the clearing, Art saw

gunsmoke, heard three shots, and instantaneously heard Link's bullet go whipping through the cedar limbs just above his head. Instinctively Art dropped to the ground, trying to keep track of all three men.

Malin had a plan. He figured that Link would try to catch him by galloping along the edge of the clearing to cut him off. Riding at a dead run, Malin pulled his horse up suddenly and wheeled around to take another shot. The Keystone man would run right into it.

But Link had already seen how Malin was using the smoke to hide behind while he made him worry about hitting Art by mistake. Maybe he could use Malin's ploy in turn. His first impulse, just like Malin had figured, was to race him to the top of the clearing and cut him off there, but, instead, he turned Messenger toward the tree in the middle.

Malin didn't see Link where he expected him to be. He wheeled around in time to spot the big black horse coming around the ponderosa. Link fired a shot, the deafening *boom!* filling the clearing, the smoke obscuring him. Malin fired in return, despite not having a clear target. His options now were to run into the smoke, which is what the Keystone man would expect, to stand his ground and keep firing, which seemed suicidal all of a sudden, or to turn and make a dash for cover. Unfortunately for him, he chose wrong.

Malin jerked the reins over hard, putting the horse and himself off balance for a split second, and putting his gun arm on the wrong side. And while he was trying to reverse direction, Messenger closed the distance. The big black came at him like it was after a wild steer, crashing shoulder to haunch with Malin's horse, sending it toppling over sideward and spilling Malin to the ground. Dazed by the fall, the outlaw scrambled for his Scofield, which had fallen into the grass. He grabbed it up and turned on his knees, clumsily off balance, but Link was nowhere to be seen.

Malin stood up, wincing at the pain shooting through his ankle, and broke the gun open to replace the burnt cartridges. He swore at his horse as he reached up for the saddle horn and felt more pain in his shoulder.

Link galloped to where Art was standing. He stopped to reload. "You all right?" he asked Art.

"No thanks to *you!*" Art said. "That shot of yours damn' near parted my hair!"

"You still got a fix on that other bastard?"

"Yeah, I can see him. He's still over there, waitin' his turn, I guess."

"Well, watch him. Here comes Malin again."

Malin came at a gallop, bending low over his horse to make himself less of a target, shooting at the two Keystone men as fast as he could cock and fire. Link touched his heels to Messenger and he sprang away along the line of trees. Another shot boomed as Art sighted along his Winchester, but Malin had doubled back again into the smoke.

Malin rode back the way he had come, slapping the side lever of his revolver on his thigh to open the gun and eject the fired cartridges. When he reached the cedars and turned again, he shifted the Scofield to his rein hand and refilled the cylinder.

Across the meadow, Link eased Messenger to a walk. He knew where Malin was, just as he knew he would probably try to repeat the same move, using noise and smoke to cloak himself every time he charged and fired. And he wouldn't let himself get cornered again, either. It was just a matter of time before one of Malin's shots hit Messenger or himself.

*What would* I *do, if I was Malin?* Link asked himself. *Just*

272

*what he's doin'*, he answered. *Keep charging in, blast away, run away again. Try to shoot the other horse, then make a fast charge at the man on foot. It's a cavalry tactic. Maybe Malin picked it up during the war.*

Link rode back to the ponderosa so he could use it for cover while he looked to see where Malin was. Sure enough. He was back at the end of the meadow, getting ready to do it again. Link thought a minute. Maybe he didn't need to play the game by Malin's rules, after all. He looked for the other man, Army. The light haze of smoke still hung on the air and made it hard to see, but Link was pretty sure the man hadn't moved. Good. He could concentrate on Malin, then.

Malin jogged forward, looking around, saving his horse and his shots until he got closer. But he knew where Link was. Right behind that big ponderosa. Being a man for fair play and honor and all that fancy-pants horseshit, the Keystone cowpuncher would hold his fire and wouldn't shoot from ambush. So he could ride even closer to that tree before making his charge. With any luck he'd get that damned horse down with the next shot or two.

He never expected what happened next. The man on the black horse came out from behind the tree, and fired without any warning. *Boom! Boom! Boom!* the three heavy shots thundered at him, gun smoke rolling away. One slug ripped flesh just below his ribs. His horse flinched like it had been hit, too.

*Boom! Boom! Boom!*

Three more shots. One hit the saddle and he heard one go whizzing past his ear. All Malin could see was the white cloud drift on the grass around the tree, and, as it cleared, the Keystone man was gone.

After firing his sixth shot, Link jammed the Colt back

into his holster and bent low over Messenger, racing for the deep afternoon shadows on the west side of the clearing. He urged Messenger back into the trees, ducking under the branches as they went. Before the smoke cleared, and before Malin's ears could hear anything again, Link and Messenger were safe in the cover of the cedars. Link dismounted and tied Messenger behind the trees, then drew out Garth's short Winchester carbine. It was a sweetheart of a gun, almost brand new. A light .30-30 caliber, good for deer or coyotes. And being almost brand new, it shot the new smokeless cartridges. The next time he took a shot at Malin, the outlaw wouldn't be able to tell where it came from.

Link kept low and stayed behind the cedars, planning his firing positions. This big thick tree would do. Then it would be a safe, short run to that place over there, where two trees leaned together, then to that other big one farther on. He spotted a good-size rock beyond that as well. It would be good cover, if he were lucky enough to get that far. Maybe shooting from cover wasn't what some men would call a fair fight, but it was still a long way from being a sure thing. Riding out there to face that maniac would be nothing but stupid.

And Malin was not a stupid man, either, not by a long chalk. He wasn't about to ride out into the open. Malin turned his horse toward safety instead, behind the giant ponderosa. From there, he thought he'd be able to sneak a look at where the Keystone cowboy was, but the Keystone cowboy was nowhere to be seen. Malin squinted down the length of the clearing, hoping to see Army, to see if Army had a clear shot at either of the other two. But there was only the grass, the haze of gunsmoke, and the surrounding shadows.

Suddenly Malin felt high and exposed sitting there on his horse. He took another quick look around and swung down out of the saddle. He dropped the reins to the ground so the horse would stay put and got himself closer to the trunk of the tree. He moved cautiously, slowly, looking all around. Still nothing.

*Whang!*

The rifle shot exploded the dirt and grass just under the dropped reins, and the horse threw up its head and bolted. Malin made a jump for the dragging reins, but he came down on his injured ankle and fell, face first, into the grass as the horse ran off. He cursed in a whining voice as he dragged himself back to the tree. He had no idea where that shot had come from. Maybe Pendragon had decided to deal himself in.

"Two against one, is it?" Malin yelled out into the emptiness of the clearing. "What'd y'do, ambush Army? Now you're both comin' after me?"

Silence.

"I kinda expected *better* of you, Pendragon!" he yelled.

Silence.

*"Awww!"* he screamed. "Y'can both of y'go t'hell and take that whore with you!"

This time there was no silence. Link's voice came across the clearing from somewhere in the cedar shadows. "Malin, you go on ahead!" Link called out. "You go first. An' tell old Nick I'll be there directly."

"Where's Pendragon?" Malin demanded.

"Dunno!" Link replied. "Keepin' an eye on your partner, I expect. It's just you and me, remember?"

Link punctuated his sentence by snapping off a shot that tore the bark just over where Malin was hiding. As soon as the bullet was on its way, he changed position by dashing to the two leaning trees.

"T'ain't fair, Lochlin!" Malin cried out. "You got a rifle an' I'm down to my sidearm here. Lemme catch up my horse and get my Henry, at least."

"Damn' shame about that!" Link called back. "You go ahead and run for your horse. I see him standin' over there a ways. Hell, you might make it. I might miss. It might even be I wouldn't shoot a man in the back. Then again, you ain't much of a man, are you?"

Link got off another shot from the .30-30, and this time Malin saw where it came from. It chipped the tree, just like before; the Keystone cowpuncher was only playing with him, trying to scare him. Maybe he was figuring on doing this until he gave up and threw out his gun. Maybe he'd made a mistake, giving away his position like that. *Or,* Malin thought, *maybe I just will throw my gun and let him come close. He don't know about the hide-out gun in my armpit holster or about the Derringer in my boot.*

Malin pulled himself to a standing position. The bullet wound under his ribs was hurting like hell. He took six cartridges from his belt and transferred them to his front pocket to make it faster to reload. He made sure he had six live ones in the cylinder. He didn't have to throw his gun down, not yet. Since he knew where that cowboy was, he could charge him on foot, do the same thing as before. The Keystone man was bound to stand up and come out in the open to finish it, would probably try to get to him before he could reload. Didn't figure on a hide-out gun. *Time to see what was what,* Malin decided.

Holding his wound with one hand and the Scofield in the other, Malin eased around to the other side of the tree and judged the distance between himself and the wall of dark cedars. Less than fifty yards. There was a bush off there to the right that would give a little cover. . . .

*Whang!*

He ducked involuntarily as the bullet ripped bark above him. Seemed like he saw a little rifle smoke that time, too. Slightly different place. And then he saw something he could not believe, at least not at first. Lochlin had stepped out of the cover of the trees and out of the shadows, walking well clear of them. Malin sneered. He almost had to laugh. That horseshit about honor and fair play again. He knew none of the Keystone boys would ambush a man or hide behind a tree and just shoot a man down. Couldn't do it. It was their weakness.

This was going to hurt his ankle, probably hurt like hell, but he knew it would work. Same as before, only without a horse, and it would work, especially with both of them on foot. All he had to do was charge hard and keep shooting to throw the other man's aim off.

Malin started at a limping, gimping run toward Link, trying to aim as he went. His first shot went high, but the gunsmoke helped hide him a little. His second shot felt better, like he had placed it where Link stood. But it made the smoke worse, obscuring both men. Halfway across the open ground, he fired the third shot and it, too, felt like it had gone home. And so far he hadn't heard any answering fire. Maybe the cowboy's rifle had jammed. Maybe he was running back into cover. Or maybe he'd got him.

Malin fired a fourth time and kept limping forward as fast as he could, but there was no way he could know he was firing into empty space.

Link had dropped flat the instant Malin opened fire. He lay prone, in the open, steadying the carbine like a sharpshooter, aiming at the smoke, waiting for his shot. He heard the booms of the Scofield going off and heard the crash of the big bullets breaking through the limbs of the cedars just behind him. He breathed evenly and slowly, making himself wait it out. He had decided to bring Malin down, but not kill him. He'd cripple him and they would take him to trial for his cattle stealing, the civilized way.

Five shots, and then there came just the very lightest breath of a breeze to lift the haze of gunsmoke from the ground. It was just enough to show the shadow of Malin's legs. Link squeezed the trigger. His bullet shattered Malin's injured ankle, bringing the outlaw sprawling like a poleaxed steer.

Link could not be certain, afterward, nor would he ever be certain, but it was probably because Malin fell so quickly to the ground that Link's next shot into the white haze, also intended to break a leg, smashed into the side of his neck, instead. It cut muscle and bone together, leaving Flynt's lifeless head dangling to one side like that of a man hanging from a gallows.

Then there was silence all over the meadow. Crouched under his tree, Army suddenly felt very alone, far from anything he might call home. He had heard a shot, then Malin curse with pain as he fell, then another shot. Now the gunshot echoes died away, the small drift of breeze erased the gunsmoke haze from the meadow, and Army saw a tall man on a tall black horse riding toward him through the evening. It was too late to run. He stood up and put down his rifle, then unbuckled his gun belt. Throwing it away, he sat down, cross-legged, to wait, the way he had seen prisoners do it during the war.

The evening was wearing on as three men topped the hill, but still there was plenty of light to show a glint of metal on the vest of the man who sat on his horse waiting for them. The two beside him also wore badges, and both of them held their Winchesters upright, butt plates resting on their thighs.

"Bob Roberts," Art Pendragon stated as he rode up and extended his hand.

The marshal took it. "Pendragon," he said.

"You're a long way from your swivel chair," Art said.

"Seems like long," Bob Roberts agreed. "Meet my deputies. Abe Brown, Tex Ginshall"

The two deputies nodded to Art.

"You know my man, Link," Art stated. "This one here is one of Flynt Malin's boys. So what brings you to the Keystone?"

"The district court decided to give me more work," Roberts said. "Extended my district by about half. But they did give me an extra man."

"I see," Art said. "Glad to be in your jurisdiction, then."

"We've been looking for legal cause to go into that Gorre Valley place," Bob went on. "We're looking into all this rustling that's been going on. So, a few days ago, right out of the blue, here came a pair of weasels who said they'd been Flynt Malin's hired guns. Only, one day, when they were guarding the pass, some bunch of citizens jumped 'em from behind. They lit out and never looked back. Wanted protection, in case a posse was on their heels. Anyway, the sheriff has 'em locked up and they're ready to swear that they were eyewitnesses when Flynt Malin killed your man Keaton."

"*Malin* killed Keaton?" Art asked.

"So they say. After your man's gun was empty, Malin chased him into the trees, rode him down, shot him. Plus, those two will swear it was him that planned that kidnapping. He'll hang for sure. All we need is to find him. Bob

Riley indicated we'd likely find you and Malin out here somewhere."

"You found us," Art said. "And you'll find Malin lyin' in a clearing back there a ways. He's dead."

"Dead?"

"Dead as a man can get. We were just headin' to his camp to send a wagon back for him. But there's no need of you goin' all that way to see a dead body. Let's let his boys fetch him. Then you can confirm he's dead. Meanwhile, why don't you and your deputies come on back to the house for some supper? I can tell you all about it, then." Art looked at Link. "Maybe you'd go on into Malin's camp and tell 'em what happened," he said. "If you see Riley or any of the men, tell them I want that bunch of cattle gone through. If any animal has a brand that even *looks* suspicious, it stays here until we find an owner. Tell Malin's gang to pack up. And tell 'em they need to find a couple of men to take a wagon and go collect their boss. I expect Henry Malin will want his son's body back."

Link welcomed the assignment. He still felt the blood running hot through his veins and the hard tension along his muscles. As he had in former times, he was quick and dangerous, set apart from the other men by what he had just done and carrying a certain smell of death. And so he rode into the Malin camp, alone, and he could see by looking at the rope corral and the picket line that half the horses were gone. Some of the roundup tents looked empty, too. Off in the distance, three horsemen were herding cattle westward. Link thought about going after them, but then decided there was plenty of time to catch them later, if Art wanted to.

He rode between the two rows of tents to the end, where he found a man he hadn't seen before, a young man who looked like someone he could trust with an important message. Link rode up to him and sat regarding him for a moment before he spoke. "All right," he said at last. "Flynt Malin's dead. The marshal's arrested his sidekick. Now, I'm puttin' *you* in charge around here." Link spoke it loudly, loud enough to leave no one in doubt. "You get a wagon and a couple of your boys. Then I want you to go up toward our bunkhouse, and ask somebody to point out the way to the clearing in the cedars, the one with the big ponderosa in it. When you get there, you'll find your boss. Pick up his horse, too. It's been shot, but not bad. Come back to the bunkhouse and wait there until the marshal gets a look at the body, then you take it back to Gorre. Savvy?"

The young man nodded. "What's gonna happen to us?" he asked.

"Right now, nothing," Link replied. "Unless you try to run off. You wait for the marshal, and he'll tell you what he's going to do."

As Link rode on out the other side of the camp, he heard murmuring behind him and knew that Flynt's remaining men were glad for the reprieve he had given them. That's the way it generally went with these outlaw gangs. You catch the leaders, or kill them, and all of a sudden the outlaws seem to turn into just plain cowhands and farm boys again. The marshal would have warrants for some of them, maybe, and maybe he'd go into Gorre and look for stolen cattle. But the days of the Flynt Malin gang were over with.

From her living room window, Gwen saw the group of horsemen in the distance, apparently discussing something. Then the big black horse split off from the group, and, as the rest of them came closer, she saw that it was Art and the marshal and the deputies. Counting people quickly, she went to the kitchen to alert Mary to the fact that there would be guests for supper. Link and Art were both safe!

She heard the men on the front lawn, and looked out in time to see the hostler leading the horses away. The man between the two deputies had his hands bound. Art and the marshal stood and talked by the gate, then mounted the front porch and stood there as if waiting for a few of the others to join them, and kept on talking. She did not want to interrupt, but couldn't help herself. She opened the front door and rushed to hug her husband.

"Oh, darling!" she said. "I'm glad you're all right! Are you hurt? Is it over? Oh, it doesn't matter. I'm just so glad you're all right!"

"Not a scratch on me," Art said. "Link got a little scratch, more like a welt. Not even worth mentioning. And, yes, it's all over now. I guess you met Bob Roberts?"

"Hello, again, Mister Roberts." She smiled at the marshal.

"Ma'am," he replied, removing his hat.

"I just wanted to tell Art I'm glad he's safe. And Link. Wasn't he with you just now?"

"Yes," Art said. "He's just gone to give some instructions to Flynt Malin's men. I expect he'll be here to join us before long."

"And Flynt Malin . . . ?" Gwen said.

"He's dead."

In the long silence, no one knew exactly what to say. There was no cause for joy, no reason for laughter, and yet, at the same time, there was a feeling that a very bad time was now over and done with.

"Well, Mary is fixing some supper," Gwen finally said. "No hurry, though. You men go ahead and talk and clean up. I'm going up to my room for a few minutes just to say a thanksgiving prayer because you're safe." She gave Art another hug, then slipped back through the door and vanished into the darkening interior of the house.

"I'll just have my men go get supper at your cook house, if that's all right," the marshal said.

"Sure. The cook'll feed your prisoner, too. Now, what say we have a drink before we eat?" Art said. "Come on in."

Restless, Link rode toward the glow and rising smudge of the blacksmith's forge. Soon he saw the broad back of the man standing at the anvil and heard the steady ringing of a heavy hammer on hot steel. He tied Messenger to the wagon and stepped under the shelter of the canvas. The blacksmith gestured with his tongs at a leather bottle and metal cup standing on a stump nearby.

"The cup's for you," he said.

Link took it up and found it already filled with wine. It wasn't sweet, yet neither was it dry and sour.

When Thompson finished hammering and put the steel back into the fire, Link spoke.

"You told the truth about that Gorre Valley," he said. "Didn't find many folks with much hope up there."

Thompson put down his tools, wiped his brow with his bandanna and filled a cup for himself. "But that's not the whole truth, cowboy. Not the whole truth. Hope, it's a peculiar commodity. Working without any hope is like trying to carry water in a grain sack."

"Flynt Malin's dead. Maybe folks at Gorre can get some kind of life back now."

"Maybe," Thompson said.

Link saw three steel rods in the coals, glowing faintly red. He had never seen the blacksmith's forge with more than one piece of steel in it at a time. Thompson reached up and worked the bellows, making sparks dance up the flue, turning the coals the color of new cherries. The three rods began to take on the hue of sunrise.

"Getting near the end, do you think?" Link asked.

"Might be," the blacksmith said. "Maybe three links left. Maybe one, if it's the right one."

Link finished his wine and set his cup back on the stump.

"Pick me out a piece of steel there," Thompson said. He picked up the tongs and pointed at the forge.

Link studied on it. All three pieces looked alike. All three looked ready for the anvil, all red-yellow with heat shimmering off them. He found himself hoping there wasn't any difference, that they'd all turn out the same. But at the same time, he hoped he would choose rightly, and hoped something serious wouldn't happen if he chose wrongly. Link had been around smithies almost all his life and had done his fair share of horseshoeing. He knew the ways of the forge; he knew he had to choose soon. There is a point in time when the metal is ready for the hammer and the anvil, ready to be shaped into its final state of being, to become what it was intended to become. If taken too early, or left too long in the fire, it will resist the hammer.

"That one, I reckon," he said, pointing at the one on the right.

The blacksmith seized it in his tongs and slapped it down on the face of the anvil. *Whang! Whang! Whang!* went the big hammer. Sparks of metal flew until Link was forced to take a few steps backward.

Thompson put the bar on the anvil's horn, and again his massive arm rose and fell against the tractable steel, forcing it to bend around the horn, forcing it into an oval shape. He saw it cooling, so he pushed it back under the glowing coals to heat again while he reached down for the end of the great chain lying behind the anvil stump.

Link marveled at the speed with which Evan Thompson worked. Out came the oval of steel, out from the fire of the forge to meet the white powder flux he threw upon it from a bag. The blacksmith thrust the glowing oval into place at the end of the chain, and, with four blows so heavy that they made the ground shake, his hammer welded the link closed.

As the ringing of anvil and hammer died away into the dark of the distant hills, the roar of the forge fire subsided. The two men stood watching as the steel link turned brown, then gray, then blue-black. Thompson threw water on it when the time was right, timing it perfectly so it would be neither too soft nor too brittle.

"Never did learn how to judge that," Link said. "I always seem to end up with something too brittle. Too hard."

"Few men are meant for smithing," Thompson said.

"Was that the last link, then? Is it finished?"

"Could be," Thompson said. "Could be. Time will tell."

A cold wind came up suddenly, like the chilling drafts that sometimes rise from a creek bottom in deep shade.

Gwen knelt at her bedside as she had always done since she was a little girl and offered up her prayer of thanks that Art and Link had come safely through their horrible encounter with Flynt Malin. She offered up a prayer for Malin's soul, and asked that he be forgiven, as all should be forgiven. She asked forgiveness for Link. She prayed for the people in Gorre. Finally she prayed for the health and keeping of all souls on the Keystone Ranch, prayed strength for Art in the coming days. She did not have it in herself to pray for what she wanted most; she did not even have it in herself to mention her love for Link, not even to God.

When she had finished and serenity had returned to the house and its surroundings, she went to her north window and looked out. The darkness was now nearly complete. She could not be certain where sky and horizon met. The window glass reflected only her own image illuminated by the dresser lamp and the candle next to the bed. At other times, such impenetrable darkness had made her feel alone, isolated, surrounded by the unknown, fearful. But tonight she was not feeling loneliness, but hope; whether it was because of the candle's reflection, or her reflection looking back at her, she did not know. What she *did* know was that out there, beyond the reflections, Link was thinking of her.

# About the Author

James C. Work was born in Colorado where his family had lived for three generations. His mother's grandparents were in Leadville and Cripple Creek during the gold rush days, while his father's forebears were pioneer farmers on Colorado's eastern plains. He grew up in Estes Park and attended Colorado State University and the University of New Mexico, and holds degrees from both. He now teaches literature at Colorado State University.

Western American literature first heard of Work in 1984 when he took on the job of restoring Jack Schaefer's novel *Shane* for the University of Nebraska Press. Since then he has published *Prose and Poetry of the American West*, an anthology which won the Colorado Seminars in Literature Annual Book Award. Of the 100 or so essays he has written, a sampling can be found in *Following Where the River Begins*. This work won the Charles Redd Award in Western Studies. He was also the editor of a collection of short stories entitled *Gunfight!* which includes many stories by Western favorites. *Ride South to Purgatory* (Five Star Westerns, 1999), the first book in his Keystone Ranch saga, was his first Western novel, followed by *Ride West to Dawn* (Five Star Westerns, 2001), *Ride to Banshee Cañon* (Five Star Westerns, 2002), and *The Dead Ride Alone* (Five Star Westerns, 2004). His next Five Star Western will be *The Water Dreamer*.